Sacri'Sanguis

Sacri'Sanguis

LeAnne Hart

Book One

Salvation of Cylendri

Amegreen Publishing, LLC

To request permissions, contact the publisher at r.leanne@leannehartauthor.info.

Paperback ISBN: 979-8-9986436-0-6
Ebook ISBN: 979-8-9986436-1-3

First paperback edition May 2025.

Cover Art & Typography by George Cotronis
Map by LeAnne Hart

Printed by IngramSpark in the USA.

Amegreen Publishing, LLC
San Tan Valley, AZ 85149

Aqu'immensi

Aquanalis

Castellum In'Caelo

Lapidis

The Crypta

Est'Alda

Castle Oblitori

Mira'Lyn

Between/Other Realms:
The Citadel (Crossroads)
Atri'anima (Spirit)
Ess'magis (Divine)
Infernus (Demon)

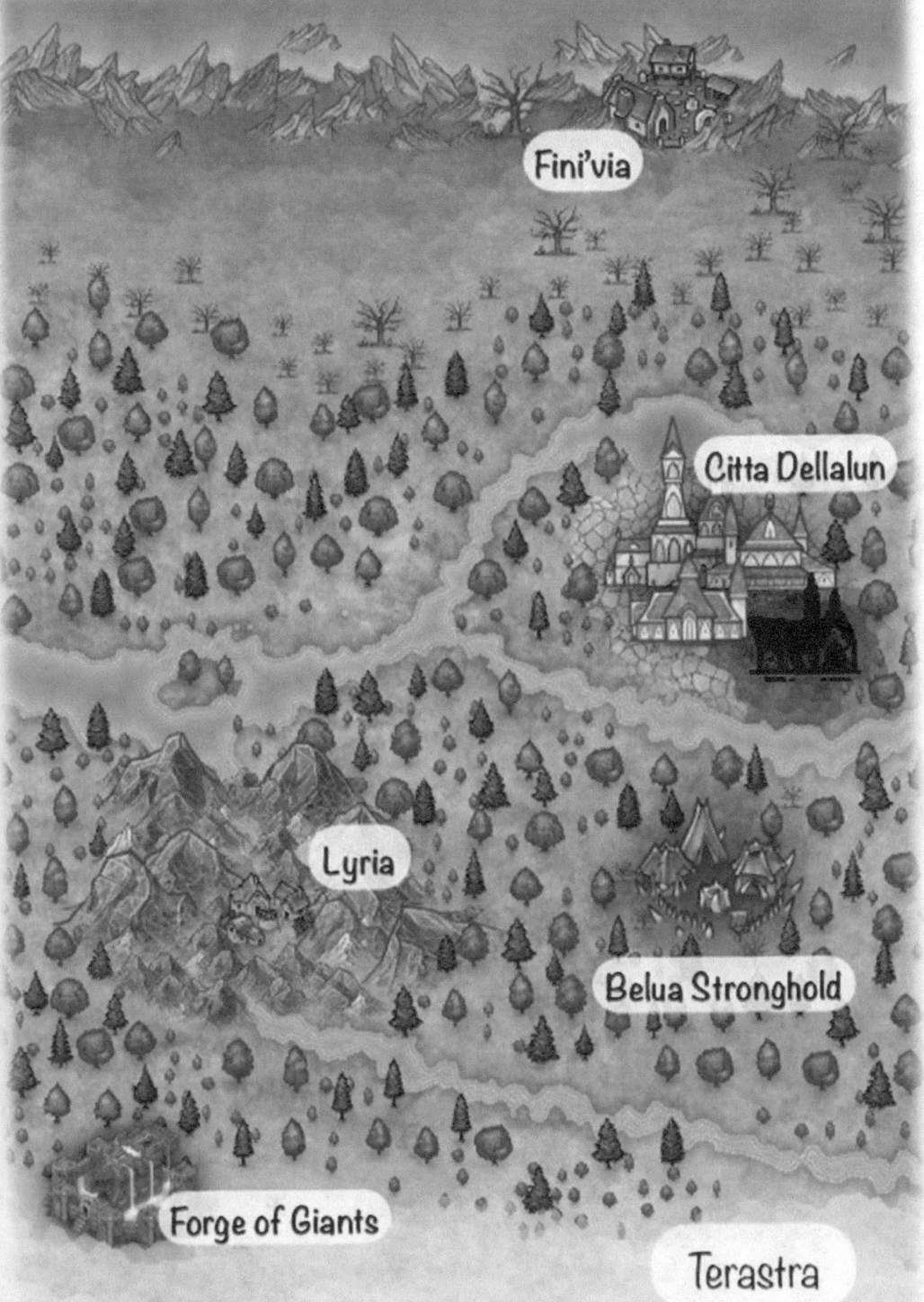

Fini'via

Citta Dellalun

Lyria

Belua Stronghold

Forge of Giants

Terastra

Table of Contents

For Iz,

who knew I had this story in me long before I did.

And for every girl who has ever been afraid of her
untapped power. Embrace it, use it to its full
potential, and even the Gods will tremble before it.

Prologue

A Coming Storm

Gondyr waited just outside Itsayea, the only metropolis in the southern desert of Terastra, under cover of night. He made himself comfortable on a large rock in the small oasis that sat about a quarter mile from the main entrance while considering what information this mysterious contact might have. It was odd they wanted to meet out here instead of inside the city walls, and the request had simply appeared on the curio in his room that morning, but the sense of urgency in the note was too enticing to ignore. As he read one of his new books, a silent heaviness filled the air, and his eyes shot up to find a creature floating before him in long, deep-hooded robes of burnt umber, the edges torn and tattered. Startled, he dropped his book in the sand. The creature bent over and reached out a withered bony hand, picked up the book, and handed it back to him.

"You must be the one who left the note," Gondyr stated as he put the book in his waist pouch.

"You must not linger in the desert any longer," the creature spoke, its

raspy voice seemingly disconnected from its body. *"You must take the elf North, for the sake of every Realm."*

Gondyr stared at the being, unable to see its face beneath the hood. "What do you mean?" he asked warily.

"The key to salvation lies within her. In the coming storm, Solaris will stand in defiance of Ess'Magis, convincing his siblings to overthrow the natural order. They must not be allowed to enter the Realm of The Divine. Your journey begins in three days' time. Travel to where North meets South and find the Forge of Giants. Destroy the weapon that would pierce the veil; disrupt the Demigods' plans." The creature pulled a piece of parchment from its robes and handed it to Gondyr. *"You will find a Stone at the crossroad of Realms, and from there she will plan your rebellion."*

He studied it for a few moments before reading one line aloud, *"we seek the Citadel as refuge from the storm?* What the fuck does this mean?" he asked curtly, but when he looked up, the creature was gone.

One

The Rebellion Rises

We have to get in there and stop him now!" Gondyr yelled over the crackling lightning and thunder from the storm raging overhead, his thick red hair matted down in his face as rain plummeted from the dark sky. Kara ran behind him fighting through a horde of Risen, demons pulled from the depths of Infernus by Mormagi...Death Mages.

"I know!" she yelled back, slicing through two of them with her daggers, "but these bastards won't stop coming!" Gondyr swung his smaller axe, hitting a large horned demon in its calf, but lost his grip as the monster turned widely and flung him back behind Kara. She finished off the demon, and a few more, with an exploding potion from her belt that sent pieces of charcoal flesh flying, which then disappeared mid-air, sending them back to the Demon Realm.

Suddenly, a great crack split through the air and Aleric unleashed a massive spell of blue light that cut through the horde, taking most of them out. Gondyr finished off the stragglers while Kara broke the Summoning Crystal that brought them to this Realm, then ran to Aleric, his long, sapphire blue robes splayed around him as he crouched on the ground. The spell had been an immensely powerful one. Even the silver filigree that adorned the fabric and usually swirled with magic had lost its sparkle.

"I am alright," Aleric sighed heavily, "I just need a moment. Go...you need to get to Solaris before he finishes that weapon!" Kara looked at Gondyr, and he nodded in agreement. She took off up the stairs that led inside to the forge. A great stone room with huge pillars and three massive pools of liquid fire in the ground stood before her as she made it into the main room. They fed an even larger, raised pool at the back of the space through a series of large channels that crisscrossed the floor. The unmistakable sound of metal hitting metal echoed off the walls and she saw Solaris standing at the main pool, his back mostly to her, hammering a massive blade. He hadn't heard her come in, she had the advantage and didn't hesitate.

She made her way across the room swift & nimble, finding a path that kept her directly behind him, and when she was within range, she deftly threw one of her poison-tipped daggers straight into the fleshy part of his lower back on the left side. He wailed, the hammer went flying across the room, slamming into one of the pillars as he lost his grip on the blade he was crafting, and it slid into a channel of liquid fire below him. The place shook from the impact.

She knew the dagger wouldn't do much damage, it barely penetrated his skin, which looked more like blacked scar tissue from severe burns than mere flesh, veins of red fire stark against the sooty flesh. And the poison wasn't nearly strong enough to take down a Demigod, but it was enough to distract him and destroy the blade. But they still had a hilt somewhere, and if this forge remained, then he could simply craft another. The only other forge large enough for him to use was The God Forge in Ess'Magis, the Realm of The Divine, and the High Gods sure as hell weren't going to let Solaris use it.

She had to bring this whole place down, right now. As she looked around for a weak point, she spotted Gondyr and Aleric making their way into the room. Solaris turned in a rage and locked his red-orange eyes on her. The liquid all around the room bubbled and sloshed with his fury, and he started towards her. Jumping across the channel to the left of her, she worked her way to the pillar the hammer had hit, knowing it had to have done enough damage for them to bring it down.

"We've got to take down that pillar!" she shouted as she jumped from one side of a channel to another, narrowly missing the pops and small waves of the molten rivers inside. Solaris was much bigger, and clumsier...he was struggling to catch up with her, but she knew she only had a brief head start, and he had strong magic that he wasn't resorting to yet because he needed this place to remain standing.

She pulled an explosive potion from her pouch and quickly tied it to a dagger, shouted "Aleric, I need wings!" and leapt for the huge crack that the hammer had left behind. A flash of blue lit up the room as the spell hit her and icy blue wings sprung from her back. She flew right for the crack, jammed the dagger inside, then flew down to the other side of the room where they were waiting. She turned quickly, threw another dagger at the potion mid-flight, and yelled, "let's go!" as she sped past them pulling Gondyr with her, Aleric quickly on her heels. Solaris was not far behind.

5

The explosion rocked the entire structure, and she could hear the crashing of stone on stone behind them, then the hiss of ice-cold rain hitting molten fire. Solaris yelled after them, streams of fire magic shooting past Kara, but they were already outside, her wings beginning to fade. She let go of Gondyr so he could roll and get to a run, then touched down and sprinted as the wings disappeared. Aleric was just ahead of them waiting with his translucent blue hand on the Travel Stone. She got there first and reached her hand out for Gondyr who grabbed it a second later. The next moment, as Solaris burst from the crumbling structure just before it collapsed, they were back at the Citadel.

"Fuck!" Gondyr exclaimed as he hit hard and rolled across the ground. Aleric just floated as Spirits are wont to do, and Kara's elven reflexes almost always landed her on her feet.

"I really hate those damn Stones sometimes." He grunted. Kara laughed and sat on the soft earth, wiping sweat from her brow. She took a deep breath in, held it for a moment, then exhaled.

Gondyr collected himself and stood. "Did we just do that?" he asked incredulously, dusting off his battle-worn armor.

"We did," Aleric replied, a stunned look on his ghostly features.

"He dropped the blade in the fire, and we brought down the forge. I don't know how much time that buys us, but Solaris can't complete his weapon, not unless he finds a way into Ess'Magis." Kara sighed. They had time, a lot more than they had this morning. But she had a lot of work to do, starting with a visit to the Nymphs.

6

Kara sat at the head of the boat with one oar, Gondyr at the back with the other, as they made their way up Cylendri River headed for Aquanalis, the City on the Water. Kara was excited, she had never been there before. There were so many stories of the islands that rose up from the center of the river, home to the Nymphs. But entry required an invitation, and luckily Gondyr knew their Sovereign.

"How much further?" she asked.

"Not much," Gondyr replied. "We're getting close."

"I don't see anything," she said puzzled. *"Shouldn't there be these great islands, coming out of the water and reaching for the sky like a haphazard stack of rocks?"* she thought.

"You won't, until we pass through the ward - Aquanalis is one of the most well-known, but best kept secrets in the Realms. The ward is the most powerful ever created. Without an invitation, you paddle straight into a dense and disorienting fog that comes out of nowhere and end up going back the way you came."

As he said this, the air around them sizzled and shimmered, and for a few moments she heard a high-pitched buzz in her ears. Just as it was getting to be too much to bear, everything went silent and she looked up to see the City on the Water looming in front of her, far more impressive than she had imagined.

There were great tree roots shooting up from the riverbed and snaking towards the sky through at least ten islands of varying sizes, connecting them. They teemed with life - creatures and insects unlike she had ever seen buzzing, flitting, and running about; colorful flowers and plants sprung from every crevice; a pale-yellow magic freckled the roots and tree branches, lending light as they made their way in just beneath one floating island and to the center where the main mass sat on the water. As they reached the edge of the island, she noticed a small group of the most beautiful beings she had ever laid eyes on waiting for them. Nymphs weren't common in the cities or even smaller villages; they preferred to stay away from the world and tend their home here. They certainly weren't found in the southern deserts where she had spent the last twenty or so years. Kara had never met one.

Gondyr gave one last push with his paddle, and the boat slid up on the land. Two Nymphs grabbed it and pulled it the rest of the way out of the water with ease. They were surprisingly strong for their slight size and frame, most of them closer in height to a dwarf like Gondyr than herself. They climbed out of the boat, and he greeted one of the welcoming party with a deep bow. Kara assumed this was their Sovereign as she stood with an air of authority. Her milky white skin didn't carry a blemish, scar, or mark anywhere Kara could see. Long silken dark hair streaked with white was pulled back from her face, decorated with a crown of glowing white flowers. Large, crystal blue eyes peered at Kara, eyes like jewels swirling with boundless wisdom. Her features were delicate and perfectly balanced. She wore a simple gown of woven leaves and flowers created from the earth itself, that wrapped around her neck and flowed down her body, barely covering her breasts, leaving her back, chest, and arms exposed. Kara had never seen such an exquisite creature in all her years.

8

"Kara, this is Vitellina, High Priestess of the Nymphs," Gondyr said as he made another bow. Kara bowed her head. "Vitellina, this is Kara."

"Welcome to Aquanalis, Kara." Vitellina spoke, but her lips never parted; she was speaking inside Kara's mind. She didn't know the Nymphs were telepaths!

"Thank you for allowing me into your home, High Priestess," Kara spoke aloud. "It's truly breathtaking."

Vitellina smiled and gestured for them to follow her. As they made their way up a winding tangle of roots to the next island, Kara noticed another Nymph stealing shy glances at her who looked remarkably like the High Priestess. The sunlight shimmered in her jet-black hair that was dotted with the same white flowers, though considerably shorter, and her blue eyes weren't nearly as deep, but Kara guessed they were related. She had a band of woven flowers around her chest and wore a skirt of sorts made from leaves that angled, leaving her right leg almost fully exposed.

They stepped off the root onto a large island, at the center of which sat a massive tree trunk the size of a great stone tower with a hole in the middle. Not a hole that had been carved or cut but had been separated by magic like a curtain of wood pushed back on either side, inviting you into the tree. The arch was speckled with glowing white flowers and the yellow sparkle of light magic. As they made their way inside, Kara was surprised to find it a dwelling of sorts. There were large mushrooms to serve as seating, small flat columns of hardened earth pulled up to make tables, and hanging branches that intertwined to create stairs up through the center of the trunk. A couple more smaller curtains of wood served as doorways to

9

other rooms on the ground level including what looked like a kitchen and a bedroom. No fires burned here, just clusters of light magic. There was no metal either that she could see. It reminded her of her elven home, and she sighed.

Vitellina gestured for them to sit at a circle of mushrooms around a large earth-table to the left of the entrance. Kara and Gondyr situated themselves, Gondyr struggling a bit due to his stout stature. They were surprisingly comfortable, though Kara did feel a bit strange sitting cross-legged on a mushroom.

The High Priestess and two other Nymphs sat with them. *"This is my daughter, Dahlia,"* Vitellina gestured to the young Nymph who had been looking feverishly at Kara on the way up, *"and this is my con'sial, Lilum."* She gestured to the other Nymph, whose eyes were a brilliant shade of rose pink. One of the only things that Kara knew about Nymphs was that they were all female, though she wasn't entirely sure how they procreated. Gondyr had to feel out of place.

"Now," she spoke telepathically, *"the message from Gondyr spoke of the Demigods, and a plot against Ess'Magis involving the Mag'nicelo, the great Veil between Realms. We do not like to involve ourselves in the wars of mortals, however, the ward that shields us from the rest of this Realm is connected to that Veil, so we have chosen to grant you an audience. Please, tell us what you know."*

Kara looked at Gondyr, and he assured her with a nod and smile. "Thank you, High Priestess," Kara began, "for inviting us into your home, and for speaking with us. We learned of a plan by the Demigods to remove

10

the Mag'nicelo and ignite a war with the High Gods. They have demanded access to the Realm of The Divine and to be allowed to rule alongside their parents. The High Gods have clearly refused – we know full well their children are not equipped to lead as their mixed blood lends to emotional outbursts and unchecked arrogance."

"You are not wrong," Vitellina interjected.

Kara nodded and continued, "the refusal has enraged the Demigods, Solaris in particular. And now his focus is on us. Just a few days ago, we interrupted him as he was crafting a blade for a weapon that could tear through the Mag'nicelo. We brought down The Forge of Giants; the only one outside of The God Forge that he could use. We aren't sure what their next move is, but we know they will now have to rethink their approach, or risk losing everything trying to access it. This has given us time to gain support and put together a team to try and stop them." She paused here to allow the High Priestess and the others to digest all she had told them.

"This is most disturbing," Vitellina finally said. *"And we cannot ignore the effect that such an act would have on our home, on our people."* She looked at Lilum, and Kara sensed they were speaking telepathically. Gondyr winked at Kara, and she wondered if he could hear them somehow.

A few minutes of awkward silence later, Vitellina looked back to Kara, *"we agree that aid should be provided when the time comes, and we would like to offer an emissary to join your team. That will allow us to remain informed."*

Dahlia spoke for the first time, out loud, "I would like to volunteer," she

11

said plainly. Kara could see the excitement in her eyes, this young Nymph clearly wanted to explore beyond the confines of her home. Vitellina looked at her daughter incredulously, the first break in her stoic facade that Kara had seen. These lulls in the conversation where they spoke to only each other telepathically was driving Kara crazy. She could tell they were arguing, and wanted to hear it. Having the High Priestess' daughter would lend a lot of credibility to their cause. But she sat still and silent, keeping that desire hidden.

"Dahlia believes that she could be an asset to your team and would like to prove herself worthy of being daughter to the High Priestess. I believe she is just chasing glory and excitement," Vitellina told Kara. *"What do you think?"*

Kara wasn't sure what to say. She took a few moments to collect her thoughts, then spoke, "I do not presume to know you, your people, or your daughter," she began. "I can appreciate your hesitation to send her out into the world, but I also understand her desire to leave home and prove herself. I have been in her place, and while I am thankful that my mother wanted me to remain safe and close, I would have resented her for trying to keep me from living the life I wanted to live. She let me go, and I will be forever grateful that she did, regardless of the trials this life has put me through. I can see Dahlia's eagerness, and I assure you I will teach her how to temper that with humility and grace. She would be a great asset for our team and our cause, but this choice is not mine to make," Kara finished.

The room grew silent as the High Priestess considered Kara's words carefully. The tension hung in the air, each of them waiting to hear if they would have what they wanted and needed.

12

Vitellina finally spoke, *"I give my blessing. Dahlia will accompany you on this journey and keep us apprised of the situation so we can be ready."* Kara, Gondyr, and Dahlia all collectively sighed in relief, letting go of the breath they each had been holding.

"We would be grateful if you would stay this night in Aquanalis, so we can discuss your plans further and Dahlia can prepare to leave." Both Kara and Gondyr bowed their heads in agreement. They spent the evening among the Nymphs, sharing stories, learning more about the elusive race. Kara was fascinated, making mental notes to ask Dahlia questions later. As she laid her head down on a bed of moss and dirt near the top of the islands, staring up at a sky full of brilliant stars through the trees, she spoke to Gondyr.

"Our next stop is one I am not looking forward to," she sighed.

"Dellalun...the Vipers," Gondyr replied with a yawn.

"Time to face my past. I pray Marciela is in good spirits...she could stop us dead in our tracks." She spoke of the First Fang, leader of the Viper Faction and one of the deadliest assassins to have ever lived. "Let's hope we can find a way to get her something she wants; the Vipers aren't known for charity."

Gondyr grunted, and she knew he was asleep, leaving her alone with her thoughts.

Two

Rescuing a Viper

Kara's heart raced as she and Gondyr walked through Dellalun, making their way to The Den. It had been almost twenty years since she walked these cobblestone streets, and no matter how prepared she thought she was, it overwhelmed her. She never expected she'd be back in her second home, much less heading straight for her old Faction, the one she had abandoned, to ask for their help in a war against Gods. Doing her best to keep her outward composure calm so as not to alarm the two Assassins who were escorting them, they strode past the ornate Whitestone buildings of the Vipers District that housed most of their ranks and before long, The Den was in sight. She continued to take deep, even breaths, but this was going to be tricky.

They reached the doors to the foyer, two more Vipers standing guard. Upon seeing the group approaching, the guards opened the doors and allowed them inside. The scent of limoncello hit her like a wave of nausea, and the memories flooded in. The Den was, for all intents and purposes, a brothel and gambling house. The rich, the desperate, the depraved, and the lonely wayward travelers spent their time here partaking in the finest foods, drinks, and lovers that money, or information, could buy. It was lavish, all gold and emerald greens, and filled with every luxurious comfort one could possibly imagine. The Den provided the Vipers with money and secrets from across the Mortal Realm, affording them a power that no other Faction could boast.

As the Vipers led them through the public areas in The Den, Kara remembered how much she hated being down here. The stink of debauchery and pretension that drenched these walls disgusted her. She had always kept herself to the upper floors, Viper-only territory, and never wandered down to the low levels unless she had to. None of it suited her.

They made their way up the three flights of main stairs meant for the patrons, then slipped behind a painting off the third-floor hall to use a private staircase for accessing the upper floors. A memory punctuated her thoughts – once finding a drunken diplomat in this staircase after he had snuck in behind a recruit who hadn't been stealthy enough to slip through unnoticed. Luckily, he didn't remember anything when he awoke in his room the next day, having been slipped a little something in his morning coffee.

At the top of the staircase, they went through a door and were inside the heart of The Den. An open room with ample upholstered chairs and sofas everywhere, and tables with candles and trays of coffee. This is where the Vipers gathered and socialized during the day. Since it was nearly dusk, it was empty, with most of them being out on marks or gathering intel elsewhere. They snaked through the room and headed for a door at the back. The First Fang's office - in a few moments, she would be standing face to face with Marciela, her old friend, whom she hadn't seen in two decades. Kara steeled herself.

They walked into the office to find a large ornate desk at the very center - perfectly organized and not a thing out of place. Floor to ceiling shelves of books lined the walls, except on the right, which sat a stunning fireplace and a lavish seating area. Marciela stood behind the desk holding a piece of parchment, looking up at the group as they entered. Her intense black eyes moved from the Vipers, to Gondyr, and finally to Kara. She kept her eyes on Kara for longer than was comfortable, but Kara held her gaze. Marciela didn't make time for uncertainty and Kara wouldn't show her any. Then she put down the parchment and made her way around the desk.

"Right on time," Marciela stated with her heavy accent. Her dark wild curls were streaked with gray now and she had a lot more wrinkles, but Kara could see that she was just as sharp as ever. And punctuality had always been particularly important to her.

"Thank you for meeting with us," Kara replied. Marciela stared at her again for a few moments and Kara felt exposed.

"Gondyr's letter was...intriguing to say the least. You can leave us," she told the two Vipers who had escorted them, and they left. "Please, sit."

They all settled in chairs around the fireplace, though Kara couldn't quite get comfortable, perching herself at the edge of the cushion, back straight and hands in her lap.

"Tell me, how can the Vipers help?" Marciela asked, matching Kara's body language. Always right to the point. She hadn't changed.

16

"The Demigods are plotting to tear down the Mag'nicelo in a power play for the Realm of The Divine. The rest of Cylendri would become the battleground. Dellalun would fall, The Den would be destroyed, and the Vipers would be eradicated, or imprisoned. You have a stake in this fight, and we need an Assassin to help us. Can we count on the Vipers?" she asked. Straight to the point.

"It just so happens that I was vaguely aware of the situation, and you are correct. This is more than just a mere squabble, it's bigger than just the Vipers. I would not trust this job to just anyone. Unfortunately, the Viper I have in mind is not here. He hasn't been here in over five years, and I'm not sure he would even be up for it," she said quietly as a shadow passed briefly over her face. Kara didn't like where this was going. "My grandson and Second Fang, Lucian, has been imprisoned by a very powerful Mormagi - in the Crypta."

Kara's heart stopped momentarily. She could see that Marciela was studying her, so Kara fought back the nausea in her gut and waited for Marciela to continue.

"Our attempts to free him have been unsuccessful at best. I want my grandson back. If you can free him and bring him home, then you can have any Viper you wish to help win this war."

"The *Crypta*?" Gondyr asked sharply. "No one can get out of that place, much less get in *and* back out alive."

"I'll do it," Kara said, without hesitation.
Gondyr looked at her incredulously. "And how are you going to do

17

that?" he asked.

"We have a Nymph and a Necromancer," she started.

Marciela lifted an eyebrow at her, not expecting to hear that. "Really?"

"Yes," Kara replied. "We have the High Priestess' daughter on our team, so we'll have a glimmer to shield us, and one of the Undeads most knowledgeable Spirits. though this is going to be increasingly difficult. We need a way in, we need to know where Lucian is being held, and we need a way out." She could tell that Gondyr couldn't believe they were discussing this, but he held his tongue.

"We can help with that," Marciela said. She got up and went to one of the bookshelves, pulling out a small, folded piece of parchment, and handed it to Kara. "I won't tell you how we came by this, but it is a map of the Crypta. We have marked all possible entrances, the cells including Lucian's, and the Travel Stone inside that will be your way out. You'll have to decide which entrance you would like to use; we haven't had any luck getting through any of them. Then you need to find his cell, bring down the ward, get him out, and get to the Stone. I wish you luck," she finished.

Kara knew that was the end of the conversation, so she stood and looked at Gondyr, who followed suit. "Thank you, First Fang," she said. "We'll see you again soon."

***

Kara, Dahlia, and Aleric made their way through the upper halls of the Crypta as quietly as possible. They were under a glimmer, which shielded

18

them from sight and most tracing magic, but they still had to keep to the shadows and less populated areas, so it was slow going. They had to get down to the cells, two floors below, and find Lucian. Luckily, the Travel Stone they would use to get out of here was on the same floor, near to where they'd find him. Kara recognized that as another torture tactic, a way out right down the hall from the cells, just barely out of reach. But, even if a prisoner could somehow get to it, they couldn't even use it.

Kara had heard stories of the Crypta, almost everyone had. It was the worst and most terrifying place on this side of Infernus, which it was rumored to be linked to somewhere in the bowels of this massive prison. The whole thing was dark and ominous, carved right out of the earth with only red flame torches to lend any light. The walls appeared alive, as if it were flesh dripping with dark blood. You could hear the cries and screams from prisoners being tortured, experimented on, and beaten in the chambers below them. It made Kara's skin crawl. Every instinct in her wanted to just rip through these monsters, but she had to stay focused.

They found a quiet hallway that curved and appeared to head down to the next level, so they continued in silence, a mix of fury and horror heavy in the air. Dahlia was learning a lot about the world beyond the water in a brief time, and Kara wished this wasn't the impression they were making, but they needed her, and she needed to understand what they were fighting against. The Mormagi would side with the Demigods, without question, if they hadn't already.

They got lucky and found that this hall also led down to the cell level, but they weren't anywhere near Lucian's. She had hoped that she would only need Dahlia with her as the more people they had to work with, the more dangerous this became. But they needed Aleric's Spirit Magic. The wards on the cells would likely be more complex than Kara could handle, and there was no telling what condition they would find Lucian in.

They stopped in a small alcove at the bottom of the hallway so Kara could check the map. As she worked through how they would get to Lucian's cell, a couple of Mormagi came around the corner and stood a couple feet from them, talking. Dahlia And Kara held their breath. The Mages were clothed in red hooded robes, partially obscuring their gaunt pale faces with sunken eyes akin to black holes flecked with blood spray, and pale, thin lips. They looked like walking death, and Kara despised them.

"She wants him brought up to the Chamber again tonight, she's got plans for that Spirit of Wrath," one of them said.

"I still don't know how she managed to capture a fucking Viper," the other one replied. They were talking about Lucian. "And that thing she put in him is fucking creepy - I don't like when it talks to me."

"We'll come back for him later, let's go get something to eat," the first one stated flatly, like they weren't just casually discussing torture.

Kara's eyes were white hot with rage. *"What the* fuck *did they 'put in him'? Did they say, 'Spirit of Wrath'?!"* she asked Dahlia, whose eyes were wide with horror, but the Nymph didn't respond. They waited for the two to be out of earshot, then she showed Dahlia and Aleric the path they needed to take. Dahlia spoke telepathically between them, relaying their thoughts to each other.

"If it's true about the Spirit, Aleric will be able to sense him as we get closer, get a feel for his condition," she told Kara, even the voice in her head shaking with fear. "We'll need to work together very quickly as soon as we have a chance to take down the ward," she told Aleric, "I won't be able to hold onto the glimmer while we do that, and it will start to dissipate."

"As soon as it's down, you do your best to get that glimmer back up," Kara replied to Dahlia, "and Aleric can go with me into the cell to get Lucian. We only have one shot at this, and we don't want these bastards having three more prisoners to experiment on. The Travel Stone is at the end of the hall here, to the right. We head straight for it once we have Lucian, got it?" Dahlia nodded and relayed the message. It was now or never.

They moved slowly down the corridor, groans and whimpers coming from almost every cell they passed. These weren't just any cells, they were large pits dug into the earth below their feet, black holes of unyielding despair. No bars, no grates, nothing to stop a prisoner from climbing out...except the holes were on the ceiling of the cell, well out of reach, and a ward woven across it to cancel out magic.

"Aleric has him," Dahlia said just before they got halfway down the corridor, "his breathing is shallow, but he's awake, and aware."

"Good, he won't be quite as difficult to move," Kara replied.

They neared the cell Lucian was in, and a small group of Mormagi came passing through the hall. Once Kara couldn't hear them anymore, she signaled for Aleric and Dahlia to get the ward down while she kept guard. Almost immediately, the glimmer around them waned just a bit, Dahlia

21

fighting to balance her magics. She was more powerful than Kara had given her credit for. As they worked to unravel the intricate ward, Dahlia had to divert more magic there and the glimmer was starting to fail.

Just before they were all fully exposed, Kara could hear another Death Mage coming from around the corner. She was ready to strike as its head came into view, but they finished with the ward just in time, and Dahlia got the glimmer back up before it saw them. They held their breath again as it walked dangerously close, then paused for a moment before continuing. The tricky part was over, but they had to get out of here now.

Kara signaled, and she and Aleric jumped into the hole. It was like being swallowed by every terrible, dark, unimaginable tragedy the world had ever seen...it was more than pitch black; it was a void. Kara was disoriented almost immediately. Luckily, Aleric was a Spirit, so he brightened his pale blue glow and Kara could make out a figure sitting on the ground a few feet in front of them. No chains, no ropes, nothing tying him down.

"That bitch didn't get her fill last night?" a deep, raspy voice with a thick Dellalunian accent growled from the darkness. Kara saw a pair of icy blue eyes look up at her, and then a different voice hissed, *"Not mages...someone new."* A Wrath Spirit...Kara felt her eyes getting hot with her rage. She had to calm down, nobody needed her to lose her grip in here.

"Who the *fuck* are you?" Lucian asked.

"Kara and Aleric. And you're Lucian. We don't have time for more, let's go." She shot back at him. "Can that thing in you fly?" she asked.

22

"Yes!" the Spirit hissed.

"Good. Aleric, give me wings and then help him out of here. I'll grab Dahlia. Head for the Stone."

A flash of blue light and she was in the air. She headed straight up and through the hole, to Dahlia's surprise, and grabbed the Nymph around her waist. As she turned and angled towards the exit, she looked back to see Lucian burst from the hole with great smoky black wings that looked like they were dripping icy blue ink, eyes filled with blue fury, and Aleric flew sharply up behind him. They were all in the air and right around the corner from their exit before any Mormagi realized what was happening. As they got closer to the Stone, Kara slowed.

"Hang on tight to me Dahlia, I have to let go of you!" she shouted. Dahlia squeezed her arms and legs around her as Kara grabbed Lucian's hand on her right and then reached her left hand out for the Stone. Aleric met her there, both putting their hands on it at the same moment, and they were gone.

They didn't go to the Citadel, they went to Dellalun. Kara had a promise to keep, and she wanted Lucian to be in familiar surroundings after being in that nightmare. He had those Viper reflexes, and landed on his feet as they came through, same as Kara. Dahlia was still clinging to her.

"Dahlia, you can let go..." Kara said, amused.

"Oh," Dahlia giggled, "right." She climbed down off Kara and dusted herself off, a blush on her cheeks.

23

"Everyone alright?" Kara asked the group.

"Never better," Aleric smiled.

"I could be better..." Lucian winced and crumpled to the ground. Aleric lifted him off the ground with his magic, and they headed for The Den. She didn't lead them to the main entrance, instead going down near the docks around the back, heading for a secret entrance in the private gardens. As they approached, the Viper patrolling the area caught sight of them, and tensed. She knew he had a dagger in each hand.

"*Flessial, Adatil, Ni'Riveael,*" she said quietly, showing she knew the Viper Creed. The guard didn't move.

"We have Lucian. We have the Second Fang, and we need to get him inside *now*," she pressed, trying to keep her voice low and pointing to the floating body. The guard finally broke and waved them over. He let them through and was about to tell Kara where to take him, but she cut him off, "I know where I'm going. Is the First Fang here?" she asked.

"No..." the guard started.

"Well, have someone go get her from the Manor," Kara was getting frustrated, "and then get back to your post."

"Yes...ma'am," the guard stuttered, and he was off. Kara led them up to the top floor, where the common room was. They laid Lucian on one of the big, deep green sofas and waited for Marciela. Kara was exhausted. They were in and out without a drop of bloodshed, but the strength it took to

24

keep from ripping through every Death Mage in that hellhole had depleted her. She nearly let the lighting explode when she saw what they had done to Lucian.

She looked over at him. He was dressed in nothing but a ragged pair of torn trousers, unshaven and disheveled. She could see all the bruises at various stages of healing, fresh cuts and scratches, and healed scars all over his body. His chest rose and fell, but his breaths were still very shallow. He likely had internal wounds, as well. It broke her to see him like this...it was not at all the reunion she would have hoped for.

"Dulci puer'mea," a voice whispered behind her. Marciela walked in from the shadows, looking over her grandson with a mix of pity and fury in her eyes. "What did they do to you?" She sat at his side on the couch and lifted his head into her lap, stroking his long, thick hair.

"You're not going to like it...one of those Death Mages crammed a fucking Spirit of Wrath inside him," Kara said. Maricela looked up at her, tears forming in her obsidian eyes, and Kara used her last bit of strength to hold herself together. She had never seen the First Fang cry.

"We'll give you some time...send for me when you're ready to talk," Kara said quietly, and they got up to leave. Marciela grabbed her hand and looked up at her.

"Thank you, Kara, thank all of you, for bringing him home. The Vipers are in your debt, as am I..." Marciela trailed off.

"Of course," Kara replied, squeezing her hand, "take care of him." With that, they headed for the Travel Stone and back to the Citadel.

Three

City of Stone

Three days had passed since their foray into the Crypta, but Kara hadn't stopped thinking about Lucian. She needed a serious distraction, and she needed it now. By some divine grace, a knock at the door pulled her from her thoughts.

"Come in," she said.

The door opened and Gondyr walked through. "Good morning. Are you ready for another adventure?" he asked playfully.

"Well, it can't be any worse than my last one," she jokingly replied.

"Fair enough. I've got a contact who might be interested in joining the team. He's asked to meet in Lapidis...looks like I get to go home, too," he said with a smile.

"I'm ready when you are," Kara said excitedly. She was itching to get out of the Citadel.

"Meet you at the Stone in an hour, I've got to get a few things together," he replied.

He left and Kara was again alone with her thoughts. She sat at the edge of her bed and stared out the small window in her room at the trees that surrounded the Citadel. All she wanted at that moment was to see Lucian, to know he was going to be alright. And to find that vile creature who had tortured, beaten, and experimented on him. Even as a Viper, Kara didn't pride herself on killing. Once she had become an Ammodytes and was able to choose her marks instead of being handed whatever was available, she only took those jobs that were focused on true monsters - murderers, abusers, soulless creatures who preyed on the innocent and weak. She wanted to be more than just an assassin; she wanted to strike fear in every Death Mage and demon worshipper in Cylendri and make them atone for their crimes against the people.

"I'm sure Lucian will have something to say about that, but he's not going to take her down without me..." she thought aloud. "Little Luca," she sighed. He wasn't so little anymore, and she had no idea how she was going to deal with seeing him again.

***

Gondyr led Kara through the mines that made up most of Lapidis, the sound of metal banging against stone echoing through the corridors as they made their way to the city in the very center, beneath the earth. Kara had been here only twice before, both when she was a Viper. Once for simple information, the other to fulfil a mark on a particularly nasty dwarf who had

28

made his gold by luring youngling elves away from their villages to be captured and enslaved by a group of Mormagi. She made sure he paid dearly for his many sins.

It was still a remarkable sight. The Dwarves had been here for centuries and had carved out this massive city to live in as they mined around it for gems and metals. It was easy to get lost in the mining shafts and corridors, though. They were hot and it would get hard to breathe in some of the more cramped paths. If you weren't careful, one misstep could lead to disaster. She was glad to have Gondyr with her.

"When we get to the city, just keep close to me," Gondyr told her, "the tavern isn't far, but we're not exactly going to have a warm welcome."

"Do I need to be worried?" she asked.

"No, nothing I can't handle. But you know my kin, they hate outsiders," he replied with a sour tone. Gondyr was quite different from most Dwarves she had known. He didn't hold the same contempt for other races as his brethren. She supposed that's why he saved her all those years ago and had been with her ever since. They shared a unique bond steeped in a great love for all life, and a fervent desire to eliminate those who would destroy it.

They squeezed through a final crack in the wall at the end of a long corridor and stepped out into an immense cavern. Her lungs filled with a deep breath of cool air and the lights of Stone City glittered before them. Great columns and bridges and structures all made of cold, hard stone filled the center of the cave, rising from the depths, and an intricate web of railcar tracks crisscrossed the space, leading from the city to the outer mines and back. Thousands of little yellow flames from torches dotted the city, as well as large fires from the forges and communal areas. As they worked their way across the largest bridge she had ever been on, she looked down and saw nothing but deep, dark black below her. She had had her fill of voids at this point, but at least this was not echoing with agonizing screams and cries.

They entered the bustling city, moving through groups of dwarves, and she kept as close to Gondyr as possible so as not to lose him in the chaos, feeling the disdain of side eye glances and downright nasty looks. They wound through the great stone halls and staircases, up and back down, until they reached a small tavern in a less populated area of the city. As they stepped inside, Kara noticed there weren't many patrons, just a couple of dwarves at a table in one corner at the back, and a few seated alone at the bar. To the right sat a single dwarf at a small table by themselves, their back to Gondyr and Kara. Gondyr grunted, and they both headed in that direction.

She made her way around the table, Gondyr behind her, and as she turned, she thought she was seeing double. The dwarf seated at the table was the spitting image of Gondyr - they were nearly identical. The same reddish-gold hair and beard, both shaggy and unkempt with a peppering of gray; the same somber deep brown eyes with flecks of gold in them; the same round and weathered face, though the stranger looked like he spent a lot more time scowling than Gondyr. Kara's surprise must have been plain on her face because Gondyr just laughed and said, "Nalor, good to see you brother!" with a slap on Nalor's back. Nalor just grunted and smiled slightly.

"Are you *twins*?" Kara asked warily.

"Indeed," Gondyr replied, "though I'm the better-looking brother," he joked with a wink. They sat down and Nalor barely moved. He clearly didn't share Gondyr's sense of humor or more cheery disposition, a byproduct of living underground for most of one's life.

"Thanks for coming brother," Nalor started, his voice gruffer and grittier than Gondyr's, "though I'm not sure it was a good idea to bring the elf."

"My name is Kara, and I'd prefer if you use it...or I can just call you 'the dwarf' if you'd rather?" she said sharply. Gondyr laughed again, and Nalor cracked a small smile.

"You've got grit, I'll give you that...Kara," Nalor replied.

"So, what did you drag me all the way down here for?" Gondyr inquired.

"I heard you've gotten yourself into quite a mess. Something about Demigods, and associating with elves, nymphs, and necromancers. You didn't think I'd let you have all the fun, did you?" Nalor asked. Kara tried not to take it personally, this was a dwarven thing, and if he was interested in joining the cause then he had to know he'd be hanging around the likes of her. "I'm sure you could use another dwarf," he looked at Kara and winked, "my brother may be prettier than me, but I'm a much better blacksmith and fighter!" They all laughed. It felt good to laugh, especially after the last few days.

"Well, I'm sold," Kara smirked, and Nalor shot a full smile back.

31

"Excellent!" Gondyr exclaimed, "less work for me to do! Now, I haven't had a good pint of Deep Mead in ages, let's order a round and we'll catch you up." After a few rounds of the strong, dark, and bitter Mead brewed with hops and mugwort, they had filled Nalor in and Kara was about to suggest they leave when an important looking dwarf with an entourage of armed guards walked into the tavern and turned straight for them. His thick black hair was slicked back haphazardly, and he glared at them with dark, beady eyes.

"Nalor! You didn't really think I wouldn't notice outsiders in my city, did you?" he exclaimed. Kara looked from Gondyr to Nalor, and their faces were a clear sign this was trouble. The newcomer strode up and stood at the edge of their table, glaring at Kara. "Especially if they happen to be a duplicitous elf, and a deserter."

"Gymmlor," Nalor replied, "hasn't my brother served his time? Is twenty years in exile not enough?"

"Served his fucking time? He was only 'in exile' because he left, not because we put him there," Gymmlor growled, staring at Gondyr. "He hasn't paid for that. He strolls back into this city and was just going to slither back out with you and this repulsive snake without so much as a fucking word for my father?"

Kara could feel the power slamming against its cage. "Excuse me? Who the fuck do you think you are?" She would not be insulted by this arrogant little shit with an array of jewels around his neck, and a big gut that said he hadn't seen battle in an exceedingly long time, if ever. Her imposing presence towered over him, daggers in hand ready to teach this creatin a

32

lesson.

"Kara, please," Gondyr pleaded with her.

"Yes *Kara*, mustn't stick your forked tongue where it doesn't belong," Gymmlor snarled.

"Gymmlor, that's enough. Your problem is with me, and I'm leaving," Gondyr replied, his usually pleasant smile replaced with a scowl. They headed for the door, pushing through the group of thugs.

"Next time you show your face in Lapidis, it will be your last!" Gymmlor shouted after them.

After they made it back across the bridge and through the mines, headed for the Travel Stone, Kara finally had to ask, "is one of you going to tell me what the hell that was about back there?"

"That little bastard is the unfortunate offspring of Rhygan, our Stone Sovereign," Nalor replied, "and he thinks he owns the fucking city."

"If his father has something he wants to say to me, he knows he can find me," Gondyr said from ahead of her. She knew enough to leave it at that. Gondyr had been abandoned in that Belua cage and had never seen himself as a deserter. They left him to die, he owed them nothing.

***

It had been almost a week, and Kara had grown quite impatient waiting for word from Dellalun. Most of her nights were spent pacing in her room or reading in the library with some snacks if she could manage to get her mind off Lucian for long enough. She wanted to know if he was recovering, and they needed to figure out their next move. There was still the meetings with the Tree Dwellers Faction and the Gryphons that had to be arranged. Getting an audience with both had proven even more difficult than the Nymphs.

Aleric had gone to provide an update to the Undead Faction and see if they had any more intel on the Demigods to share. Having contacts who could slide between Realms was immensely helpful, but Spirits aren't known for their patience and can be notoriously difficult to track down when you need to talk to them. He had been gone for days. And the dwarven twins had been catching up, drinking mead, and getting in pissing contests, both literally and figuratively, so things had stalled. The Citadel felt like a pit of thick, unrelenting mud in which she had become stuck.

Dahlia and Kara had at least had time to learn more about each other's homes and cultures, which was enjoyable. The Nymphs were fascinating, and every time they finished a conversation, Kara found she had even more questions to ask. She did finally find out that they were born from earth and magic, forgoing the pleasures of the flesh, which she still couldn't quite wrap her head around. Dahlia had explained it as a seed created from a very complex spell that could take years to perfect, then planted in the ground of the main island that sat atop the water, which eventually grows into a great big flower and when it blooms, a young Nymph is inside. While Kara appreciated the beauty and simplicity in that, she almost pitied them for never experiencing sex. It wasn't always great, but when it was...well, it was surely on the list of things worth fighting for.

Dahlia was a sweet thing - smart, strong, and undeniably stunning. And she clearly had an infatuation with Kara. Any opportunity she got to talk with her or touch her, Dahlia was taking. While normally Kara wouldn't be opposed to showing a beautiful girl some of the finer things in this world, and a Nymph would be a fun new experience, she had no desire for it. Ever since Lucian had crashed back into her world, he had dominated her every thought, no matter how hard she fought against it.

Another restless night had stolen sleep from her and, sick of lying in her bed staring up at the stone ceiling of her room, she got up before the sunrise, threw on some trousers, then headed to the kitchen. A cup of tea and a couple of berry tarts would do her good. She lost herself within the process - preparing the dough and berry filling, a mix of gooseberries, elderberries, and cinnamon, with a hint of lemon; meticulously cutting, stuffing, and shaping the small treats before putting them in the wood-fired stove; boiling the water over the open fire, and creating a tea blend of rosehip, orange, and jasmine with cinnamon and ginger root shavings; steeping the tea in a small cheesecloth pouch, until it was just strong enough. When she was done, she sat at the table, poured some tea in her cup over a spoon with honey on it, and took a bite of one of the tarts. Closing her eyes and chewing slowly, she savored the flavor, letting the warm filling roll over her tongue before sipping the tea, a perfect complement for the tarts. She leaned back into the chair and just tried to enjoy the simple moment. But the smell of cooking always woke everyone up, and before long Dahlia, Gondyr, and Nalor all made their way to the kitchen for breakfast. Dahlia, a tired frown on her face, was not one for talking in the morning, something she shared with Nalor. But Gondyr had always been a little too perky as soon as he awoke, which was usually too much for Kara. Today, she didn't mind. The company was welcomed, as

35

was the conversation.

"Good morning, Kara," he said cheerfully, "it smells delightful!"

"Berry tarts, I made plenty. Help yourselves," she gestured for the kettle, "and there's tea." Dahlia snatched up the kettle and poured herself a cup of tea, Nalor and Gondyr going for the tarts. They each grabbed three and got themselves some spring water before settling down at the table. As Dahlia took her first drink, she moaned slightly, and Kara smiled. It was damn good tea.

"Usually, I don't like berries," Nalor started, then took a bite, "but you make magic with these tarts."

"Thank you Nalor. They're an elven family secret," she winked.

"Oh, a raven came this morning with a letter," Gondyr mumbled with a mouth full of tart. He pulled a piece of parchment from his nightshirt and handed it to Kara. She did her best to keep her eagerness in check as she grabbed the letter and opened it:

Kara,

Lucian is mending well, and I'd like to speak.
Please come to the Dellalun Manor as soon as possible and bring this letter.

Marciela

"Finally," she sighed aloud, forgetting she had an audience. Expectant faces around the table stared at her. "News from Dellalun, Marciela would like to speak," she said, composing herself. "I can make this trip alone; it won't take long. I'm going to gather my things and head out. Enjoy the tea and tarts!" Her voice echoed as she left the kitchen, not giving any of them a chance to respond.

Four

Coffee and Lavender

Kara walked through the nearly empty Market District of Dellalun, which wasn't surprising. Most of the commerce in this city began just before sunset and the stalls would be teeming with activity then. Everything about this place was so different from the life she had grown up in, which is what had drawn her to it all those years ago. Dellalun Manor came into view as she turned the corner out of the markets back into the Vipers District. A deep breath helped steady her nerves before she headed up the stairs that led around the sides of an ornate fountain, and straight for the front door. She had been to the manor many times, but almost never through the main entry. Two Vipers stood guard, same as with the Den. They wore the traditional black and jewel green leathers, wrapped and stitched to be as flexible as possible, with hidden pockets throughout for an array of daggers and blades. A simple green belt at the waist held a small crossbow, and a few different potions in glass bottles, some for health, some for damage.

She handed one of them the letter, and he rubbed a thumb on the top left corner - he was checking for the invisible, heat-activated seal. It appeared a moment later, and the other guard opened the door to allow her in. The manor was one of the most beautiful buildings in all Dellalun, at least to Kara. It was the perfect balance of comfort and style. Maricela always had an eye for decor, and it shined here. Muted taupe and cream colors on the walls, floors, and tapestries provided the base, while stark shades of natural greens and splashes of black offered a dramatic flair, without being lavish or overstated. As with all that Maricela put her hands on, everything was in its right place, and none of it had changed much.

As she walked slowly through the foyer, taking it all in, her eyes moved to the stairs, and her breath caught in her throat...Lucian stood at the top, leaning against one of the pillars with a cup of coffee in one hand, its rich aroma invading her senses, and he was staring at her. Even though she left the Vipers almost twenty years ago, that was a face she had never forgotten, and he had grown into quite a man. Little Luca, heir to the Dellalunian Dynasty, a mischievous boy and devilish young assassin. He was nineteen and barely off to complete his first solo mark the last time she saw him. Now he was a hardened, brooding figure, as if chiseled from stone that had weathered too many storms. At six-foot-three, he stood a good nine inches taller than her with thick, black, slightly tousled hair - perfectly messy, a few strands falling naturally across his eyes, accompanied by the rugged shadow of a beard on his strong jaw. His features were sharp and intense with thick, expressive eyebrows and eyes like obsidian glass. When he looked at you, it felt as if those eyes were unraveling every mystery locked deep within your soul.

He wore a loose, silky green robe that complimented his warm olive skin and simple black trousers with no shoes. The robe hung perfectly on his broad shoulders, opening to expose his well-defined chest where the head of an intricate snake tattoo that wrapped around his left arm and

39

down across his heart was on display. Her eyes slid briefly down his body and back up to his smirking face as she tried desperately to keep the blush from her cheeks. Before she could start up the stairs, Marciela came around from a room to the left of them to greet her.

"That was sure quick," she said with a smile as she reached for Kara, pulled her in, and kissed her cheek, "I sent the raven just last night."

"The Travel Stones make it easier," Kara replied, happy to see her old friend in such good spirits.

"I noticed you didn't have a dwarf with you last time either," she gave Kara a sly look, "I'm assuming you have a Stone Charm, then? How ever did you come by one?" Oh, she was still sharp as ever.

"A girl has to keep some secrets for herself," Kara winked. And as Marciela studied her face for a moment, Kara could tell she was starting to make some connections. But if the First Fang had figured it out, she didn't say a word. She simply smiled and gestured for the stairs. "Shall we?" Kara started up the stairs, caught between the eyes of one of her oldest friends, and the man who was enslaving her every free thought. Why does everything have to be so damn tricky?

All three of them silently made their way to Marciela's office, Lucian's eyes burning holes into Kara's back the whole way. It was excruciating as she fought the overwhelming urge to glance at him, fearing that he would see right through her. After what felt like an eternity, they finally reached the office, which was set up similarly to the one at The Den, though less opulent, following the more muted tone of the Manor.

Marciela went behind the desk and sat as Kara sat herself across the desk in one of the two chairs there. Lucian went to stand by one of the large windows behind Marciela, overlooking the Manor's courtyard, and stared out nonchalantly. A wave of relief washed over her now that his eyes were no longer caressing her skin.

"As you can see, Lucian is faring much better," Marciela started, glancing at him, "but I haven't discussed the situation with him yet." He looked back at her, his left eyebrow sharply raised.

"Oh, stop brooding," she snapped at him, "you know you have her to thank for even standing here, you could show a little gratitude." His features softened, and he cracked a charming half-smile turning his eyes to Kara again.

"You're right," he replied, his throaty voice like warm honey rolling over sharp rocks, "and thank you, Kara." She returned the smirk, doing her best to remain indifferent.

"You're welcome, Lucian. It's good to see you are recovering." The fire rose in her, and she looked away from his intense stare back to Marciela.

"As for the situation, we've made a bit of progress. We went to Lapidis and recruited a second dwarf, Gondyr's brother. Our Necromancer is visiting with the Undead Faction to see if they have any leads for us. And we have plans to meet with the Gryphons and the Tree Dwellers soon," she told Marciela.

"What situation?" Lucian finally asked.

41

"It would seem that the Demigods have grown restless with their exile from Ess'Magis," Marciela told him, "and are plotting against the High Gods, putting us all in great danger." On hearing this, he moved to the chair next to Kara and sat down, clearly distressed by this news. "Kara is building a team and gathering support from the Factions." She looked down her nose at him, "your rescue secured the Vipers support," she finished.

He looked from Marciela to Kara as he digested what she told him, his eyes shimmering with that icy blue. The tension was palpable. The heat coming off him lent heaviness to the air between them and she inhaled the intoxicating scent of coffee and lavender that lingered on his skin. It was breaking her focus.

"Who is she recruiting from the Vipers?" he asked the First Fang, not taking his eyes off Kara.

"That depends." Kara spoke instead. She was getting a little frustrated with his attitude, though.

"On?" He asked as he gave her that little half-smile again.

"You," she replied, holding his stare. Marciela was watching this unfold, and Kara sensed she was equally frustrated, though slightly amused under her calm, collected mask.

"We had hoped that you would be up for it, Lucian," Marciela finally broke the tension, "but we could volunteer any of the Ammodytes." Those were the top Vipers, the Pit Leaders and most well-trained, deadliest assassins in the Mortal Realm, excluding the two Fangs.

"That won't be necessary," Lucian replied, "I've got a debt to pay. I'll gather my things and meet you at the Travel Stone...don't leave without me." With that, he got up and left.

"Lucian is a good man, and one of the best Vipers I've ever seen. But he's been through a lot..." Marciela faltered for just a moment, then collected herself, "even before the prison. He's angry, he's broken, and that Spirit is complicating matters. Please keep him safe. Don't let him make irrational decisions." She looked at Kara with sadness in her eyes. "I am only allowing this because I know he won't work through it wallowing around here all day, and he can't go back to The Den until we agree that he's ready."

"You have my word," Kara simply replied.

***

As Lucian filled a small pack with clothes and provisions and gingerly put on his leathers for the first time in five years, he couldn't keep his mind from wandering to the elf. Her eyes were unlike any he'd ever seen. Bright opal irises that shone stark against black pools, framed by full violet eyelashes and shimmering scars of branching electricity, likely from a wayward spell that left its mark. She wouldn't have to lift a finger to kill, those eyes could stare daggers into the heart of any man. And something about her was so familiar, but he couldn't put his finger on it.

She was also beautiful...truly breathtaking. Clothed in a thin, white top that left little to the imagination draped off one well-toned shoulder, and black pants that hugged her legs. They highlighted a lean, but powerful

43

silhouette decorated with the markings of her clan and conquests, sprinkled with battle scars covering supple, sun-kissed skin. Long wavy locks of deep violet framed her face, punctuated only by the slightly curved points of her ears, and cascaded down to the middle of her back. Her features were somehow both sharp and soft, a striking balance of lines and curves. Lips akin to ripe pink berries, high commanding cheekbones, an expressive brow...but those eyes. They burned with white hot fire, and he was mesmerized.

"She's clearly a force to be reckoned with...not just anyone could stroll into the Crypta and walk out with one of The Mormagi's prized prisoners unscathed," he thought aloud. He could sense a real depth within her, a story weaved with tragedy, loss, and regret. One much like his own...and he found himself drawn to her, even as he knew he shouldn't be. He couldn't be. It wasn't like he had much to offer her anyways.

"She...excites us!" Ira suddenly hissed.

Lucian sighed. He should be better at controlling his feelings. Especially now...he had a mark to fulfill, and a debt to pay. He didn't have time for distractions. And having a spirit parasite feeding on his emotions was a serious distraction.

"Leave it be Ira," he told the Spirit, "I've got a job to do, and you need to keep it in your fucking pants." Ira just laughed inside his head. He finished dressing, still sore but in far better shape than he'd been for quite some time, grabbed his pack, and headed out.

***

Kara waited by the Stone anxiously. She paced back and forth in front of the great rock, with its veins of golden magic like thin molten rivers that sparkled when a dwarf or wearer of a Stone Charm drew near. Lost in a sea of conflicting thoughts, she jumped with a start when Lucian came up out of nowhere.

"You wouldn't last a day in the Vipers," he laughed. She just looked at him, eyes squinted, and brow furrowed, clearly annoyed.

"Maybe in another life," she quipped with a sly smile, then put her left hand on the Stone, grabbing his arm with her right hand, and they were gone.

They landed in the center of the Citadel's courtyard, both on their feet, and Lucian looked around. She loved watching each new person take it in - this place was truly remarkable. A large tower to the north served as the most communal area as it contained multiple floors of bedrooms. The library and kitchen were on either side of the tower, long curved rooms with high ceilings, and then the stables past the library and the small blacksmiths forge past the kitchen completed the circle around the courtyard, which had a training area, a fire pit, and a spot with canopies over large branches staked in the ground for extra stores of supplies.

Her favorite thing was that it technically existed at the crossroads between Realms, so it had its own magic. Rooms appeared, grew, and changed to suit the needs of whoever occupied them. You could see the shimmer of magic on everything, which included the land around it. A thick of trees spread all the way around, and within it a beautiful spring, boasting multiple pools and small channels of cool sparkling water.

"Not a bad base of operation," Lucian said, clearly impressed.

"It's really not," she replied and started walking to the north, "the tower is where you'll find a room. Be warned, the rooms change the longer you stay in them. And the kitchen resupplies itself with basic items regularly, so we try not to take too much from the surrounding forest. There's a spring out past the library to the west where you can bathe, and further up we gather water from. We all help with the cooking and upkeep. Oh, and don't touch Nalor's forge unless you desire fewer fingers." She was only half-joking. She led him inside, a small seating area with couches and a fireplace in the very center, and a staircase spiraling to the left up, around the interior edge of the tower. "Library to the left next to the stairs, kitchen to the right. You won't be able to open a door to a bedroom that doesn't belong to you without an invitation, so find an open one. Lunch is in a couple of hours, and the newest recruit has the honor of cooking their first meal here. I doubt Maricela raised a boy who can't cook, so I'm sure you'll do fine." She gave him a little wink and headed upstairs to her room.

***

'This is going to be tricky...' Lucian thought to himself as he watched her walk up the stairs and disappear around the corner. He stood there for a moment, making sure she was gone, then headed for the kitchen.

"We like her," Ira hissed. Lucian really hated having the Spirit in his head right now and just ignored him. He walked into the kitchen and looked around. To his surprise, he found a kettle, a small jug of spring water, and coffee beans on the dining table. He was just thinking about making a fresh pot.

"Well, that's convenient," he murmured. After setting his pack down in one of the chairs, he got to work on the coffee, doing his best to keep focused on that and not allowing his mind to wander where it shouldn't. As the coffee brewed in the kettle, Lucian walked around the kitchen, taking stock of the spices and ingredients at his disposal, and started to plan lunch. Giard'in Capallina...he hadn't made it in so long, and it was one of his favorites. He had everything he needed - pasta dough, tomatoes, basil, lemon, garlic, red peppers, black peppercorn, and butter. He knew that elves and nymphs were vegetarians, choosing not to ingest other animals, but the dwarves would likely appreciate a nice meat stuffed roll to go with it. He found Lepri'dae meat, and some additional spices for those.

The Necromancer was a mystery - Ira loved meat, but does an incorporeal being eat or drink? He pondered on that as he enjoyed a hot cup of coffee, which was better than he expected, though he would need to get a proper kettle set soon. As he sat in a chair, the aroma brought two nearly identical dwarves into the kitchen, followed by the nymph from the night of his rescue. He had known another nymph once, lithe little thing. But this one seemed much younger and far more innocent. Her big eyes didn't hold a lot of wisdom or depth. This world wouldn't take long to change all of that, but he was not interested in being a 'teacher'. He would have to watch his thoughts more carefully, he knew they were telepathic.

"The assassin, I presume," Gondyr greeted Lucian with a smile.

"Did you make extra coffee?" Nalor grunted.

Dahlia didn't say anything, just grabbed a couple of what looked like berry tarts off the table and went to sit in one of the large windows facing out into the forest, as far as she could be while still within earshot.

"Yes, in the kettle," Lucian replied.

"Apologies for my brother, he's not really good at mornings...or afternoons," Gondyr laughed, "I'm Gondyr, and he's Nalor. Dahlia is over by the window." Lucian was surprised by the dwarves' cheerful disposition; he'd never met one who wasn't permanently sour.

"I've never been great at mornings myself," Lucian smirked, and lifted his cup.

"Oh good, you're all here...mostly," Kara said as she entered the room behind the brothers, "where's Aleric?"

"In the library!" a voice shouted from the other room, and only Kara caught Dahlia mouthing the words in sync. Lucian saw her laugh to herself, and that pang of familiarity hit him again. A moment later, in floated the Necromancer, tome in hand.

"Ah, Lucian. It's good to see you up and about!" Aleric smiled.

"I have you, Dahlia, and Kara to thank for that," Lucian replied with that sly half smile as he started cutting the pasta dough in long strips so it would be ready for lunch. "I am wondering, Aleric...do you eat? Just so I know how much to prepare..." he asked hesitantly.

"I don't, unfortunately," Aleric replied, "though I like to have a cup of tea every now and again, purely for nostalgia. I don't require fuel or

48

hydration, so it's not worth the waste."

"Do you have a sense of taste? And smell?" Lucian was fascinated. He'd never had the chance to have a conversation with a Spirit like this before.

"I have both, but without a digestive tract, well it just kind of falls on the floor," Aleric laughed.

"Good to know," Lucian said and continued with his pasta preparations.

"Alright, since we're all here," Kara started as she poured a cup of spring water, "we received a letter this morning from the Tree Dwellers while I was gone. They need our help locating a group of elves that went out to investigate a strange magical interference in Cylendri Forest and have yet to return. If we can help, we will gain an audience with their Sovereign." She took a long drink of her water before continuing, "Dahlia, Lucian, I'd like you both to accompany me, assuming you're up for it," she looked at Lucian.

"I'm ready," he replied.

"Good. We'll have lunch and head out afterwards." Kara finished her water, and continued, "Gondyr, any luck with the Gryphons?"

"Nothing yet," Gondyr frowned.

"We can't wait much longer for a response...if we haven't received one by the time we return from the forest, then I say we just go to the Castellum In'Caelo and see what happens," she replied. Gondyr nodded in agreement. "Aleric, how did it go with the Undead?"

"It went well. We have a Spirit contact that is gathering some intel for us, and we should have an update on the Demigods movements very soon. We do know that Solaris is no longer trapped at the Forge of Giants, his sister Terranis was able to free him. So, I imagine they are devising a new plan as we speak."

"At least we will soon know their next move," Kara frowned. "I will be in the library going over a map of the Tree Dwellers domain in Cylendri Forest until lunch is ready if anyone needs me," she announced, then left.

Lucian continued his prep work as the rest of the group dispersed. He could tell that Kara was frustrated, but she had been thrust into the role of leader and was making the best of it. He wanted to get caught up on all the details with her, but now wasn't the time. And being alone with her didn't seem like a great idea, given his and Ira's apparent desires. It felt good to be useful again, especially in the kitchen, and to be talking to anyone other than Mormagi or Ira, though. As he cut the tomatoes and zucchini, chopped the basil, red peppers, and garlic, and ground the black peppercorn, he put all of it in a large pot with the melted butter, cooked pasta, and lemon over the fire to heat and release the flavors.

***

The aroma wafting into the library was divine, and Kara's stomach rumbled, the single berry tart from that morning had barely satiated her.

50

She made her way back to the kitchen, and found Lucian over the fire, having a taste of whatever it was that perked up her senses.

"It's nearly ready," he said without looking up. She really couldn't sneak up on him.

"It smells incredible," she replied, pouring a cup of spring water and finding a seat at the table. He turned that wicked gaze on her, exuding a perfectly crafted charm that would have already broken a dewy-eyed girl, and she felt the fire rise within. *'Tricky, tricky...'* she thought as the rest of the team gathered in the kitchen.

Five

The Well of Magic

ahlia, Kara, and Lucian made their way through the dense forest from the Travel Stone nearest to Est'alda, The First Tree, home of the Tree Dwellers. It was almost a two-day hike. They were to meet an emissary who could lead them to the camp of the missing elves. If all went well, they would have their audience with the Sovereign that night. But things rarely went well.

"I don't understand how anyone can want to live in this," Lucian growled, clearly uncomfortable in his leathers, "the insects, the elements...the lack of coffee."

"It's too hot!" Ira added in disgust.

"Our bodies are born from the earth and return to it when our spirits leave this Realm," Dahlia replied sharply, the first time she had spoken to Lucian as far as Kara knew, "some of us have a deep respect for that."

Lucian stopped and looked at her for a moment, then smiled slightly.

"Fair enough," he simply said.

The forest began to thin out and the air sizzled with magic, which told Kara they were getting close. She reached a curtain of vines and branches and pulled them back to reveal a gap they could squeeze through. On the other side was Est'alda, a massive expanse of branches and dwellings high up in the canopy that grew from one tree with a trunk the size of The Den in Dellalun. This tree had stood for millennia, since the First Elves, and had been home to the Tree Dwellers for as long. They were agile, nimble archers and Elemental Mages. Not entirely different from Kara, though a bit smaller in stature with larger ears. They made incredible assassins, and she had known a few during her time with the Vipers.

As soon as they were through the thicket of trees and the pressure of the ward dissipated, the emissary was waiting there for them. She was a few inches shorter than Kara and wore a loose belted tunic of pale green linen, earthy brown skintight trousers, a bow nearly as big as her strapped to her back, and a quiver of arrows at her side. Her long white hair was pulled up in a tight bun on top of her head. An intricate weave of tree roots pale brown in color adorned her arms and shoulders and tapered off as they reached her sharp jaw. These were similar to Kara's clan markings, indicating that her family held the title of Protectors of the Great Tree and its inhabitants.

"The camp is west, this way," she said and started walking. Kara shot a puzzled look at Lucian and Dahlia, then turned to follow the archer.

"We were told the elves had come out here to investigate a magical interference. How did they know what they were looking for?" Kara asked the archer.

"They didn't know what," she replied curtly, "simply where."

Kara waited for her to continue, but when she didn't, Kara then asked, "do you see these types of interference often?"

"No."

"Okay, so an anomaly. That's tricky..." Kara thought aloud.

"Exactly."

Kara looked to her right at Lucian, who was wearing his frustration all over his face, and to Dahlia on her left, who was still marveling at The First Tree and not paying attention. *'These two,'* she thought. He might be one of the greatest assassins the Vipers had seen, but he surely couldn't hide his more volatile emotions if his life depended on it. And she was in a constant mood swing from disdain to elation...you almost never knew what you would get out of her at any given moment.

"Up here, in the tree line," the archer pointed ahead. Kara could make out a couple of tents among the trunks. They approached the camp slowly, looking around for evidence and taking stock. Three tents, three packs, a cold fire. As Kara moved around the edge of the camp, she noticed a scrap of parchment a few feet from one of the tents, and a couple more scraps a little further...a trail.

"Over here," she called to the rest as she knelt and picked up the single

54

piece. It had lines on it like a drawing, and one word. There were drag marks that disturbed the earth, as well.

"We need to grab those other pieces," she said, giving the parchment to Lucian, "and look for more or see if these drag marks lead us anywhere." She went and picked up the other three pieces of parchment - same lines, curving and intersecting.

"I don't recognize this word," Lucian said as he looked at the piece she had handed him.

"Mai'ngolo..." Kara started but was cut off.

"...the Well of Magic," the archer finished, a shadow crossing her face.

"And these pieces look like part of a map...I'm assuming this is not good," Kara frowned.

"Not good at all," the archer replied.

"We have a direction, let's go." And the group headed off along the drag marks, looking for more signs of them. Kara found a few more pieces of the torn parchment as they walked, and realized whoever was being dragged had torn this and scattered it. It looked like about half of the map. The drag marks ended, and Kara lost the trail, but if someone was after the Well of Magic, all they needed to do was get to it.

"The trail is gone. We need to get to the Well, it's the only lead we have," she told the archer.

"I can't take you to the Well," was her sharp reply.

"Why not?" Kara was getting tired of this.

"Because I don't know where it is," she told Kara. "But we must find them. One of those elves is the Sovereign's daughter, and one of the only Tree Dwellers who does know the location of the Well. This is her map."

"Fuck," Kara sighed, "so how do we find them?"

"We have to speak with Nae'lin," the archer said, "I need to take you to Est'alda."

As they headed for The First Tree, Kara could feel the knot in her stomach growing. Something was very wrong here. Whatever, or whoever had taken the elves, was clearly after some immensely powerful old magic, which made them extremely dangerous. She had only ever heard of the Mai'ngolo as a youngling when her father had told her the story of the First Elves. The legend went that the High Gods created a race of pure beings who would live for a thousand years and help maintain the balance between Realms. They would live in nature and serve the High Gods as conduits for the great magic that held the Realms together. But after a few generations, the First Elves grew tired of their "enslavement" and demanded a choice - to be tied to the old magic, or to be free to explore the world beyond it. To ensure there was no disruption of the balance, the High Gods granted their request but advised that those who denied the old magic would never again be able to access it. All elves were descended from these two groups - the Tree Dwellers, who still retained the old magic, and the Independent Clans, who broke away from it. According to her father, Kara was descended from the latter. Nowadays, any Tree Dweller who chooses to leave Est'alda permanently will also lose their ties to the old magic permanently, which is why the only family who knows the location of the Well is the Elder family, they keep the secrets of the First Elves, and the Well holds the old magic.

They reached The First Tree and began their ascent to the top where the Elder family resided. They climbed on branches that intertwined to create stairs, like those in Aquanalis. They passed large dwellings and shared areas built right into the tree that got smaller and more sparse the higher they climbed. As they reached the top, only one dwelling remained, built on top of a great knot of branches.

"Wait here," the archer told them, "I'll be back in a moment," and she headed into the dwelling.

"I only know of the Well from legends and bedtime stories told to children. What is it truly?" Lucian finally asked.

"It's the place where the old magic is held, the magic of the First Elves, that both binds everything together and separates the Realms. It's tied to the Mag'nicelo, to Ess'Magis, to everything. This is not good, not good at all," Kara explained.

"Then we know this has something to do with the Demigods," Lucian said, "who else would be interested in the old magic?"

"Exactly," Kara replied.

The archer came back and gestured for them to follow her. They made their way inside and Kara could feel the pulse of old magic all around her. She looked at Dahlia and asked telepathically, *"do you feel that?"*

"I do," Dahlia replied wearing a look of awe mingled with hesitation.

In the center of the dwelling stood the most regal elf Kara had ever seen adorned in flowing, pale green linen robes decorated with swirls of leaves and branches, and long silver hair that nearly touched the ground, his skin practically glowing. He had the slightest wrinkles around his sage green eyes, a sign of his great age, and wore a crown of simple, but beautifully woven twigs. Kara bowed deeply, gesturing for Dahlia and Lucian to do the same. The Sovereign bowed his head ever so slightly in acceptance and Kara waited for him to speak.

"Sel'arin brings grave news," he began, "and we have to move quickly."

"Agreed. I understand that this knowledge is not given lightly, but without knowing the location of the Mai'ngolo, we cannot hope to find your missing elves or what is behind their disappearance. However, we do have a theory and would have spoken with you about this after we returned with them," Kara explained. "The Demigods..." she let that hang in the air for a moment before continuing, "they are plotting to take control of the Realm of The Divine. We have interrupted their plans, and in their desperation, they may be trying to access the old magic to use against their parents." She could see the fear and apprehension in Nae'lin's piercing gaze.

"That is...disturbing indeed," he finally replied. "We will provide you with a map to the Mai'ngolo, and a few of our best Archers to accompany

58

you."

Sel'arin spoke up, "I volunteer."

Nae'lin bowed his head slightly, granting his permission, and said to her, "please choose two more Archers, and head out immediately. Here is the map," he handed her a small piece of parchment.

They held each other's eyes as she took the map and said, "I will give my life to protect the Mai'ngolo and our people, if necessary."

With that, they headed back down the tree, all somber in mood. About halfway down, Sel'arin stopped to speak with a group of elves, and two of them joined the group. When they reached the ground, Sel'arin introduced everyone.

"This is Kara, Dahlia, and Lucian," she said to her fellow Archers, then turned to Kara, "and this is Balin and Ev'lina, two of our best Archers and strongest Elemental Mages. The Mai'ngolo is about a half day's hike from here. We will not stop again until we reach it. Is everyone ready?"

"Yes," they all said in unison.

"Good, let's get going." And they were off.

***

They reached a clearing in the woods well after night had fallen, and Sel'arin finally allowed them to stop for a moment. The powerful magic here

59

sizzled deep in her bones. She realized they must be close to the Well.

As if reading her thoughts, Sel'arin said, "we're not far, it's just ahead. I need to find the entrance point, so take a brief rest...we could have a fight in front of us."

As Kara looked around the clearing, she noticed scorch marks on some of the trees to the left. She walked over to them and discovered there were traces of Death Magic.

"Wait!" she shouted to Sel'arin, who turned to look at her. "Mormagi...they've been here. Look," Kara pointed at the reddish black marks. Sel'arin and the others made their way to her. Kara put her right hand on the marks, and flashes of furious red magic pounded her mind.

"Fuck!" she exclaimed, pulling her hand back quickly. "They were trying to find the entrance, but I don't think they were successful," she told the group. "They've got to be close by...probably waiting for someone to come looking for the Elves and open the path." Her eyes burned with swirling electricity, and Sel'arin looked at her sharply.

"Are you sure?" Balin asked hesitantly.

"Without a doubt," Kara replied, as Balin and Sel'arin exchanged a strange look.

"Then we need to spread out, find them," Sel'arin finally said. "Balin, you go with Dahlia that way; Lucian with me; Kara and Ev'lina, you go that way." She looked at Balin and Ev'lina, "use your horn if you find

60

something."

The three groups headed off in their respective directions, moving slowly, but diligently. After a few minutes of silent searching, Ev'lina asked quietly, "what happened when you touched the tree?"

"It's hard to explain," Kara began, "like visions, but more feeling than seeing. I could feel the anger, the frustrations, and see the flashes of red magic." The archer squinted her eyes at Kara, but didn't say anything else.

Before long, they saw movement up ahead, red robes gliding between the trees. Ev'lina lifted the small horn around her neck, but Kara stopped her. "We have the advantage, they haven't seen us," she whispered. "Let's get closer first and see what we're dealing with."

They crept closer, light as feathers making almost no sound, and could see there were at least a dozen Mormagi, likely more. They were setting up a Summoning Crystal. Off to the side a bit was a warded cage with the three elves inside, clearly wounded.

"We have to break that crystal, before we have a horde of Risen to deal with, too," Kara whispered. "I'll go straight for it, and you blow that horn as soon as I get close." Ev'lina nodded.

Kara headed around to the right a bit, giving herself a direct line to the Crystal, as the Mormagi moved into place to activate it. Then she burst into a full sprint. As she neared the Crystal, she heard the horn blow, which distracted the Death Mages and gave her the few seconds she needed to close the gap. She slammed a dagger into the great stone, shattering it. The next moment, red streaks of magic were zipping through the air, and an arrow flew right past her, hitting one of those bastards right in the eye. Her dagger sliced through another one before it could blast a spell at Ev'lina, black blood pouring from the wound as it crumpled to the forest floor. Then Lucian came bursting through the trees, Ira's wings carrying him, and two daggers flew from his hands into another Mormagi close to Kara, hitting the Death Mage in the heart and gut.

The next few minutes were a flurry of arrows, daggers, and spells. Red streaked through the air, hitting Balin and knocking him to the ground. Dahlia ran to him and wrapped the wound in a golden healing spell. A tree sprung to life with a flash of green from Sel'arin and branches swung to hit a Death Mage across the head before it tried to hit Dahlia with his magic. Lucian flew to Kara and picked her up off the ground, then threw her into the largest Death Mage, and she shoved a dagger right into his throat. He fell with a great thud that shook the ground. She was up and running a moment later, headed for the last two Mormagi, the earth lifting below her thanks to Ev'lina. Kara leapt over them, spinning forward in the air and dropping an exploding potion between them that blew them in opposite directions as she landed deftly on the ground. Then everything grew quiet.

Balin was still down, but Kara could see he was moving. "Is he okay?" she asked Dahlia.

"He will be," Dahlia replied.

Kara then went to the cage. "Dahlia, come help me with this ward." Kara had learned a bit of Ward Magic from her mother as a child, but this one was more complex than she could handle on her own. They worked

62

together to get the ward down and unlocked the cage. The elves inside were all alive, thankfully, but they were in bad shape. The rest of the group made their way over, Balin being helped by Lucian.

"We need to get them back to Est'alda now," Kara said. "Is there a faster way?" she asked Sel'arin.

"I don't know..." Sel'arin trailed off, the worry clear on her face.

"I can carry two of them," Lucian offered, "but I don't know the way back."

"Ev'lina and I can try to create a gust of wind for you to ride that will carry you straight back," Sel'arin offered, "but it's tricky, and could falter the further you get from us." At that moment, a great winged beast flew into the clearing where they stood and landed before them in a rush of wind. It was the largest owl Kara had ever seen. It easily stood nine feet tall, with large reddish orange eyes, pale yellow and brown feathers with dark red streaks, sharp ear tufts streaked with black that shot out from each side of its face, a sharp black beak, and huge black talons. It stared at Kara, and she stared back in awe.

"*Aqui'noctua!*" Sel'arin exclaimed quietly, "I haven't seen one since I was a youngling..." The owl fluffed its feathers and hooted - a deep, resounding '*oouh-oouh*' - then lifted a talon and clicked it.

"Can you...carry them?" Kara asked, not sure if it would understand her. But it clacked its beak and lifted its wings in response.

63

"Alright," Kara said, still unsure, "Lucian, you grab two of these elves here." He came over and picked two of them up from the ground. They were relatively small compared to him, so he held one in each arm with ease.

"And..." she continued, talking to the owl, "can you carry this one and Balin back to Est'alda?" The owl clacked its beak again, and opened one of its talons for Balin to climb in. He looked up in wonder as he situated himself in the great predator's claw.

"Balin, tell them what happened. We'll do our best to move quickly going back the long way," Kara told him. Balin nodded.

"Lucian, be careful," she said thoughtfully, "and stay with the owl...if you just fly into Est'alda, they might try to shoot you down. But if you show up with this beast carrying Balin, you'll have a better chance." Lucian simply winked, his eyes glowing blue, and took off into the sky. The owl picked up the other limp elf surprisingly gently and took off after Lucian.

"I can't believe we just saw the great Aqui'noctua," Ev'lina said, still bewildered.

"Neither can I," Sel'arin agreed.

"I didn't think they were real..." Kara stammered. "My father loved to tell stories when we were younglings, especially about the forest creatures, but he always made it seem like they were fairytales," she explained. "Okay, we've got to get moving, we have a long hike ahead of us. Let's go."

Six

Amalthia de Lyria

By the time they reached Est'alda, Kara was depleted. The archers were in better shape. Elves had incredible stamina, but Kara had been traveling for the better part of three days now and had had to fight in the process. Her body strained to keep itself upright as they climbed to the largest part of the tree, the lowest layer of branches. They found Lucian and Dahlia speaking with a group of Tree Dwellers outside one of the dwellings.

"There you are," Lucian sighed in relief as he locked eyes with Kara, and she smiled weakly. He quickly made his way over to her, catching her as she suddenly collapsed in his arms.

***

Kara had just fallen into him, so he picked her up and carried her into the dwelling, an infirmary of sorts, Dahlia close behind.

"Is she alright?" Dahlia asked, clear worry in her voice.

"She doesn't look injured, I think she's just exhausted," Lucian replied as he laid her on a moss bed and checked her for wounds. "Help me remove some of this," he said, and lifted her up to a seated position while Dahlia undid her belt and removed any daggers she could find. As he laid her back down, he looked at her face and that pang of familiarity hit him yet again. "I'll stay with her; you go talk to Sel'arin and then get some rest yourself. When she wakes, we'll speak with the Sovereign." Dahlia smiled at him shyly and left the room.

Lucian made himself comfortable against the wall next to Kara, and watched her sleep for a time, her rhythmic breaths soothing his weary bones. She was...different. Unlike anyone he had ever known...or maybe he had known her in another life, he chuckled to himself. What he did know was that he wanted her, though he didn't understand why he was so immediately drawn to her. It was as if she was always there, but just at the edges of his furthest memories, tugging at his desire. When he heard that horn blow in the forest, he knew she was in trouble, and he didn't even hesitate. Neither did Ira, which was strange. It was as if he and the Spirit finally agreed on something. He leaned his head back against the wall and closed his eyes, pining for a cup of coffee. He knew that it would look strange to the Tree Dwellers if he didn't at least appear to be sleeping, so he could rest here awhile, and be here when she awoke.

***

Kara woke up to sunlight on her face. She was a little disoriented, and didn't quite know where she was. As the room came into focus around her and she sat up, she saw Lucian resting against the wall next to her, letting her eyes fall over him for a few moments, just taking him in during a rare moment of peace.

"It's not polite to stare," he said suddenly, that sly smile on his perfect face as his eyes opened to meet hers. Kara blushed, and she knew he had seen it. She looked down at herself, then around for her daggers she could feel were missing from within her leathers, and her belt.

"They're in the basket there," Lucian stated, then asked, "how are you feeling?"

"I'm...good," she replied, reaching for the basket, "thanks...for staying with me, and for saving my life back there. I guess we're even," she laughed.

"I still owe you my life," he said to her as they both got up, and she set about putting her daggers back and belt on, "you did more than just throw a couple of daggers at some walking corpses, you pulled me out of a five-year hell that I had given up hope of ever leaving." She looked up at him and saw just a hint of the man he hid beneath. "I may never be able to repay that debt," he said with conviction as he studied her face, almost as if he were looking for something. She could see that he was desperately sifting through his memories, searching for the place in his life that she had once stood.

"How long was I out?" she asked, changing the subject and looking down again, adjusting her belt to avoid his intense stare.

"Not long, a few hours. You clearly needed it," he laughed.

"Yeah...it was a long day," then she remembered the Tree Dwellers they had found. "How are the elves?" she asked, looking around.

"They're going to be fine...over there," he said, pointing to the other side of the room. Three elves lay out on moss beds, with bandages wrapped around various parts of their bodies. But they were alive, and they would be okay. She did what she came here to do and got more intel than expected.

"We need to speak with Nae'lin," she said, "he needs to get sentries out near that Well, more will come for it."

"Yes, he's already done that, and he's expecting us," he gestured for her to lead through the doorway.

They made the climb back to the top of the tree, though Kara wasn't expecting the warm welcome they received on their second ascension. Tree Elves were everywhere, smiling and waving at them, speaking elvish blessings as they passed, and thanking both Kara and Lucian. It was overwhelming but she did her best to accept them all with a gracious smile. They reached the top, and Dahlia was there, deep in conversation with Sel'arin. They cut the conversation off as soon as Kara came into view.

"Oh, blessed Dea," Dahlia said, hugging Kara, "I was so worried."

"I'm okay Dahlia," Kara smiled, "just needed a little rest."

"Glad you're feeling better," Sel'arin smiled. "Nae'lin is waiting for us inside." They all went into the Elder Families dwelling once more, and the Sovereign was in the exact same spot. His face, however, was softer and kinder.

"The heroes of Est'alda!" he exclaimed, and moved to meet them, taking Kara's hands in his. "Thank you, for protecting the Mai'ngolo, and for bringing our young elves back home," he said, looking to both Lucian and Dahlia, as well, "all of you."

"We are grateful we found them alive, and found the cause of the disturbance...also, for the kindness of the Tree Dwellers," she replied with a smile.

"Of course, you are always welcome here," he started, releasing her hands, and folding his hands in front of him. "Now, we have patrols in place for the Well, so we can hold the line there. However, I believe you have a great task that lies ahead, and I would like to send Sel'arin with you to aid in the protection of our home from the Demigods. Should they succeed in their plans, all Cylendri would fall, swiftly and with great devastation. She is one of our strongest Protectors, and will be an asset I can assure you," he finished.

"We will be lucky to have her, if this is what she wants," Kara said, looking to Sel'arin for her agreement. Sel'arin simply nodded, but that was enough for Kara, she could see the resolve in the archer's eyes. "Alright, then we have more work to do. We will be sure to update you on our progress when we can, and please do the same with any movements around the Well. That is now also part of my responsibility." She bowed to Nae'lin, who returned the bow in full.

"And I thought you might want to use the Travel Stone at the base of the tree this time," Nae'lin said with a smile. Kara looked at him quizzically. "It is one of only two untraceable Stones that I know of," he told her, "we do not like to announce its presence."

"That would be wonderful," Kara laughed.

***

There she was, Amalthia de Lyria, the Viper with Nine Lives. Of course, he hadn't realized it was her when she fell through the ceiling of his cell to rescue him, nor in the days that followed as he desperately searched within his memories. But after seeing her in action a few days ago, he knew she had to be. She was a Viper legend - you couldn't throw a stone in Dellalun without hitting someone who had a story about her. Whether she was a hero, or a villain depended on which stories you chose to believe. And he didn't believe any of them.

But there she was, living another life by the name Kara, and she had rescued him, saved the life he had been certain was over. So, what should he believe? As she and Sel'arin worked around the kitchen, her warm and slightly raspy voice filling the space, he could feel Ira stirring in the back of his mind, equally intrigued and curious by this revelation.

"Nine Lives?" The Wrath Spirit asked.

"I'll tell you later!" Lucian responded sharply under his breath. He was not about to have a chat with his spirit parasite while they were ten feet away. He leaned back in his chair, feet up on one of the large windowsills, looking out into the trees. *'I should visit the spring later, I need a bath,'* he thought to himself. As Ira pricked at his head, wanting to know more about her, he realized that Kara and Sel'arin had stopped talking and were now looking right at him expectantly. He had missed something...

***

"Lucian?" She had pulled him from some deep thoughts, she could tell. His dark hooded eyes sizzled with flecks of icy blue; he and Ira had been having a conversation. The blue faded as he realized she was saying his name, and he came back into full focus.

After a moment, he finally spoke. "I am sorry, Ira was asking about lunch. Spirits have a rather ravenous appetite," he smirked with a little curl of his lip and a raised eyebrow. *"Fuck,"* she thought to herself, *"I wish he would stop doing that."*

"Sel'arin was telling me she has some recipes she'd like to try. Do you mind if she makes lunch?" Kara asked again.

"Yes!" Sel'arin exclaimed. "I have a great one for spiced root and mushroom hand pies!"

"Yes! Hand Pies!" Ira hissed. *"I'm starving!"*

"Dammit, you'll get lunch! Now calm down!" Lucian growled with that thick, throaty accent. She wondered how many hearts that voice had broken over the years.

"Okay...I'll, um, get started then..." Sel'arin stammered, and she quickly went about collecting tools from around the kitchen and laying out ingredients.

"Unless you need help..." Kara started in, but Lucian cut her off.

"I'll help - it keeps Ira quiet when he gets to watch me cook. You can go."

"Alright. I'll be in the library, let me know when it's time to eat." Kara said as she left, a slight thorn in her mood at being told to *'go'*.

As she sat alone, surrounded by flickers of yellow candlelight, she tried desperately to reel in her wandering thoughts and keep her mind on the book she had pulled from the shelf. She must've read the same line a dozen times; she couldn't stay focused on the words as her mind pondered over the last couple of decades. Over what Lucian had seen in that time, what he had done, and how he had ended up in that prison. He had been through so much even before the Crypta, starting back when he was just a boy of nine and his parents were murdered by the vengeful mate of a mark his mother had completed. That's when he had come to live with Marciela, and while he guarded his secrets well, his haunted eyes betrayed him. She knew she shouldn't care, she should let go of this feverish desire to untangle the webs strangling his soul, to unwrap him one layer at a time until all that he was laid bare before her, but she couldn't shake the longing for him. Tricky, tricky. She shifted her thoughts again. At least the team was coming together nicely. Kara felt unsure what she was doing most of the time, but she had assembled an impressive group thus far and was starting to feel a bit better about their chances against the Demigods.

There was Lucian, of course. His years of training in blades, potions, and stealth were an absolute asset to the team, though Ira, and her obsessive thoughts, did complicate matters.

Then Aleric, the Spirit and Necromancer. For such a strikingly haunting appearance, he was exceedingly kind, and well-spoken, which Kara had come to genuinely appreciate over the years. He possessed a wealth of knowledge, both of magic and the histories, and his ability to traverse between Realms gave them a huge advantage.

Dahlia, the Nymph and Mage of Light, who had a sharp mind. Her dry wit and humor balanced her great heart. As a Ward and Healer who also possessed the gift of telepathy and the power of Glimmer Magic, they were lucky to have her on their side.

Sel'arin, the Tree Dwelling elf and Archer who was an expert acrobatic and well versed in Elemental Magic. Her cheery disposition brought much-needed light to the Citadel, and helped soften the moodiness of some of the other members.

Nalor, the Dwarven Bruiser of the Stones Faction, with an impressive array of weapons and armor. Master blacksmith and weapons specialist, who kept to himself at his forge a lot of the time, but whose sourness had sweetened in recent days.

And Gondyr - her friend, her mentor, and the reason she was in this mess to begin with. They had struck a blow at the Demigods early when they impeded Solaris trying to craft the blade and foiled whatever the Mormagi were trying to do at the Mai'ngolo. But she still needed to go to

Castellum In'Caelo and meet with the Gryphons. She had needed a few days to refocus and plan their next move after Est'alda, but Kara knew it was time. They would head out in the morning. Tonight, she would go out to the spring and bathe herself, she definitely needed it.

Seven

Tia & Luca

The night settled in, and the Citadel fell quiet as everyone retired to their rooms. Lucian made his way quietly down the stairs and out to the courtyard, then through the back of the stables, headed for the spring. The moon was large in the cloudless sky, lending plenty of light for the walk through the trees. At night, the glow of magic around this place was more visible, and everything shimmered with it. As he got closer to the spring, a splash in the water stopped him in his tracks. He moved quickly behind the tree ahead of him and looked around to see a naked Kara, wet and bathed in moonlight, facing slightly away from him. His heart stopped and his eyes followed the graceful line from her neck down her left shoulder and over the curves of her body as she stood waist-deep in the water.

"*Fuck*," he whispered as he finally let go of his breath. He stood there for a while, watching her as she swam through the spring, utterly mesmerized, and when she went underwater, he took the opportunity to move to a different spot so she wouldn't pass him when she headed back to the Citadel. Hidden in the shadows, he sat in silence and watched as she emerged from the spring, put on her nightshirt, grabbed her pack, and went

75

back through the forest. Once he was sure she was gone, he made his way to the edge of the pool.

"Who? Is she?" Ira hissed.

"Dammit Ira, why are you so fucking curious?" Lucian responded sharply.

"How could we not be?" Ira asked.

"Fine. The Viper with Nine Lives," he started as he undressed and got into the water, a round bar of lavender soap in hand, "the story of that name goes way back, before she disappeared from Dellalun. She was said to be more feline than Viper, armed with unique prowess that gave her a deadly edge over her marks. And she had cheated death on a few occasions over her years with the Faction." He paused as he washed his face and dunked below the surface to rinse.

"Her last job was a mark on Nero, just before he and his Belua invaded and left half the city a blackened pile of rubble. Rumor has it she died on that mission...twice. The mark was never completed, and Amalthia de Lyria was not heard from again. No one knows exactly what happened, though that didn't stop the stories from swirling throughout the city. One such story claimed that she was last seen with a group of prisoners that she had freed from the camp carrying her body, lifeless and bloodied, out of the Belua stronghold and into Cylendri Forest. People speculated for years on whether she survived that job, and if so, where she could have gone. But no one ever found out."

Ira had quietly listened to the story, clearly enthralled, then asked, *"How? How do you...know it's her?"*

Lucian still couldn't put his finger on why she was so fucking familiar. Surely, he'd never forget those eyes...but every time he grabbed a tendril of memory to trace back, it slipped from his grasp. He'd been at it for days, ever since she returned to The Den and asked for the Vipers aid. She clearly didn't wear the traditional black and green leathers of the Faction, opting instead for a custom deep purple, but she was masterful with daggers, and hid them in her armor the same as he did. She was fast and agile, which wasn't unusual for an elf, but there was something methodical about it that reminded him of the assassins. He was sure he had never known an elf with violet hair, that color didn't exist in the race at all, and yet, her features tugged at his memories, just out of view. Ira could feel his frustration and knew to leave it at that, for now.

Lucian finished cleaning himself, got dressed, and headed back to the Citadel, straight to the kitchen to brew a pot of coffee. Having retired his shirt to a chair, he stood by the fire to warm up and dry off while it brewed, then poured a cup, savoring that first drink. The door to the kitchen creaked open and there she was, ripping him from his mind. Their eyes locked as she stepped into the light, both clearly surprised to see the other. He and Ira both tensed.

"Oh, I didn't think anyone would be in here..." she stated hesitantly. "I was just going to grab a snack."

He watched as she made her way across the room to the pantry, drinking her in. The pale blue night shirt barely covered the curves of her

77

body, just enough to make his desire boil with need. She disappeared into the pantry, allowing him the chance to compose himself, and came back out a moment later with some dried fruits in hand. He stood motionless as she pulled out the chair at the far end of the dining table and sat, leaned back, legs crossed, and studied him as she ate a slice of dried apple. Even the way her lips parted, and her tongue took the piece of fruit into her mouth aroused him. It was fortuitous that he was standing behind a chair at that moment.

***

She had hoped her restlessness would not be noticed by the others as she slipped downstairs to the kitchen. Sleep had regularly eluded her even before this, but ever since Solaris had been trapped in the forge when she and Gondyr stopped him from finishing his weapon, she could not sleep without the Demigods invading her mind. She had been careful to keep that information close to the chest. She didn't want the others to think they were manipulating her. There were more images and random flashes than anything, but she was still cautious. As she stepped into the kitchen, she found Lucian enjoying a cup of what could only be strong coffee, and it stopped her in her tracks. When their eyes met, she saw a flash of something...not fear or anger. Desire maybe? He looked even more haunted standing in the low light from the fireplace, shadows dancing across his bare torso, his snake tattoo almost alive, appearing as though it slithered up his arm. His hair was wet, which meant he had just been out at the spring - she knew she had smelled coffee and lavender as she headed back to the tower, but she didn't see him out there. *"Had he been watching me?"* she thought to herself curiously.

78

She made her way to the pantry, grabbed a handful of dried fruits, and seated herself at the dining table, noticing the air was thick with tension. Hers? His? She wasn't sure. But she finally broke the silence.

"Why aren't you asleep? And why are you drinking coffee in the middle of the night?"

"I..." he started. "I don't sleep much. Else Ira would wreak havoc, especially in the kitchen. But why aren't you asleep? Are you secretly also harboring a spirit?" He asked with that sly smile.

Kara laughed and ate a couple of dried berries before answering. "Something like that," she stated coyly. "Is that why you took the first open room right next to the stairs, so you could be up all-night making coffee without alerting anyone as you sneak around?"

"Yes," he said, that sharpness back in his voice. He hadn't moved from that spot since she walked in, and she was sure he was trying to keep her from seeing too much of him. His walls were high and thick, he had surely spent many years building them to protect himself from anyone ever getting too close. This somehow made her desire for him even stronger. What was he hiding from? He would blame the Spirit, but she knew these defenses were in place long before the Crypta. They sat in silence for a time, and she could hear his deep, even breaths over the cackling fire. It somehow soothed the disharmony that had rooted within her. She knew he was studying her, perhaps trying to uncover her place in his memories. She wondered if he had pieced together who she was in her previous life, and if he had, what he thought of her now.

As if reading her mind, he spoke again. "You know, there's a Dellalun legend that speaks of an elven assassin who cheated death and disappeared from the Vipers. It's said she died and was brought back to life in her own body by a spell that left lightning in her veins and made her an outcast from even her own elven clan. I wonder, have you heard this tale?" His tone was curious and light, but the look on his face betrayed his thoughts. He knew it was her, and she felt the blush rise to her cheeks.

"I have," she stated calmly, hoping he could not see her slight panic in the dim room. She knew it was only a matter of time, but she still wasn't prepared for this conversation. "Do you believe such tales?" She questioned as she ate a piece of dried melon. He finally moved from his spot across the table, making his way to the chair in front of her. He sat down, never taking his eyes off hers, and crossed his arms over his chest, coffee in one hand. He took a long sip before leaning back and answering.

"Usually? No. But here you sit, Amalthia de Lyria. A ghost. A fairytale. Living a completely different life." His brow furrowed and she had to steady her breath. "So, what am I to believe?" He asked, taking another drink. The scent of rich coffee and lavender invaded her senses as she fought the overwhelming urge to crawl on top of him at that moment. He had figured her out, but it would seem he still hadn't put the whole puzzle together.

"I wouldn't dare tell you what to believe. But I also won't lie...I was once a Viper," she admitted, "and I did die that day." She tore her eyes from him as she said it, not wanting to see the look of disgust and disappointment he would surely give her. She had abandoned her cause, her family, her mark. No matter what happened that day, the Vipers would never have forgiven her mistakes and never have allowed them to go unpunished. So, she built

80

herself another new life, the life of an outcast...no clan, no faction, no family, no home, no purpose beyond survival. And she never could have imagined that Marciela's grandson, of all the souls in Cylendri, would find her.

***

Lucian had his answer, and yet he still couldn't believe it. As he weighed the truth she had just laid before him, he saw her armor fall briefly. She was scared, afraid to face him in that moment, afraid he would despise the woman she once was. But how could he? Her story was no different from his...he had made a terrible mistake, and it had cost him dearly. He had not completed his mark either, instead becoming a prisoner and test subject for that fucking Mage. If anyone understood, it was him.

As she avoided his gaze by picking through the fruit left in her hand, he noticed just how breathtaking he found her. It wasn't her body, desirable as that was. It was something much deeper, it was something within her heart that he could sense beyond the powerful facade she showed the world. She was just as lost as he, yet fought so fiercely to help others find their way, even knowing she may never again find hers. He admired and respected her.

He set his coffee on the table, slid to the edge of his chair to be closer to her, and gently lifted her chin to again meet her hesitant eyes. "As far as I'm concerned, that was a different life. Whoever you were, whatever you did or didn't do, it doesn't matter anymore. You are here, Kara. This is your life now, and I promise I won't ever hold who you may have been before against you," he smiled. Not that guarded, sly smirk he gave everyone. This was a genuine smile that softened his face and shone brightly in his eyes, and he could see her nervousness melting away.

As she looked back at him, allowing every one of her defenses to fall, the curve of her lips caused a distant memory to puncture his mind like a spear. He had known her! It was the same unmistakable look of affection that first ignited his boyhood passions. His breath caught in his throat as the flood of memories now came in waves, crashing against him. She was there when Marciela took him in as a young boy after his mother and father were murdered. She was there when he was initiated as an Ursinii Viper, and again as an Aspis inducted into his first Pit. She had been there throughout his Shadow Viper training as a Walser until he became a Berus about to gain his first solo Mark - she had shown him how to throw a dagger with deadly precision, how to hide his blades within his leathers, how to brew the perfect exploding potion. She had helped to shape the assassin he now was. How the fuck could he have forgotten her?! And how could he not have known it was her the minute he saw her? What else had that fucking monster in the Crypta stolen from him?

It was, in part, the eyes - those were quite different then. Still beautiful, but not the striking eyes sizzling with power they are now. The spell that saved her life must have changed them. And she didn't go by Amalthia or Kara back then. But now that he saw her, now that he knew it was her, he realized that otherwise she hadn't changed too much. Her hair was white and much shorter before, and she didn't have as many tattoos or scars. But that was twenty years ago, and she had hardly aged. Then he remembered - elven blood. They, like Nymphs, aged impossibly slow compared to humans and dwarves.

***

Kara looked deep into Lucian's eyes as he studied her. And as she did, she saw something else...a flash of recognition. He finally remembered her. She could see him working through it as his eyes searched her face for the faint scar his dagger had left on her cheek the last time she had seen him during a rousing bout of training before his first assignment. They sat there in tense silence, his hand still holding her chin, close enough to share a breath, but he wasn't breathing.

"Tia?" He finally whispered.

"Luca." She whispered back.

His hand dropped, but he held her gaze. "How is this possible?" He was still piecing it together. "They told me you left. I returned to find you gone, and all they told me was that you left. No goodbye, no explanation. You were just...gone. You could have been dead for all I knew, and apparently you were! I was so angry..."

The pain in his voice pierced her heart. She had never wanted to hurt him, but she couldn't have known when she left Dellalun to handle the mark that she would not return. Then it hit her – she was responsible for at least part of the pain and loss that caused him to build his walls as he did. She had abandoned him, without so much as a word, and he had never known why. He must have blamed himself, tormented by the thought that his mentor didn't care for him as he cared for her. A single tear fell down her cheek, over the scar he'd left, and her regret was surely plain on her face.

83

"Oh, my sweet Tia," he said calmly as he wiped away the tear, "you didn't leave. You were lost."

"I'm so sorry Lucian...after what happened, I knew I couldn't return to the Vipers. They wouldn't understand, they wouldn't let me come home. I lost everything that day, and I honestly believed that I would never see you again. As far as the Vipers were concerned, Tia was dead, and she would stay dead." He stood up, the anger within rising to the surface. His eyes glowed that icy blue, wings sprung from his back, and Ira made a full appearance.

"She lied to you!" He spat. And for a moment Kara thought he was talking about her.

"I...I didn't lie..." she stammered, but he cut her off again.

"No! Marciela...she lied! She knew...and she lied!" Ira was taking it personally, and Lucian was struggling to gain control.

"We don't know what she knew. But we are going to find out." Lucian growled. Even as his eyes went back to normal, and the wings retracted, she could see he was still furious.

"All she could have known, if anything, was that I died. Perhaps she was trying to save you from that pain by allowing you to believe I was still out there somewhere..."

***

84

At that moment he pulled her up from the chair, wrapped her in his arms, and held her tightly to him. He had believed a lie for twenty years, a lie that had shrouded his heart in stone, and now that he knew the truth, he would not let her get away from him again. Her warmth crashed against his body, a warmth he had all but forgotten even existed in this cruel world. But she was here, they were together, and nothing else mattered.

Eight

A Treacherous Climb

Gondyr met Lucian and Kara at the Stone in the courtyard the next morning, both clearly restless. They were up most of the night, talking in the kitchen. She had been so frightened of him figuring out who she really was from the moment their paths again crossed, but he had taken it unexpectedly well. There was so much more to him than she could have known, and while the tension between them was still strong, part of it had alleviated. She felt more focused, and ready for the next task.

"To the Fortress in the Sky," Gondyr said as they all put their hands on the Stone and were gone. They appeared a few moments later at the base of an ancient staircase that zig-zagged up a steep and rocky mountainside. The stairs led to a great fortress at the top of the mountain, Castellum In'Caelo. The Gryphons made their home here, and you had to brave the trek up the mountain to reach them. The further you got up the stairs, the more dangerous it became - ice, wind and snow reduced grip and visibility, while jagged rocks punctured the path that you would have to climb over. But compared to her last few adventures, this looked like a breeze to Kara. And while Lucian couldn't use his wings due to the wards here, he was a

Viper, he could handle this. Gondyr might struggle, though.

"I never thought I'd make this climb again," Gondyr sighed, and Kara remembered that he had started training as a Gryphon many years ago, before they met. But he didn't finish his training, and never took the *Alis Aquilae*, the vows that made one a full-fledged Gryphon. He had never told her why, and almost never spoke of those years. "No use delaying it, let's go." They began the ascent, Gondyr leading, followed by Kara and then Lucian, finding themselves climbing another great structure to ask for aid in this rebellion.

The first leg of the climb wasn't too bad, but the air got colder and thinner as they made their way, making it difficult to breathe at times. After a while, they came upon a broken section of the stairs and had to use the jagged, icy rocks against the mountain to climb across and reach the stairs on the other side. One misstep or misplaced hand meant almost certain death at this height. Gondyr was surprisingly nimble as he worked across the rocks and made it to the stairs first. Kara could hear Lucian grunting behind her, following the same route, slow and steady. They all made it across, and continued up the steep, slim path.

They were a little more than halfway when the snow began, adding a layer of difficulty to their climb. Big, fluffy snowflakes fell, making every step that much more dangerous. And the staircase was mostly just rocks jutting out from the mountain at this point. One in particular as they were nearing the top gave little in the way of deep hand holes or flat edges to rely on. Kara thought she had a good grip on it as she reached across a large crack to the other side, but her right hand slipped. If Lucian hadn't been there to catch her wrist as she fell, that would have been it. She hit the rocks below

87

with her chest as he struggled to hold on to her, and grabbed a sharp edge, cutting her left hand, but she held it tight and got a good footing. Lucian lifted her as she pushed up and found a hand hole in the rock he was hanging onto, blood pouring from her hand, then pulled her into him so she could get herself readjusted on the rock and quickly wrap her hand with a small cloth from her pack before trying again. Gondyr looked back and waited for them both to get across. "You alright?" he asked warily.

"I'm fine, thanks to Lucian, just a little scratch," she looked back and smiled at him. He returned the smile with a wink. They continued up, taking it a bit slower, and made it to the top a brief time later. Gondyr got there first and helped pull Kara up over the ledge from the last large rock, and then they pulled Lucian up together. They all sat there for a few moments, catching their breath. "Well, that was something," Kara laughed, "how many times have you done that Gondyr?"

"Too many," he replied with a sigh.

"Once is too many," Lucian chimed in.

"Which is why we don't get many visitors," a voice behind them spoke, deep and smooth. Kara jumped up and turned to find three Gryphon warriors in full armor standing at the gate of a massive stone rampart. They looked to be two humans and a dwarf, whose armor gleamed in the snow and great white wings speckled with earthy browns that nearly touched the ground arched from their backs. The one at the front had dark, tanned skin, short dark hair peppered with white that balanced the brightness of his wings, and sharp golden eyes. He looked to be Terastralis, from the southern deserts of Cylendri. Kara and Gondyr had spent a number of years in those lands after leaving the North, and knew they were some of the strongest warriors in all the Realms. Resilient, resolute, and disciplined from birth - they made the best Gryphons.

"You mind telling me why you're standing on our threshold?" He asked, eyes trained on Kara.

But Gondyr stepped forward and spoke, "We sent requests for an audience, and got a little worried when we didn't receive a response, so we thought we'd just check in, make sure everything was alright," he said with a smile. Kara got the feeling that the Gryphon was not amused.

"You climbed the Path just to...check in?" he asked incredulously.

"Why don't you go get the Lord Gryphon and tell him Gondyr is at the gate." The Gryphon narrowed his eyes at Gondyr, who held his smile as he spoke.

Without breaking eye contact, the Gryphon simply said, "Pytra," and the female, also Terastralis with darker skin, a single braid of long onyx hair, and golden eyes, turned and flew into the sky, disappearing over the wall. "You still haven't told me why you're here," he continued.

"We'll just wait for Rowan, if you don't mind," Gondyr replied, "that way I don't have to repeat myself." Kara and Lucian exchanged tense glances. They didn't need to be antagonizing the Gryphons; they needed their help. But Gondyr's words hung in the air as they all stood silently in the cold snow. A few minutes later, Pytra returned with another Gryphon, a human who looked to have some Belula in his blood due to his great stature. He

89

wore his thick midnight curls loose around his face, falling right at his broad shoulders, and his large golden eyes sparkled with ferocity against his olive skin. His armor was embellished with intricate gold that laced around all the edges of each piece and met in the center of his breastplate as a great golden sun. The Lord Gryphon, Rowan, landed lightly for his massive size, a scowl fixed on Gondyr.

"In all my years," he started, "I've never seen a dead man still walking around in his own skin." His words added a layer of tension to the air around them, and Kara put both hands on her daggers.

"Because dead men don't," Gondyr replied, "but free men do." Furtive glances were exchanged all around as these two men stared each other down. Then, to everyone's surprise, a deep bellowing laugh erupted from Rowan. He moved to Gondyr, lifted him off the ground, and gave him a great big hug. Kara glanced at Lucian, a look of perplexity on his face.

"It's good to see you, old friend!" Rowan smiled wide as he put Gondyr down.

"And you," Gondyr replied, clearly amused, "though I could've done without that pointless climb," he laughed. The three Gryphons, Kara, and Lucian were all still tense, hands on weapons, ready to strike.

"Stand down Markus, Pytra, Doramyr," Rowan said, "we have guests."

"Kara, Lucian, this is Lord Gryphon Rowan. You can let go of your daggers," he winked at Kara, "Rowan, this is Kara and Lucian."

"You always did keep strange friends," Rowan replied. "Please, come in out of the snow, you must be tired, and hungry after the climb." Rowan and Gondyr led, heading through the massive gate, followed by Kara and Lucian, and finally Markus. Pytra and the dwarf Doramyr stayed behind, standing guard. Kara took stock of everything as they made their way through the courtyard and into the Fortress. Two great towers stood to the left and the right, connected to the main hall by small bridges about halfway up. The main hall itself rose up into the sky, an impressive stone structure with large windows and walkways around the outside. Gryphons were going about their work, some younglings without wings training in the courtyard, others carrying provisions and tending the stables. Kara wondered how they got horses up and down from here as they passed by. They headed inside the main hall where great fires burned along the walls offering warmth and light. There were grand staircases to the left and right, and large tables in three lines down the center with food and tomes and parchment scattered around them, Gryphons seated throughout eating or studying. They followed Rowan and Gondyr to the right and up the staircase on that side. Kara could feel Markus' eyes on her back, like he could see inside her, straight to the caged power. As if sensing her discomfort, Lucian put his hand in the small of her back and moved to the left a bit, putting himself between her and Markus. She knew if Markus could sense that in her, he damn well could sense Ira...but Lucian didn't seem to be bothered. She was grateful for his calming presence.

They weaved through the halls of the great Fortress, Rowan and Gondyr talking, catching up on the many years since they last saw each other, as the rest of the group silently followed. Eventually, they reached a large room with three desks on each side, shelves of books and tables with different weapons and trinkets on them behind the desks, and a great table

91

in the center with a map of Cylendri spread across the top. Two fires warmed the space, one in each of the rear corners, and candelabras with candles at various stages of burning sat on a few of the tables and desks. There were chairs scattered around the center table, and Rowan gestured for everyone to find a seat.

"While I'm happy to see you Gondyr," Rowan began as they all got situated, "I'm concerned this is not a social visit."

"Your concern is valid," Gondyr replied. "Did you not receive my letters?"

"We did not. We have had a problem with the ravens as of late, something is affecting our wards here and causing the birds to change course unexpectedly, more than half of them avoiding the Fortress at all costs, while others have been thrown off course and into the stone walls," Rowan explained, his eyes narrow and brow furrowed, "I've never seen anything like it."

"We might have an explanation," Kara finally spoke. This was her responsibility, and she knew it was time for her to establish herself to the Lord Gryphon. He looked at her now, studying her closely as this was the first good look that he got at her. She was used to it by now, it was the same look she was always being given, one mixed with fear and uncertainty. "That's why we're here."

"And who are you in this story?" Rowan asked her.

"The bearer of bad news, it would seem," she replied.

Rowan laughed. "Great leaders usually are," he said. "What bad news have you brought to us?"

"The fate of the world is at stake," Kara started, "as the Demigods have declared war on Ess'Magis and the High Gods. We have managed to disrupt their early plans, but eventually they will succeed if we don't do something to stop them. So, we are assembling a team and bringing the Factions together to fight." Rowan's smile had faded into a scowl at hearing this.

"What plans have you disrupted?" he asked. Kara told them of Solaris at the forge and the weapon they stopped him from creating, as well as the fight outside the Mai'ngolo. He and Markus listened intently and looked at each other when she finished talking.

"That certainly explains the problem with the ravens," Markus finally said, "the wards are tied to the Mag'nicelo, and if there's a disruption to the balance, it would surely affect any magical barriers." *Except for the Citadel,* Kara thought to herself. She hadn't really considered it until this moment, but the magic there seemed to be unaffected. She needed to have Aleric investigate that.

"We could use a Gryphon on our team, and the aid of the Faction. Not only are you the greatest warriors in Cylendri, but your access to the Histories could be a great asset in the search for a solution on how to stop the Demigods," Kara said.

Rowan weighed her words as he thought, and replied, "this isn't a fight we could avoid even if we wanted to. You have the support of the Gryphons. As for the team," he looked at Markus, "I believe you would be the best asset we could offer."

"I agree," Markus simply said, bowing his head slightly.

"Then you have what you came for," Rowan told them, "please go enjoy some food and some rest for the night, we have plenty of room for all of you," he smiled and stood.

"I'd like to see the Library, Lord Gryphon," Kara requested, "if possible."

"Of course!" he exclaimed, "and *'Rowan'* is fine."

"Wonderful," she replied with a smile, "though I would like to eat first." They left the office and headed back downstairs to the main hall. Rowan set them up at a table near one of the fires with meats and cheese, fruits, vegetables, and mead of various flavors. Kara was famished but did her best to eat slowly and deliberately. Gondyr tore into his food, as dwarves do, and Lucian savored each bite with a smile, stealing glances at Kara.

"I'll head to the Library after this," Kara said between sips of tart, spiced Rootmead, "I want to speak to the Historians and see if they can find any information to help us. Plus, I've always wanted to see the Library of Cylendri," she smiled.

"Be careful," Gondyr said with a laugh, "if I know you, you'll not want to leave. I'll find us a few beds while you do that."

"I'd like to go with you," Lucian told Kara, and she looked at him puzzled. "You're not the only one who doesn't want to pass up the opportunity to visit the Histories," he smiled.

"Fair enough," she replied, and they finished eating in comfortable silence.

***

Lucian couldn't believe he was about to see the Library of Cylendri, the most detailed and dynamic collection of information in the Mortal Realm. Documents dating as far back as the First Elves - clan lineages and family trees and Faction histories, journals, tomes, and musings collected over thousands of years. The Den had the second largest collection, and it was but a tiny fraction of what the Library housed. As he followed Kara and another Gryphon, he could feel her excitement matching his, connecting them, and it was amazing. Now that he knew she was Tia, everything made more sense. His desire for her, his familiarity with her, his need to protect her and be near her...he had loved her since he was just a boy and had compared every subsequent lover in his life to her. Now, by some strange and unbelievable twist of fate, they were here about to witness something very few had access to, something they had both wanted to see their whole lives. It filled him with hope, a sensation he had not felt in an extraordinarily long time.

Ahead of them was a great arched door, a good ten feet tall at its peak, dark wood adorned with an intricate floral and vine design made of black iron set into the gray stone wall. They reached the door, and the Gryphon pulled it open as Kara and Lucian walked through and found themselves in the largest collection either of them had ever seen. A cavernous round space with at least four levels above them, walls lined with floor to ceiling shelves filled with books, and two additional rows in rings going in towards the center, which was a large spiral staircase, also lined with bookshelves around the inside. They must be in one of the towers. There was no fire burning here, instead balls of light magic were settled in small stone braziers throughout the space. There were small desks and chairs, as well as a few metal and wood ladders for reaching the higher shelves, making a maze of the pathways through and between the shelves. You could see young, wingless Gryphons copywriting older texts at some of the desks, and much older Gryphons, their wings clipped permanently, moving through the rows or reading in the chairs. He glanced over at Kara and smiled at the look of absolute delight on her face.

Taking his hand in hers, she pulled him to the stairs, abandoning all pretense and just being in the moment with him. They climbed the staircase, stopping along the way to look at books on the shelves around the center, and at each floor to see even more rows and rows of volumes. They made it to the top floor, a smaller space with an even more quiet and still ambience than the rest of the Library. There weren't any large shelves here, just a spread of larger desks covered in books and parchments, and glass display cases holding what Lucian could only assume were exceedingly rare or special tomes. The floors were lined with deep red carpets, the walls with earthy tapestries, minimizing the echoes you would normally have in a space like this. Kara still had his hand as they made their way around the room slowly, looking at each book under the glass.

"This is unbelievable," she said, pure joy in her voice, as she ran a finger lightly down the glass of a case holding *Est'alda L'Gen'isi*, The Creation of the First Tree. One of the oldest known books in all the Realms.

96

"That is quite a volume," a voice spoke from behind them. They turned to see a weathered human Gryphon, pure white hair and a lifetime of wrinkles creasing his olive skin. He, like the others in the Library, wore a simple long linen tunic, belted at the waist with brown leather, and walked lightly on bare feet. It was hard to imagine this man as a warrior, but his deep golden eyes held the wisdom of several lifetimes. "I was granted the rare opportunity to read it in my youth," he said with a smile, "a truly inspiring story." Lucian could tell Kara was about to burst with questions. "What an honor!" she managed to squeak out before putting the lid back on her eagerness.

The Historian smiled, "I am Carmine, the Head Curator. Is there something you were looking for?" he asked.

"Yes, actually. Are there...any volumes here about the Demigods, particularly focused on any weaknesses or...weapons that could damage them?" she said hesitantly. "Oh, I'm Kara, and this is Lucian." Carmine looked down his nose at her, as if searching her very soul for the truth of her intentions.

"Anything to do with the Demigods will be under lock and key in the Sanctuary, a hiding place for the relics and histories of the Realm of The Divine. We don't allow access to that to outsiders, or almost anyone for that matter," he finally told them.

"I wouldn't dare ask for access, Carmine. I do think, however, that you should speak with your Lord Gryphon, and he will tell you what you need to be looking for," she said confidently. Lucian enjoyed watching her be diplomatic - when they really needed it, she led without the reluctance he saw in her when they were alone.

"I will do that," he replied, smiling again. "You are welcome to peruse the Library as long as you'd like, and don't hesitate to ask any further questions you may find here." And he left them alone.

"Well, that was ominous," Lucian smirked.

"It went about as I expected it to...you can't just start asking how to hurt a Demigod without raising some eyebrows," she replied playfully. "Do you want to stay for a bit?"

"Absolutely," he replied. He could spend a lifetime here, with her, and be a happy man.

Nine

The Snake, Betrayed

They eventually made their way back to the beds Gondyr had claimed for them, him snoring loudly in a deep sleep by the time they crawled into theirs. After the climb and the excitement of the Library, she was ready for a little rest, though she knew Lucian would likely be awake all night and wished she could help him sleep. The heavenly smells of breakfast coming from the kitchens pulled Kara from her slumber the next morning.

"How was the Library?" Gondyr asked cheerfully as they all dressed and packed their bags.

"It was amazing," Kara replied with a smile, "and it's possible there are texts that could help us. But it will take time. We should head back to the Citadel...after breakfast." He smiled at her, and they headed down to the main hall. Rowan and Markus were waiting for them, the rest of the Gryphons gathered for the meal around the tables.

"Good Morning friends!" Rowan greeted them, "Come sit with us at the head table." They enjoyed a hearty breakfast of spiced Verris links, baked potatoes with truffles and mushrooms, buttered rolls, and sweet Berrymead over conversation of what lay ahead. When they finished, Rowan asked to speak with Kara alone before they left. He led her out of the main hall to a small pantry past the kitchen. Once inside, just enough space for about a foot of breathing room between them, Rowan looked hard at Kara.

"I spoke with Carmine. We will be looking into the Sanctuary for anything that might help," he started, speaking barely above a whisper, "but be wary. Even places such as this have ears that shouldn't be listening." He raised an eyebrow, "I cannot stop men from chasing their desires, and some men are not satisfied with their place in this world. Do you understand?"

"I understand," she replied plainly.

"Good. Please take care of Gondyr, I have much more catching up to do with my old friend. And please ensure Markus checks in with us regularly. With the ravens being a problem, we are not receiving reports as often. I need him to be my eyes out there."

"I'll be sure he keeps you apprised. We're grateful for the help," she smiled.

"We wouldn't be doing our job otherwise," he replied, then opened the door for her to leave. They met Lucian, Gondyr, and Markus near the entrance of the Fortress, and headed out together. As they passed through the courtyard once more, Kara could see the beasts in the stables this time...Onyx Pegasi! She hadn't seen one in a long time, and they were just as majestic as ever. Markus went to one of the Pegasi and led her out into the courtyard.

"You and Lucian will ride Sable here down to the Stone, I'll carry Gondyr," he said, brushing Sable's coat.

"I'd almost rather climb the Path back down than be carried," Gondyr said with a frown.

"No, you wouldn't, my friend," Rowan laughed. Gondyr stared at him for a few moments, then cracked a smile.

"I did say *'almost'*," he replied with a wink.

"You take care of yourself out there, and we'll do what we can from here," Rowan said, then turned to Markus. "Check in before the New Moon, we should have some information." Markus nodded and helped Kara mount Sable, then Lucian behind her. She did her best to steady her breathing, but having his body against her on this magnificent beast was nearly too much to bear. She leaned forward a bit, placing her left hand on the back of Sable's neck and grabbing a small portion of mane for stability, her right hand on Sable's shoulder. Lucian put his right arm around her waist and pulled in tight, then his left hand on her hip, ever so slightly digging his fingers in.

'Not a bad way to start the day,' she thought to herself as the Pegasus got a running start, then leapt in the air and circled the courtyard before heading up over the rampart, Markus and Gondyr right behind them. Sable took them on a scenic route down the mountain in great sweeps and turns,

gliding over the trees and rocks. For just a few moments, Kara was granted reprieve from the choices constantly demanding her attention, and completely free of obligation's hefty weight. Her eyes closed and grip loosened, focusing on the experience, feeling each breath of the creature between her knees, the wind brushing across her skin as they swayed, Lucian's heartbeat against her back, steady and strong. She could've stayed here in the sky forever.

But soon they were gliding down sharply as they descended onto the Travel Stone. She braced herself for the landing, and they touched down a moment later, Sable slowing to a trot and stopping just a few feet from the Stone. Lucian dismounted, then helped Kara as Markus and Gondyr touched down next to them.

"Thank you, Sable," Kara whispered as she rubbed the muzzle of the beast, who huffed in response and pushed her head into Kara.

"She likes you," Markus smiled, "she's not usually so affectionate." He put his large hands on each side of Sable's face and brought his forehead to the bridge of her nose. "I'll be gone for a while, girl, but I'll be back. Try not to give the Wingless too much trouble." She nuzzled him, then he pulled away, giving her a final pat before she took off to the skies and back up the mountain. "Shall we then?" He said as he walked to the Stone.

***

It had been a couple of days since their return from the Fortress, and everyone seemed to be settling into the Citadel nicely. The space had

102

expanded to include a larger training ground outside, as well as a training room inside for spells and potions. There were also more bedrooms added as the main tower increased its floors. The library had doubled in length, as had the kitchen. Everyone had the space they needed to be alone or be together as they saw fit. Kara was grateful she didn't have to stay on top of anyone, everyone contributed, and no one complained about carrying part of the workload of cooking, cleaning, and tending to the Citadel. It gave her hope that they could do the same with the rest of Cylendri, unite the Factions, Clans, and Tribes, and even some of the creatures who made this place their home, as well.

As she sat in one of the kitchen windows with a cup of lavender and citrus tea looking out into the forest, Lucian came rushing in, a letter in his hand and that icy blue fire in his eyes. "We have to go to Dellalun," he said sharply, a slight panic in his voice, and gave her the parchment.

She read it and returned the look with fire of her own, "The Belua have staged another invasion? Let me get in my leathers, you go ask Markus and Sel'arin to meet us at the Stone ready for a fight." He nodded and left as she quickly headed upstairs. She got into her armor, grabbed her daggers and belt, and went back down, sliding the daggers into their slots on her arms, legs, and torso. She made it outside as Lucian, Markus, and Sel'arin were heading to the Stone, and in a few moments, they were all gone.

They arrived in Dellalun, and the streets were pure chaos. People were running in every direction, shouting, screaming, and in the distance, the rattle of explosions. Without missing a beat, Kara hit a dead run and headed straight for The Den, Lucian and the others right behind. They rounded a corner just before they were out of the Dwelling District, and were face to face with a group of Belua - gigantic creatures, half man and half beast with great curved horns on each side of their head. They were vicious, violent animals who used their size to intimidate and bully others, and Kara hated them almost as much as the Mormagi. They had invaded the city once, many years ago, and Dellalun was still recovering. This could devastate it; they had to stop them at all costs.

Kara threw a dagger into the calf of the nearest one, and he howled in pain. As he turned towards her, she leapt through the air and buried another one in his heart, then pulled it out and threw it to her left, hitting another in the eye. Markus flew in at her right, grabbing one of them by the throat and lifting him in the air before tossing the creature hard into the stone ground with a loud crack. Sel'arin put three arrows in another, and Lucian had buried his Khyber in the chest of the biggest one.

They continued through the city, taking out any Belua that crossed their path and helping the citizens get to safety until they reached The Den, where they found a Summoning Crystal, a horde of Risen, and Mormagi, the Vipers doing their best to keep it contained.

"These assholes are working together!" Kara yelled over the explosions. "Markus, you help the Vipers keep the demons busy! Sel'arin, you take out that Crystal! Lucian, we're on the Death Mages! Now!" She roared and they headed into the battle. Arrows and daggers flying past her, Kara jumped over a demon, dropping an explosion at his feet, and cut through two more with her daggers as she headed straight for the Mages. Lucian was in the air on her right, slicing through demons like butter with his blade, Ira laughing maniacally. As they got closer, one of the Mormagi turned and threw a spell straight at her. She jumped to the side, narrowly

104

escaping it, and flung a poisoned dagger right into the mage's shoulder. Kara watched its thin lips pull back into an eerie grin as it pulled the dagger out, but the poison worked quickly. It shook its head before stumbling backwards and falling to the ground. Within the moments it took Kara to get to it and retrieve the dagger, it was dead. Lucian flew over her, and then sharply dropped into a dive heading for another one of the Mages, twisting this way and that as it tossed spells at him. He used his daggers to lift it in the air through its stomach, black blood pouring to the ground, before dropping it. Sel'arin was helping clear out the rest of the horde after she shattered the Crystal when a Mormagi hit her in the side with a bolt of red. Kara ran for her as Lucian and Markus took out the last of the Death Mages.

"Sel'arin, are you alright?" Kara asked as she slid to her side.

"I'm fine, it stung a little," she said with a laugh, followed by a wince, and she grabbed her side.

"Let me see," Kara said and lifted her hand. The spell had left a large red mark that pulsed with magic. Kara pulled a small vial from her belt and handed it to Sel'arin, "drink this." As she did, the magic waned and disappeared, leaving the mark which would heal.

"Thanks," Sel'arin said, and they both got up. Lucian and Markus both came flying over, landing simultaneously.

"Is everyone okay?" Markus asked.

"Yes, we're good," Kara replied, Lucian nodding. "Let's get inside, and Markus you get a ward on the building." They headed in with the remaining

Vipers, and up the main stairs after Markus completed the ward, assuring everyone inside they were safe. They made it to the secret painting entrance and slipped in, up to the main floor where a few of the Ammodytes were waiting for them.

"That was quite a show you put on out there, Second Fang," the one in front greeted them. She was a Clan Elf, like Kara, with fiery red hair that she wore in a high ponytail, and her wide emerald eyes matched her leathers. Kara noticed a hint of adoration in the way she looked at Lucian.

"Where's the First Fang, Vivvain?" Lucian asked immediately, no preamble.

"She was taken in the fight, we only saw the Belua, we didn't know they had the fucking Death Mages with them, and one of those bastards must've snagged her in the chaos," Vivvain told him. "The Belua are holed up in the Burned District for now, but they will clear out if they got what they came for."

"Fuck!" Lucian and Ira growled together. "I want two Vipers on their movements, now. Send them to separate sides of the Burned District, I don't want them together. I need to know what direction they head, and where they move to," he looked at one of the other Ammodytes, "Now!" he yelled, and the Viper left. "Vivvain, how many did we lose in the fight?"

"Not many, we were lucky that a lot of us were present in the city when they attacked," she said, clearly shaken.

"Ok, let's get some Vipers out on the streets, helping the people and

106

ensuring none of those bastards are still lingering around. Where was Marciela taken from?"

"Her office," Vivvain said. "I'll start sending out Vipers." And she left with the other two Ammodytes.

Lucian headed for her office, while Kara told Markus and Sel'arin to stay put, then followed him. They looked around the space quietly, careful not to disturb anything. As Kara made her way around the desk, she found a parchment on the floor under the rug, a tiny corner peeking out. She pulled it out as she heard Lucian inhale sharply. He was looking at the back of one of the oversize chairs near the fireplace, a small splatter of blood that dripped onto the floor, and another splatter on the rug, as if someone had been hit in the face and fell there. His eyes were filled with deadly rage.

"I found a letter here, it was intended for us," she said walking to him, trying to calm him at least a little. "It says she had news on the Mai'ngolo and a lead on why the Mormagi were after its location. That may be why they took her if they knew she had this information." He took the letter and read it himself, the blue in his eyes lessening, but his anger still clear.

"They knew we'd come for her," Ira hissed, *"the Demigods. They tried to trap us!"*

"And they underestimated us," Lucian said with a scowl, "we won't have a chance to strike back until we figure out what information she had. Otherwise, we're just playing into their hands." Kara was glad he was thinking with a level head.

"You're right, so we need to get a few Vipers on that. We should have news from Aleric when we return to the Citadel that could help us." He looked at her finally, and she could see behind the anger was a real fear - not of anything, but for his grandmother. Belua and Mormagi were brutal to prisoners. "They need her, to get to us," she assured him.

"That doesn't mean they won't hurt her," he replied.

"Then we need to work quickly. Let's go." They headed back out to find Vivvain waiting with Markus and Sel'arin.

"What do we do next?" she asked as they approached.

"We need to know what information Marciela had for us," he showed her the letter, "and we need it soon."

"I'm on it. I'll send a raven as soon as I have something," she said and turned to leave, but Lucian grabbed her wrist. She looked in his eyes as he said, "be incredibly careful. They risked a lot to get to the First Fang for having this information, they won't think twice about eliminating you or anyone else," he finished. She held his gaze and then nodded, acknowledging the risks, and left. "Let's get back to the Citadel, and see what Aleric has for us," he said sharply.

Ten

Demigods & Distractions

So much had happened in the last six days. They had learned that Marciela was still alive and finally had a lead on where she was being held. Cassius, one of the highest-ranking Vipers, would pay for his betrayal. He had sold them out to Nero, leader of the Belua, and was responsible for Marciela's abduction. She had discovered that Aeranis, Demigod of Air & Sky, was after the Mai'ngolo as a means to access the Realm of The Divine. As the old magic was tied to everything and originated from the High Gods, the Well had a direct line to their Realm and Aeranis could pass through it undetected. The Tree Dwellers had been successful thus far in stopping the Mormagi from opening the path to its location, but the attacks were becoming more frequent, and they needed help.

Aleric had learned that Terranis, the Demigod of Earth and Rock, and Solaris, were wreaking havoc on the mines around Lapidis. They had also received a letter from the Nymphs - Aquanis, the Demigod of The Waters, was stirring up the river and the Aqu'immensi where they met just below the City on the Water, their base island now inaccessible as the levels continued to rise. If water levels were rising, that would be a severe problem for a lot of villagers who made their home on the riverbanks, as well as Dellalun, which was surrounded by Cylendri River. Markus had gone to check in with the Gryphons and see if they could spare a few warriors to help in Est'alda - hopefully, they had some good news.

Kara sat in the library, anxiously waiting for the team as she studied the information that Marciela had gotten for them. Vivvain had come through, and at least they knew more of the Demigod's plans now. It seemed like a lot of what they were doing at this point was just distractions for the team, to keep them spread thin and away from the Mai'ngolo. Kara would not allow them to succeed.

***

Lucian was the first in the library, weaving through the tables and chairs making his way directly to Kara. He needed to feel her close to him, to know that she was here, that she was real. After learning that his best friend, someone he had spent nearly his whole life with and considered his brother had betrayed everything they stood for, he was feeling more isolated than usual. She looked up and smiled at him as he approached, and it melted a bit of the icy wrath in his veins. Without speaking, he took her hands, lifted her from the chair, and pulled her into his arms. They stood there for a few moments, suspended in time.

"Is everything alright?" she asked as they pulled away, hands still around his waist, looking up at him with concern in her beautiful opal eyes.

"It's a little better now," he smiled down at her, and kissed her forehead.

"Am I interrupting?" Gondyr asked as he entered the library, a playful smile on his face.

"No sir," Kara replied, letting go of Lucian and picking up the letter she had been studying. Gondyr looked from Kara to Lucian and back, clearly amused. They weren't fooling him, Lucian knew that Gondyr was aware something was brewing between them and had likely known for a while now. They had done their best to keep their passions a secret, but Gondyr was a clever dwarf, and one of Kara's oldest friends, you couldn't get much past him. The rest of the team trickled in, including Markus who had just returned from Castellum In'Caelo, four other Gryphons in tow, and Sel'arin who had brought Ev'lina and Balin with her from Est'alda. Lucian watched as Kara slipped into her steely leadership armor and positioned herself at the head of the table.

"Now that we're all here, let's start with updates," she said flatly. "Dahlia?"

"The Nymphs need help strengthening the wards around Aquanalis and calming the waters. If the levels rise any further there, we could lose the island's foundation," Dahlia reported.

"Sel'arin? What about Est'alda and the Mai'ngolo?" Kara asked.

"The attacks around the Well's entrance have increased threefold. We need a better solution that's less reactive - though the Aqui'noctua have come out in force to aid the Elves, they won't be able to keep it up much longer."

111

"Aleric, you have news from Lapidis?"

"Yes. The Demigods are disrupting work in the mines and have caused structural damage to a small area of Stone City. Solaris punctured a hole in the earth and diverted liquid fire from the core into the city, though he miscalculated the placement and most of that fell into the chasm below. They won't be so lucky if he does it again."

"And Markus? I see you brought some reinforcements. News from the Fortress?"

"Yes, I have some information to discuss with you. This is Pytra, Doramyr, Calisto, and Kratus. They have volunteered to help wherever needed. We have also brought a few of the Pegasi with us, including Sable."

"That is some good news we needed in a sea of frustration," Kara replied. "We know what Solaris and the others are doing, they are trying to distract us so they can access the Mai'ngolo and Aeranis can use it to get into Ess'Magis. They are making a play for the God Forge. If they reach it, Solaris will be able to craft his blade while the others keep the High Gods from getting to him, and we will have no hand in that fight. We cannot allow that to happen, we need to keep the battle in our domain," she said resolutely. The room grew quiet, and Lucian could see Kara working through all their options.

"We need to maximize our efforts, so here's what we're going to do - as soon as you have your assignments, please get yourselves ready and head out immediately, we don't have time to waste here," she commanded. Everyone nodded in agreement, and she went through the assignments.

112

"Aleric, you go with Dahlia to Aquanalis. Take Ev'lina and Pytra with you, they need all the strong Ward & Elemental magic they can get, and the Nymphs will be more comfortable with females than males. Use one of the Pegasi so that you can get there quickly and avoid having to use the river. Let us know when you're ready to leave so one of us can activate the Stone." Aleric and Dahlia nodded, heading out of the Library with Ev'lina and Pytra in tow.

"Calisto, I need you and Doramyr to go with Sel'arin to Est'alda. They could use a couple of warriors to help fight off the Mormagi and will need your Ward magic to strengthen the barrier around the Well. That is our focus, if Aeranis can't break down the wards and find the entrance, then we will have created a large thorn in the Demigods' plans. Take one of the Pegasi with you, as well."

"I'm ready to leave now," Sel'arin advised, to which Calisto and Doramyr nodded. They left the Library and headed straight for the Travel Stone in the courtyard, grabbing one of the Pegasi on their way.

"Gondyr, you take Nalor, Kratus, and Balin to Lapidis. Get that hole plugged and help them fortify the city walls with Stone and Elemental Magic. Then get the Dwarves out of the mines - it's time you speak with the Stone Sovereign, they need to understand what we're dealing with and that we will need their help in the coming battles with the Demigods."

"Rhygan will give us an audience," Gondyr advised, "and we'll get his support." With that, the dwarves, Kratus, and Balin left.

"That leaves us," she said to Lucian and Markus, "and we are going to get Marciela. As far as our intel has revealed, The Belua do not know we have her location and won't be expecting us. Markus, you and Lucian will create a diversion to pull the guards away from where she's being held. I will free her and get her out on Sable. We'll head back to The Den once I have her," she instructed. "Once we've returned, we'll discuss the information you have from the Library."

"Sable and I will be at the Stone, ready and waiting," Markus replied and headed out. Kara looked at Lucian, and he could see the apprehension in her eyes.

"You're amazing, you know that?" he asked.

"I don't feel it," she replied with a sigh, "I feel like I'm just stumbling through every problem that's being thrown at us, making it all up as I go."

"That's all anyone in your position could do," he said, trying to reassure her. "But look at everything you have done. The Factions are uniting for the first time in at least three centuries. The Demigods are growing desperate, they're making mistakes and getting sloppy. The team is strong, and we trust you."

"Thank you, Lucian...I'm grateful you're here," she smiled. "Now, let's go save the First Fang."

***

Kara rode Sable through the night sky a few miles outside of Dellalun's Burned District where the beasts had invaded once before, Lucian flying on

114

her left, Markus on her right. She was headed back to the Belua Stronghold, the place where she had died and lost everything. This time though, she wouldn't miss her mark. She looked at Lucian, who nodded and broke off to head low, then at Markus who did the same. They would go to the front of the camp to pull the guards away while she crept in through the cellar to retrieve Marciela. As she approached the stronghold, she could see Markus and Lucian below, making quite a scene. Belua ran from inside the tower to join the fight, and she had her opening. Sable landed in the trees just outside the wall where the cellar door hid below the ground.

"Wait here girl. I'll be back shortly, and we'll need to get off the ground quickly," she told the Pegasus, who shook her head in acknowledgment. Kara headed for the cellar, making her way quickly and silently. Once inside, the halls were quiet, vastly different from last time. She used the shadows to her advantage, sneaking through the lower halls and past the couple Belua that remained inside, to the cells below the tower. One guard remained, though he was asleep on a pile of hay a few feet from the cell doors. She snuck up on the snoring beast and jammed a poisoned dagger in the side of his throat as she held a thick cloth in his mouth, muffling the sounds of his gurgling and struggling against the poison, which was fast. He was dead within a few moments, and she pulled the keys from his belt.

"A true Viper move if I've ever seen one," Marciela said quietly as she came from the shadows to the door of her cell, eyes trained hard on Kara.

"We have to move quickly," Kara said as she opened the door, ignoring the statement, "Lucian and Markus won't be able to hold the Belua much longer."

Without another word, Marciela followed Kara back to the cellar door along the same route she had entered, and out into the cool night air. "This way," Kara directed her. They got to Sable, and Kara helped Marciela onto the winged beast before getting up herself, then they headed up into the sky. She circled the courtyard of the stronghold just out of range of any weapons, yelled "Go!" and took off towards Dellalun. In a few moments, Lucian and Markus flew up on either side of Sable, and Kara could see the relief on Lucian's face as he looked at Marciela.

They landed on the roof of The Den, Vivvain waiting for them. She rushed over to help Marciela down and hugged her tightly. "We were so worried, First Fang," Vivvain said. Lucian was there a moment later.

"Are you hurt?" he asked as he looked her over.

"Nothing a good night's rest in my own bed can't cure," she said with a smile, pulling her grandson in for a tight hug. Kara jumped down from Sable, giving her nose a rub in gratitude, and Sable trotted over to a flowerbed to snack on the flowers there. Before she knew it, Marciela had pulled Kara into the hug with Lucian, and they all stood there for a few moments, tangled in each other's arms.

As they pulled away, Kara could see a few bruises and cuts on her old friend's face. The fire in her eyes burned at this, but Marciela looked squarely at her and said, "I'm fine, thanks to you. It would seem that the Vipers and Dellalun will be indebted to you for a long time," she smiled. Kara hugged her again.

"Okay," Marciela stated, "enough fawning over me, let's get inside.

116

Vivvain, gather the Vipers," she ordered. They all headed into the common room and waited for the rest of the Vipers to arrive, each going to Marciela to welcome her back, then thanking Kara, Lucian, and Markus for saving their leader. Once the room was full, Maricela stood in front of the fireplace and held her hands up, signaling everyone to quiet.

"Vipers, we have a traitor among us," she started, and hushed whispers trailed through the crowd. She gave it another moment before continuing, "a traitor who will not escape punishment for his crimes. But we need to find him - he will hide himself well, so ask every contact we have, call in every favor we need, and bring Cassius to me," her fury boiled just beneath the surface of her calm exterior. With that, the room quickly emptied, leaving the First and Second Fang to discuss their next move.

"Lucian, I need a few days. As soon as we find him, I will send word," Marciela said. Lucian simply nodded. Then she turned to Kara, "we will be able to focus all our efforts on the Demigods once we handle this business. I trust you discovered the information I had gathered before being taken?"

"Yes, and we have diverted some of our allies to strengthen our presence around the Mia'ngolo, so thank you," Kara replied.

"Good," Marciela sighed.

"Get some rest," Kara told her, "we'll head back to the Citadel and await your raven."

Eleven

Tia's Garden

It had been over a week since Lucian was alone with Kara. The last few days were filled with incoming reports of their team's efforts across Cylendri, and thankfully most of them were positive. Nalor had taken a nasty fall as they were repairing the hole in the wall outside Lapidis due to a rockslide from one of the tremors in the shifting earth, but he was on the mend. Doramyr returned with the Pegasus, who had been hit with a strong spell from a Death Mage that left a giant gash in her side, so Markus was tending to her, expecting a full recovery. Aleric and Dahlia were still in Aquanalis but had sent word they got things there mostly under control and would stay a little longer to ensure the wards would hold up well now that they were laced with Elemental Magic. Kara had her hands full with all of that, and Lucian did his best to stay out of the way, only helping when and where he could. But he knew they both needed a night away from it all, especially Kara. He saw the weight of everything taking its toll on her and had a plan to give her some respite.

He had asked Gondyr and Markus to make sure they were all caught up and had nothing left to handle before dusk fell in Cylendri, then advised

118

they would be gone for the night to Dellalun. Gondyr seemed quite pleased, while Markus wasn't fazed at all. Then he told Kara to meet him at the Stone at sundown and refused to tell her why when she pressed him.

He was ready to show her just how much she meant to him, and nothing had scared him so much in his life. He had never let anyone get close to him. Sure, there had been lovers, purely physical attractions that ended as quickly as they began, but not this. Even before Ira, he kept himself guarded and played the part of charming rogue to perfection. Because the only one he had ever allowed himself to feel anything for had disappeared, and no other would compare. But she found her way back to him. He still couldn't believe it. Every time he looked at her, it was like seeing her for the first time. All those years ago, he was just a lovesick boy pining for something he never thought he could have. Now he was a man, and she was within reach...he wouldn't mess it up this time.

***

Kara was tense with apprehension as she waited for Lucian at the Stone, no idea where he was taking her or why. He came out of the Citadel, with a dashing smile on his face as he made his way to her.

"Where are we going?" she asked hesitantly. He grabbed her hand and simply said, "Dellalun," as she put her hand on the Stone, and they were off. He was strangely quiet while they made their way through the busy streets of the city, hand in hand, down to the private docks off the rear gardens of The Den. Even when she asked again where they were going, he simply smiled that perfect smile at her and kept walking, never saying a word. When they arrived at the docks, a single boat sat in the water, decorated with pillows, blankets, and beautiful little lights of green and gold. There was even a picnic packed, and a bottle of wine, but no oarsman.

"What is this?" Kara asked, not sure what to make of it.

He climbed into the boat, shot her a mischievous look that melted her last bit of resolve, and reached for her hand.

"My lady?" He said sweetly.

She took his hand and stepped in. He made sure she was seated comfortably and then led the boat away from the dock. They glided through the waters around The City of Moonlight. She hadn't seen some of these parts of the city in so long, and they were still beautiful. Cool wind danced across the bare skin of her shoulders as the boat sliced through the water beneath them. She had missed this place. The days were slow and quiet, but Città Dellalun dazzled at night, filled with lights and music and the bustle of life. It was quite different from the village in Cylendri Forest where she was born, and it had called to her for years before she ever set foot on its cobblestone streets.

They made their way just outside the city, away from the array of lights to a secluded inlet with moonlight trickling in through a canopy of trees, and vines of hanging flowers. The scent of white jasmine filled the space...those were her favorite flowers. The whole place felt like a dream.

"How have I never seen this place before?" She asked, those stunning eyes filled with wonder. He guided the boat to the center of the inlet.

120

"Because it wasn't here, not like this," he answered as he secured the oar and sat down behind her. "I found this place after you left and planted everything that grows here."

She turned to face him and was met with a deep kiss...their first. It was filled with hunger, yet she knew they were both still holding back. As they pulled away, breathless and barely satiated, he took her face in his hands and smiled. "I planted each one for you. After you left, I held out hope for those first few years that you'd come back, and I could bring you here. The years in the Crypta nearly stole this place...and you...from my memories. But we're here...together. And everything is as it should be. Do you like it?"

She was speechless. All her fears, doubts, and second-guessing...and he had planted a garden for her! He had loved her even then, and if he wasn't ready to say it now, he didn't have to. This told her everything she needed to know.

"You are...*unbelievable*," she sighed, "how can this be real? How can you...be real?" She stammered. "This is the most extraordinary and beautiful thing...I can't believe you did this..."

"I would give you the whole city if you asked it of me," he smiled, brushing her hair from her face.

He grabbed the bottle of wine and poured a glass each, handing one to her as she laid herself against his body and stared up through the canopy above, taking a long sip. It was a strong, dark wine, with notes of chocolate and oak, and a plum finish. The scent of coffee and lavender on his shoulder mingled with the jasmine in the air...she loved how he always

121

smelled of coffee and lavender. His heartbeat against her back - strong, clear, steady - calmed her racing mind. And though she wanted nothing more than to climb on his lap and feel him inside her, she knew she had to wait. She was always in control, always leading, but for once she wanted someone to take the reins and lead for her.

***

As she sipped wine from the glass and gazed up at the moon peeking through the canopy, he was busy drinking her in, memorizing the lines of her face, the way her eyes lit up and her lips pursed slightly, the way her nose crinkled at the bridge when she was deep in thought, the way her chest rose and fell with each steady breath, the way that every scar on her skin told a story. He would never again let her stray too far from his mind...or his arms. No matter how deeply he desired her, he wouldn't rush this, and he could only hope that she would wait for him. What beautiful agony...he wanted to feel her, to taste her, to explore every inch of her and discover all the ways he could please her. So, he would woo her, he would cradle her heart in the center of his strength, showing her everything he'd be willing to do for only her, and then he would have her...heart, mind, body, and soul.

"If you don't want to talk about it, I understand," he started hesitantly, "but would you...would you tell me what really happened on that final job, and why you left?"

She sat up, took a deep breath, and just stared off in the distance.

"Dammit," he thought.

122

"You shouldn't have asked!" Ira hissed, and Lucian pushed the Spirit from his mind.

"I'm sorry. You don't have to tell me..." he said as he ran his fingers down her arm and took her hand in his.

"No," she replied, "I want to tell you. I just..." she turned now to look at him square in the eye, and he could see how difficult this was for her. He was so mad at himself for bringing it up.

Grippin his hand tightly, she continued, "I haven't actually told anyone. I've never spoken of it since I recovered, and I almost don't know where to start."

"Take your time," he said softly.

She inhaled deeply, held it for a moment, and released the breath slowly before beginning. "I met my contact at a small camp not far from the Belua Stronghold. He gave me a key to the cellar door underneath the tower and told me that I'd find Nero in the room at the top. A few guards stood between me and my mark...easy," she laughed, "but it went sideways so quickly. As soon as I got inside, all hell broke loose...there were Mormagi everywhere. Total chaos. It appeared the Vipers weren't the only ones trying to bring down Nero, and my contact had missed some key information. As I fought my way through the lower floors, taking Belua and Death Mages out along the way, I realized I was in way over my head. There were just too many of them. I managed to get outside and found a bunch of locked cages with prisoners in them. I know it wasn't part of the job, and maybe I should have just left them there...but I couldn't. They were being tortured..." She looked up at him with glistening eyes as she fought back the tears, "more than half of the cages were piled with bodies...some of them just parts. And if the Death Mages got their hands on those last few prisoners...I couldn't even imagine what they would do."

"I could," he said flatly. The tears came as she saw the shadow cross his face, but it was gone just as quickly. He smiled at her and wiped the tears from her face.

"By the time I got the wards down and cages open, the battle that had been raging inside the tower poured out into the courtyard, and I was in the thick of it. I fought my way towards a hole in the outer wall where the prisoners were slipping out, but I had taken a lot of hits and was losing a lot of blood. Then," she paused to take a long swig of wine, "the spell hit me, just before I reached the wall..." another deep breath, "a flash of arching, blood red light hit me right between the eyes, and everything went black. The only thing I remember was like I was floating...suspended in between Realms. Like I was in a dream, and I couldn't quite make out anything or anyone around me, just light and shadows. Then, I was ripped backwards in a flash of blue, slammed into what felt like a wall, and everything went black again. When I finally came out of the fever, it had been weeks, and the Vipers thought I was dead." She let out a sigh and reached for the wine to pour another glass. The air between them hung with heavy silence as she regained her composure. She took a long drink and looked back out across the water.

"Gondyr had been in one of those cages. He saved me...he saw me get hit and before that asshole could finish me off, he pulled me through the wall and up on a horse with the help of two other prisoners. The three of them holed up with me in a ruin on the southeast outskirts of the forest. Turns out, one of them was a Necromancer, and when that Death spell hit me, it stopped my heart...but he threw a counter-spell at nearly the same moment and managed to restart it. The impact of that almost killed me again. They cared for me until I regained consciousness, and when I was ready, we left the ruin and headed south together. I never even looked back. I couldn't, or I would have been frozen there...terrified to go home, terrified to move on. Just stuck between lives. Gondyr had given me a second chance, and I owed him everything. Besides, the magic that both took my life and gave it back...it changed me. It lives within me still; it's a part of me. I'm an oddity, a mutation. I don't fit anywhere anymore." She fell silent and looked back at him, her eyes glowing like the fire of a star, and he could tell she was gauging his reaction to the next part.

"This magic is dangerous, Luca. It's volatile, and it's exhausting trying to keep it in the cage all the time. I don't know how long I can keep it up, I don't know how or why it's living inside of me, and it scares the absolute shit out of me," she finished. He wished like hell that he could find any words of comfort or solace, but they wouldn't come. So, he simply pulled her to him and held her, his arms saying all the things he didn't know how to say.

***

His arms felt like home; the one place she was protected from the constant anguish this world threw at her. And while she knew they still had a hell of a fight ahead of them that they might not survive, she was content to just be here, to have this memory.

"So, what brought you back to the north?" He asked as he stroked her hair.

"Solaris..." she whispered. "Gondyr learned of his plans, and he knew we had to interfere."

"Is it selfish that I almost want to thank Solaris for being an asshole?" He joked. She laughed, and he squeezed her tight. A weight lifted from her as she realized she was happy that he knew the truth now. She had held those secrets for so long, believing that she would carry them to her grave.

"I understand why you didn't come back, why you thought you couldn't come back," he said tenderly, "but you did nothing wrong."

"Luca," she pulled away, staring those daggers right through him, "I abandoned my mark, I got distracted and sloppy. If I had taken Nero out, he never would have invaded Dellalun. And the Belua wouldn't have taken Marciela. I...I did everything wrong!"

"My sweet Tia...you were missing intel, you practically walked into a death trap, you saved lives, you died, and you took a bunch of those fucking monsters with you. And look at you now...leading a rebellion against the Demigods. You were always more than just a Viper, and you're not a mutation...you're a fucking warrior and a hero."

As the weight of his adoration crashed against her, she felt the desire boiling inside and couldn't stop herself. She reached up, grabbed his hair between her fingers, and smashed her mouth into his. Their hunger exploded as they devoured each other in a fit of passion, lips and tongues

126

dancing, wandering hands sliding over skin...but as she tried to pull his shirt off, he grabbed her hands abruptly and backed away.

"Wait..." he murmured breathlessly. She stared at him, confused, frustrated, and even a little angry.

"Why?" She asked, her voice pained and sharp. "I mean, what did you bring me out here for? Don't you want this? Don't you want...*me*?"

"More than you know," he assured her, "but..." he sighed, "I'm sorry, Tia. I spent the last five years alone in that black hole, and even before that..." he trailed off and looked down at her hands. "I don't want to disappoint you, I'm just not sure I'm ready yet." Now it was her turn to be his safe space, no matter how great the aching inside her.

"I understand. I really do," she said quietly as she curled back up in his lap, head against his chest, and drew his arms around her, "I can wait. I don't need more than this right here." He sighed again, and she could feel his tension waning as his heartbeat and breathing steadied. Before long, she found herself drifting to sleep.

***

He could tell she had fallen asleep and was content to let her rest. It often eluded them both, and it wasn't like he had anywhere else to be. But it also meant that Ira had time to pester him.

"I don't pester," Ira snapped.

"I'm sorry," Lucian laughed, "that's unfair. Thank you for tonight. It was nice not having another voice in my head, though I know it wasn't easy for you."

"She is...special to you...to us, now," Ira assured him. *"Ira will protect her."*

"Really?" Lucian asked incredulously.

"She...comforts Ira. She isn't...scared," Ira confessed.

"She is special...and I'm grateful. Maybe this spirit parasite thing isn't so bad after all," Lucian said with a smile.

"Hmfp...maybe. You sleep, Ira guard...and snack." Lucian allowed himself to drift off, as well.

Twelve

Past, Present, & Future

By now, the rest of the team had figured out that there was something going on between Kara & Lucian. The tension was palpable whenever they were in a room together. Every now and then, if you were paying attention, you'd catch them stealing glances, and the way he looked at Kara was unmistakable. They were practically inseparable, wherever Kara was, Lucian wasn't far behind. It was a little annoying, but also sweet. These two guarded, haunted souls found something worth fighting for...who could fault them for that? Dahlia had taken it a little harder, moping around the Citadel for a time, but even she had to admit they were perfect together. And Markus had taken quite a liking to the Nymph, so she had turned her attention to him.

Aleric and Lucian sat around the fire pit, Lucian with a coffee in hand, Aleric with a bright floral tea that Sel'arin had brewed, enjoying the warmth of the afternoon sun and some quiet company. But Lucian had been working up the nerve to ask him something, Aleric could feel it.

"She is quite unique, is she not?" Aleric asked, as nonchalantly as

129

possible while he adjusted the sleeve of his robes, "Kara, I mean."

"She is," Lucian smiled, "but I think you knew that already. I think you knew that a long time ago..." he paused to sip his coffee and weighed his next words carefully, "...when you saved her life. Not just any spellcaster could have done that. Did you know it would work?"

"No..." Aleric replied quietly. He thought back on that fateful day, when an elven assassin had saved his life, and then he nearly killed her trying to return the favor. "That spell is volatile at best, and one of the most intricate I have ever studied. There was only one previous record of it working, and it did not end nearly as well. The fury and pain that grew within overtook him, and he destroyed his entire village before he took his own life to stop it from spreading." Aleric sighed, hesitant to continue, but Lucian stared at him expectantly and Aleric knew he needed to hear this. "She was broken...in every way one can be broken. That spell restarted her heart, but it ripped her back from the Spirit Realm with such force that it snapped nearly every bone in her body. She was sick with fever, lost in the depths of her mind. I do not know if it was her elven blood, or an anomaly in her make-up, or the sheer will she possesses to prove the entire universe wrong, but something in her fought through the darkness, and she survived. When she finally awoke, I was terrified. I knew what that spell could have unleashed," Aleric sighed heavily, "but she caged it, used it as fuel...I had never witnessed such a miracle in all my years before, nor have I since. She is truly...unique."

"Thank you, Aleric, for taking that risk to save her, and for telling me this now. You will never know how grateful I am...I owe you my life, and hers," Lucian stated plainly.

"How curious the way our paths have intertwined. We were brought together for this rebellion, stitched from the stories of her past. I assume you have a history with her, as well?" Aleric pressed.

"Yes, I do," Lucian replied with a small smile. "A story for another time perhaps," he said as he saw Kara coming out of the Citadel and making her way across the courtyard.

"Indeed," Aleric smiled, "and one I should very much like to hear."

"I hope I'm not interrupting," she said coyly as she approached them, "looks like you two were having quite the conversation."

"Not at all, I was just leaving to look over the new shelf of tomes that appeared in the library last night. This Citadel is fascinating!" And with that, Aleric left them alone. Kara took the empty seat and poured herself a cup of tea from the pot on the little table.

"You and your tea," Lucian teased.

"You and your coffee," she poked back. An easy laugh escaped his throat...he found himself doing that more lately, but he didn't mind. He felt more himself than he had in years.

"Marciela wants us to have dinner tonight," she started, handing him a letter, "I'm assuming she has news on Cassius?"

"I hope so. Strange that she addressed it to you, and only you. Fuck. This...could be bad," he frowned.

"Lucian...she has to know by now. She's seen me enough times, and she was always very sharp, her age hasn't changed that. It's time to clear out these skeletons...otherwise, we'll have this hanging over our heads, and we can't afford that." She was right, of course. She usually was. But he had been dreading this...there was no telling how Marciela was going to take all of it - Tia returned, Amalthia de Lyria the Undead, her grandson in love with a mutation (while being a mutation himself) - and with Kara then being a suspected deserter, there was even more at stake. This was going to be tricky.

***

"Lucian, sit down!" Marciela said sharply. He had been pacing and lost in thought, so he didn't notice that dinner had been served. He shot her a pained look, but took his seat next to Kara, across from his grandmother. She waited for him to settle before speaking again.

"Thank you. Now, I believe we have some...mysteries to unravel this evening, " she said, looking squarely at Kara over a glass of red wine. "You, my dear, are more than just the leader of this little rebellion. Do you wish to tell me the truth, or shall we continue the charade until we've finished eating?"

"No," Kara stated calmly, "I'm ready." Marciela put down the glass and folded her hands on the table, waiting for Kara to continue.

Kara took a deep breath and got straight to the point. "I am Amalthia de Lyria, the Viper with Nine Lives and Ex-Second Fang. Twenty years ago, I abandoned my mark on the Belua leader known as Nero and fled to the

South. I deserted my family, changed my name, and walked away from a life that meant everything to me."

Lucian was holding the hilt of his Khyber so tightly that his whole arm ached. He wanted nothing more than to defend her, to tell Marciela and the Vipers to go fuck themselves if they thought they were going to punish her...but he knew he had to hold his tongue. This was her fight, and he would stand beside her no matter the consequences.

"I let the Vipers down. I let Dellalun down. Most of all, I let you down. I know I don't deserve it, and I know it will take more than a simple apology to atone for my transgressions, but I'm before you now, humbly begging for your forgiveness." She had to speak slowly to keep her voice from shaking and grabbed Lucian's hand under the table. He squeezed, letting her know he was with her, no matter what. But could she really ask him to betray his family for her? Could she honestly say that she'd be happy knowing he had to make that sacrifice? She wasn't sure she could live with herself if she did.

"Thank you, for being honest. I imagine there's a much deeper and more complex story behind your choices. And I'd quite like to hear all of it. For now, let us eat, and speak of the present and the future before we look to the past." She took a bite of meat and chewed slowly as Kara and Lucian exchanged a tense look.

"At present, we have a larger threat to combat, a mark to fulfill, and a traitor to bring in. The past and future mean nothing if we don't keep our focus on that. A lot has happened since I was taken, and I've only recently been fully briefed. Tell me Tia, how is your team faring?" Kara loosened her grip on Lucian's hand but didn't let go. Hearing the name *'Tia'* from a voice that didn't belong to him was unexpected and a bit jarring, but she steeled herself.

"It was a little uncomfortable, at first - with all of their own lives and plans and ideas - but I think we've really started to embrace each other's differences, and it's been fruitful. We've made some impressive progress with the Factions and have a lot of support for our cause. As word spreads, we only gain momentum." She was regaining her confidence...she had always loved the art of strategy; it gave her focus and purpose.

"Excellent. You know, of course, you will have the full support of Dellalun and the Vipers. I'm sure Lucian and I can agree on that. In fact, we have a...contact of sorts, with information on where the Demigods will be making their next appearance, and they have requested Kara specifically to receive that information."

"What contact?" Lucian spoke for the first time all evening. "How did we come by this request?"

If he had been a cat, every hair on his back would've been on-end. Kara could see the apprehension all over his face...and so could Marciela.

"Which leads me to the second part of the present day - this. You two. I'm no fool...you were one of my closest friends for many years," she said to Kara, "and you are my grandson," to Lucian. "I've known your hearts for a very long time, and I can't say I'm surprised. Even as a boy, he looked at you like you were the moon & stars of his whole existence. He is the man he is, in part because of you...both the good and the bad," she raised an eyebrow at Kara as she said this. "I can't stop you, but I need to know that this will not interfere with the greater good. There's too much at stake, and it won't matter what any of us want if we're all dead." She did have a way of putting things into perspective.

"You haven't answered my question," Lucian growled. "Who is the contact? And how did we come by this information?"

Marciela looked at him and frowned. "We don't know." She said slowly.

"What do you mean, *we don't know*?" He had let go of Kara's hand and she could hear the wooden handle of the chair creaking as he gripped it firmly, his eyes glowing hot with anger.

"We got a letter," she stated, pulling a piece of parchment from her pocket and sliding it across the table. Lucian grabbed it and held it open so they both could read it:

The time has come.

The bell tolls at the stroke of 9
on the evening of the Solstice.

In the gardens to the North,
you shall have your answer, Kara,
should you choose to claim it.

"Who delivered it?" Lucian asked, eyes shimmering blue.

"We don't know. It was on the desk in The Den's foyer this morning. No one saw anything." Marciela looked at Kara, "I don't need to tell you what this looks like..."

"A trap," Kara finished her thought.

"Exactly. Good to see you haven't lost your instincts, you're going to need them," Marciela said with a half-smile. But Lucian wasn't smiling. He was fighting back Ira. And they were both furious.

"This is exactly what I was talking about," Marciela frowned, "you can't do this with a clear head if you allow your emotions to control you, Lucian."

"She's right. I know you're angry...so am I." Kara said as she put her hand on his arm, and he looked into her eyes...white hot fire swirling in them. "But we have to be smart about this. Just because it's a trap, doesn't mean we won't get the information we need. We have to stay focused." His eyes still glowed, but she could see he and Ira were in agreement.

"Well," Marciela broke the tension, "that settles that. Shall we finish dinner while Tia tells me the story of how she came to be Kara, so we can put the past where it belongs and focus our attention on the Cassius problem?"

***

The next evening Dahlia, Kara, and Lucian traveled to Fini'via, a small town far north from Dellalun, at the edge of Cylendri where the rocky shores met the Aqu'immensi. It was dark, dreary, and cold - a harsh place where only the utterly lost and loneliest of souls made their home. Perfect for a liar and a traitor. Their Viper intel had revealed that Cassius was meeting someone at the ramshackle tavern that sat precariously atop a rocky overhang above the crashing waves. As they got closer to the town and the trees of the forest disappeared, Dahlia got a glimmer up around them. The dwellings and buildings were sparse, spread out and easy to navigate, and the townspeople kept their distance from each other, so the group didn't have much difficulty getting to the tavern.

Lucian saw Cassius inside through the broken window to the left of the door, sitting at the bar with a pint of mead, waiting for his contact. *"Let's wait here,"* he told Dahlia, *"I want to see who he's meeting."* She passed the message on to Kara and they huddled up, watching the inside. They weren't there long before a group of four Death Mages came walking up the road straight for the tavern. When they were close enough to get a good look at, Lucian growled low and his whole body tensed.

"That's the one who captured him, who hurt him," Dahlia told Kara, a pained look on her face. Lucian felt her trying to block out his thoughts and he did his best to calm Ira. The leader of the group had a sharp, contorted face, with stringy white hair and the trademark dead eyes, though even they seemed more severe than your run of the mill Mormagi. It wore a black robe instead of the traditional red that most of them chose. And it looked right at Kara as the group passed through the tavern door. She grabbed Lucian's arm, and he steadied himself.

"Cassius!" a gravelly voice snarled. "I hope you have good news for

137

me."

"Domi'dolori, alwaysss a pleasure," Cassius replied, bored and drunk. "As it happenssss, I don't."

"Your consistent failures never cease to amaze me. It's truly no wonder that even your precious Vipers don't want you in charge, you aren't meant to lead," the Death Mage snapped, "you're barely qualified to follow."

"Your fuckin' deal with...th'Belua is wolf shit," Cassius slurred the words, "they're gonna turn tail, jussyou watch. They let Marci...*hic*...ela get away, I didn't have a fuckin' thing to do with't."

"And yet, here you sit - whining, drinking yourself to death, blaming the rest of the Realms for your misfortunes. You fucking *child*," Domi'dolori looked out the window, right at Kara again, "you've gotten yourself into a nasty mess." It looked back at Cassius, who was still sitting at the bar with his back to them, and said ominously, "I'll be surprised if you survive the night." A flash of red flew at Kara suddenly, grazing her cheek as she turned away from it. The glimmer disappeared, and Lucian was through the window before Kara even had a chance to breathe. She and Dahlia jumped in after him, glass shattering and wood splintering around them as spells hit the walls. Lucian had one Mormagi in each hand, lifted in the air and was squeezing the life out of them. The other red-robed one was already dead on the floor, three daggers in its chest. Domi'dolori was gone, and Cassius was passed out under the bar.

"Lucian?" Kara said softly. He dropped the Death Mages and turned, wings out, pure rage in his eyes, his face twisted.

"That fucking bitch was right here, and we missed!" Ira shouted.

"I know, I'm sorry. It all happened so fast," she put her hand on his cheek, "but we have to get Cassius and get the hell out of here before more show up, okay Ira? Please?" Kara pleaded with the Spirit. He looked into her eyes and his face softened, then Lucian started to come back through. He nodded, picked up their mark, and headed out the door, Dahlia and Kara close behind.

***

They were in the common room of The Den after having returned with Cassius. Lucian had shown him mercy, though he would still pay for his crimes against the Vipers. He would be stripped of his title, his status, and all his assets. He would not have any access to the Vipers or The Den, and word of his alignment with the Mormagi and Belua would spread to every corner of Cylendri - he wouldn't have a friend in the world. He could run back to them if he wanted, but as he had failed them repeatedly, it was not likely they would show him the same kindness.

Marciela had used the last of her power as leader to absolve Amalthia of her past offenses, reinstating her as an Ammodytes Viper on the grounds that she had served her time in exile and recently paid the Vipers back in full, and then handed the legacy to Lucian - he was now First Fang, Vivvain taking the spot of Second Fang. Kara was genuinely happy for him, but a small pang of regret was stabbing her heart. Would he still want her now that he had an empire to rule? How could she make him happy when he could have anyone or anything he wanted? As they stood in The Den filled with the Vipers cheering for their new leader, Kara had never felt more

139

alone. No matter how foolish it seemed after all they had been through together, he had rejected her that night in the boat, and her heart was heavy with concern that she would be losing him all over again.

Lucian made his way through the crowd and over to where she stood with Dahlia, stopping every now and then to speak with Vipers congratulating him and offering him wine, which he politely declined. He had that smile he reserved only for her spread across his face as he neared. Her heart tightened in her chest, the way it did every time he looked at her. She had been so careful with him, she had let him lead instead of following her instincts, and for what? To protect herself? To protect him? She wished she had taken the opportunity to show just how much she wanted him when she had the chance and not allowed him stop her. He had always been important to her, but now...he was everything she wanted. Everything she needed. And she might never have that chance again.

"Enjoying the celebration?" He asked, reaching for her hand.

"It's a little overwhelming, to be honest," she smiled as he grasped her hand in his. She loved the way it felt. His hands were strong, and surprisingly soft. "I imagine the Vipers will be celebrating well into the morning, but I'll see you back at the Citadel later, right?" She asked hesitantly.

"Actually, I had something a little more...private in mind," he said with a wink. "Are you ready to get out of here?" She nodded, not sure if she should be worried or elated. She had so much she still wanted to share with him. They grabbed Dahlia and headed back to the Citadel.

140

***

It was quiet when they arrived in the stillness of the night. They all
silently headed for their rooms, Lucian telling Kara he'd be right back as she
went in hers to change. She took out her daggers, peeled off her leathers,
and threw on her favorite linen nightshirt as she heard a knock on her door.
Lucian was on the other side, and grabbed her hand before she could say
anything. She followed him outside, through the stables, again at the mercy
of his secret plans. They made their way to the spring in the woods and
stood together at the edge, their feet in the water. She looked up at the full
moon, closed her eyes, and filled her lungs with the crisp night air. Lucian
watched her for a moment, then gently kissed her shoulder, causing her to
inhale sharply. She opened her eyes and turned to him, and in that moment
he let all of his walls come down.

"I shouldn't have stopped you the other night," he whispered with a
sharp intensity, "I have wanted you since before I even knew what true
desire was." He pulled her close, bringing her mouth to his, and kissed her
with all the greed and hunger that he had been holding back from the
moment he saw her again, his wings spread wide. She removed her
nightshirt, glowing naked in the moonlight, and his breath caught in his
throat as he took in every inch of her radiance. She pressed herself against
his body, untying his trousers before he wrapped his arms around her
waist, lifted, then pulled her with him further into the water. Draping her
arms around his neck, she circled her legs around his hips, and their shared
passion ignited as he slid himself inside her. Her back arched, eyes of
white-hot fire rolling back in her head, and an exquisite moan escaped from
within her as he used his lips to explore her skin.

They spent the whole night out at the spring, lost in pure ecstasy, unlocking the desires they had chained within themselves for so long. As the sun rose, they were lying tangled together on the ground in the trees, her head on his chest and hand over his heart. He was awake, but didn't dare move...he wished they could stay here and never leave. He wished life could be this simple, this perfect. Even as he knew that for them it never would be, they would always be thrust into the fires of the world, he knew they would fight every flame together from now on. He felt her stirring beneath his arm and she looked up at him as her eyes opened, a content smile on her face.

"Good morning, *me'amata*," he said softly, and kissed her forehead, "how did you sleep?"

"Better than I have in a long time," she sighed, "maybe ever. Did you sleep at all?"

"I drifted off for a while," he smiled, "Ira's been a pretty reliable lookout as of late."

"Well, that's good, thank you Ira."

"You're welcome," the Spirit hissed, and Kara laughed.

"We should probably get dressed and head inside," she said, but didn't make a move to get up.

"Yes...but I can't do that if you don't," Lucian teased. She kissed his chest, and then reluctantly got up. He watched as she slipped into her nightshirt, completely captivated by each flex of muscle and bend of limb her body made.

She tossed his trousers to him playfully. "Your turn," she said with a sly smile. He growled as he lifted himself off the ground and pulled them on. They went through the stables, petting the Pegasi as they did, and headed around into the main hall. Gondyr was sitting at the fire with a cup of coffee, looking up as they came in. A wide smile spread across his face.

"About damn time," he said with a laugh, and Kara felt herself blushing. Gondyr winked at them as they turned and headed up the stairs.

Thirteen

A Mother Knows

"A mysterious letter, with a cryptic message, left by an invisible spirit, is supposed to tell us where the Demigods will make their next move?" Dahlia sighed. "Great."

"It's a lead, one we desperately need..." Kara started. They were gathered in the library, maps of Dellalun and scrolls scattered on the table they stood around.

"But whoever this mystery contact is, they clearly know we need this information, so they're using it to get you alone Kara...we can't allow that," Markus chimed in.

"We won't," Lucian added, "we have a plan."

"Nobody knows the city like the Vipers. We'll have them posted around the Gardens - here, here, and here," she pointed to three areas on the map, "and I won't be alone. Dahlia, we're going to need you there - you're the only one who can create a glimmer. You will keep Lucian from being seen so I have backup on the ground."

"I'll head to the training room, and start practicing," Dahlia replied, "Lucian, meet me there later so we can ensure the glimmer will be strong and hold up around you."

"Perfect. Whoever this is will be expecting an ambush, just as we are. We don't want to spook them, so everyone keeps their distance while I get the information we need. As soon as I have it, we either leave...or we fight." Kara explained. "Aleric, Markus...I need you two to meet with the Gryphons. We received a letter this morning. They have found texts of a weapon that could even the playing field in our next meeting with the Demigods."

"We're on it," Aleric stated.

"Sel'arin and Nalor, we need to check in with the Factions. See if there's anything else we can assist with...we're going to need every bit of help we can get once we have the location, and don't want to leave anything on the table to prevent that." Kara instructed.

"We'll get started right away," Sel'arin chimed in.

"Great. We've got three days until the Solstice...let's make sure we're prepared for anything." And with that, everyone headed off to their assignments. Lucian stayed behind and made his way around the table to Kara.

"I know this is our best plan of action, and you can handle yourself, but I don't like it," he said calmly as he leaned against the table next to her.

She placed a hand on his chest. "I know, and that's why you're my man on the ground. They won't get the drop on me, not with you and Ira looking out for me," she smiled.

His eyes glowed blue, and Ira spoke, *"they won't touch you."*

"I'm glad to see you two working together...it gives us an edge," she stated.

"And removes a liability," Lucian replied.

She looked up at him, her eyes dancing, and assured him, "you'll never be a liability to me, no matter what. I need you at my side, there's no one I'd rather go into battle with than you."

He smiled and kissed her deeply. "No matter what," he said as they pulled away.

"Now, go get some training in with Dahlia, I want that glimmer to be the strongest she's ever produced. I've got some preparations of my own to attend to. I'll be gone until tomorrow, but I'll fill you in when I'm back."

***

As she made her way through the curtain of vines and branches that hid the entrance to her old village from most of the Realm, she felt her panic rising. She stopped at the edge of a shimmering pool of water across from a small waterfall and took a few deep breaths.

"You can do this," she said to herself, "this war affects them, too, and they deserve the chance to fight."

She gathered her strength, stepped into the shallow blue-green waters of the pool, and made her way across to the waterfall. Even after all these years, she remembered each step, careful not to trigger the traps that lay in wait beneath the surface. When she reached the fall, she spoke the words in her native tongue to gain entry:

"Ingrassi'ato i'nami'Deavita."

The rock behind the water cracked, opening just enough for her to slide through, and there she was, overlooking Lyria Village. It hadn't changed at all; it was just as beautiful and ethereal as when she last saw it. Small hills of evergreen peppered with white, blue, and purple flowers that filled the air with sweetness. Great trees with swooping vines and arching canopies of branches that intertwined. A cool, crystal blue stream that shimmered as it snaked down into the valley below and met the village that sprawled in the clearing. It seemed somehow smaller than she remembered, even as she knew that it had grown, with new structures dotting the edges and more elves living here than ever. Some years ago, during a particularly dry season, a fire outside the mountains took some of the nearby villages, and the Lyria clan had opened their homes to the fleeing elves. They may have hidden themselves away, but they had always been a clan of aid to those in need. It filled her with a deep sense of pride to call this her clan, even if they no longer claimed her.

She made her way down the sloping hill, along the stream, and into the village. She could smell bread baking in the tavern and the Honeymead brewing in barrels around the back. There were younglings running and playing around the stream, and Patroni'usi grazing in the nearby field. The weavers were tending their looms, and the tattooist was finishing up a beautiful floral pattern on the fair face of a young elf. She smiled as she walked through the bustle but was met mostly with wide-eyed stares or hesitant glares. She expected nothing less. She had been careful to keep her gear minimal with just a small pack and switched from her armor to a less...intimidating garb of simple brown trousers, a blue belted tunic that hung off one shoulder, and boots. But she still posed a striking image, especially with violet hair and lightning in her eyes.

As she approached the village square in the center of town, a curious youngling ran up behind her, pointed to Kara's left shoulder and exclaimed, "that's a Lyria marking! Are you from our clan?" She asked with big eyes.

"I was, a long time ago..." Kara started.

But she was interrupted by a voice floating in behind her, "...a very long time ago."

She turned, and there stood Elaria de Lyria, the Sovereign of the clan in all her ageless beauty. "A face I never expected to see again," she spoke softly, but there was pain in her voice.

"Nor I..." Kara replied with a slight bow of her head, "...*mi'matia*."

Elaria folded her hands in front of her. "So, Amalthia de Lyria has returned home after all these years. There must be quite a story behind why. Shall we take this conversation somewhere with less..." she looked

148

down at the curious youngling, "...prying eyes and ears?" Elaria turned and headed for the dwelling up the hill on the other side of the village, Kara following close behind. She could already hear the whispers and gasps of her elven brethren as they made their way through the village.

As they approached the structure, Kara paused and took a sharp breath. Her childhood home loomed, and a wave of memories washed over her. Elaria went through the gate, turned and held it open. Kara collected herself and walked through, noticing the years of wear on the wood, and the bountiful garden of herbs her mother always kept on one side of the stone walk, a familiar feeling of apprehension stabbing her gut. The same feeling she had the last time she walked through this gate...to leave.

They silently made their way inside, through the front door of knotted bark, and into the main room. So little had changed. The kitchen to the left overlooking the garden, filled with cooking tools, jars of dried herbs and teas, and a large pot big enough to fit a full-grown Dwarf over a smoldering fire bubbling in the center. The sitting area and library at the back of the room, lined with shelves of tomes and scrolls that also lay scattered about a few tables, and the oversize chair of wood and moss that her father had built before she was born. Her bedroom was to the right, but the door was shut and probably locked. Her mother's room was up the staircase opposite the library. Kara removed her boots and let her toes sink into the soft, purple creeping moss that covered the floor.

Elaria was preparing a pot of tea in the kitchen as Kara walked around the space, running her fingers over the trinkets and books that had been collected over the years, the woven blankets that she had wrapped herself in as a youngling, the furniture her father had built with his own hands, and the smooth stones that made up the fireplace. She had never allowed herself to miss any of this, for fear that she wouldn't be able to stay away, but it all came flooding back.

"Come, sit," Elaria said as she put down the tray of tea and lavender biscuits on a small table between two chairs in front of the fireplace. Kara sat down opposite her mother, and they sat in silence for a few moments as they sipped the tea. It was exactly as it had always been, citrus and spiced, with notes of honey. Her mother's favorite brew...and Kara's.

"You wear the face of *mi'filia*, but it has changed. You carry another light within, a fire that was not there before. It burns in your eyes..." Elaria said plainly. "Is this why you remained gone?"

"In part, yes..."Kara started. She took another long sip of tea, delaying the inevitable.

"Most thought you had died. The rumors of Amalthia de Lyria's demise spread far and made their way even here. But a mother knows." Kara did her best to keep her face from showing the pain...but a mother knows.

"I can see," Elaria said, "but I cannot understand."

Kara steeled herself again. "I did die. And was saved...by magic. A rare mutation that manifested."

"Was it those Vipers you left us to join?" Elaria asked, a hint of anger in her tone.

"No...and yes," Kara stammered. "It happened on a job, but it wasn't the Vipers who did it. It was the combination of Death and Spirit Magic." She proceeded to tell Elaria everything, from that day and where she had been since. Her mother listened, never interrupting or asking questions, simply taking it all in. After Kara finished, she sat back and snacked on a lavender biscuit. It reminded her of Lucian, and she smiled. Elaria noticed, but didn't ask. Enough stories had been shared for today.

"So, you believed you no longer had a home here?" Elaria finally asked.

"How could I? I had left, I had denied my elven calling and ran off to become a Viper. And then this mutation...everything changed. I couldn't be seen in the North anymore. So, I ran even further. I gave up both lives that meant so much to me and created a new one."

"And what do they call you now?"

"Kara."

Her mother's eyes misted at hearing that. Kar'lina was Amalthia's older sister's name. She had died from a fever that took out nearly a quarter of the clan when they were both young.

"What has brought you back to the North, back home?" Elaria inquired.

"The Demigods. They are threatening to destroy everything in a fit of rebellion against the High Gods, demanding a seat at the table...and I'm leading a rebellion of my own against them."

"*Mi'filia*...an assassin, a deserter, a hero, and now leader of a rebellion. You never could stay out of trouble, could you?" Elaria smiled.

"I guess not," Kara laughed. "I'm here to warn the village...and to ask for help. If the Demigods succeed, even this place won't be safe. The wards that hide it will fall, and they will tear through everything. We are uniting all the Factions and Clans..."

"We have no warriors here, " Elaria interjected.

"Yes, but you have Ward Mages and Healers, both of which will surely be needed."

"I suppose..." Elaria started, but Kara cut her off.

"I'm not here to make demands...I'm here to ask for aid. That's what this clan does, that's what it stands for – Keepers of the Sacred Harmony. There will be nothing to keep if the Gods wage a war, there will be no harmony. I only wish to give them the choice...they deserve to know, and make a choice on their own," Kara said firmly. Elaria looked at her daughter with a mixture of pride and sadness. She had lost so much, lived through unimaginable nightmares, witnessed things all parents fear their children seeing...and yet she stood here a survivor, a hero, and a leader poised to try and save the world.

"You are right," Elaria said after a moment. Those were not words she heard from her mother's mouth very often even as a child, and Kara sighed in relief. They talked for a time, about how the clan had fared over the years, about Kara's father who had passed in the years after Kara left the Vipers, about some of Kara's adventures since leaving home. The hours passed as they drank tea and laughed and cried and shared stories. While Kara knew this couldn't last forever, she was grateful to be reconnecting with her roots and making amends with her mother. No one knew what would happen in the coming months, and this might be her last chance for a bit of reconciliation.

A familiar sound of bells ringing in the village square rose up and pulled them from their musings. It was nearly dinner time. The whole clan gathered and ate together every evening, and each family contributed to the meal. As Elaria was the village herbalist, her garden provided all the fresh spices and teas.

"Will you be staying tonight?" Elaria asked as she stood.

"Yes. Do you need me to gather the tea?" Kara replied.

"That would be most helpful." Elaria and Kara collected tea pouches and jars of honey in comfortable silence, placing them in grass-woven baskets, then made their way back down the hill. Tables were sprawled across the cobblestone square, with warm fires burning in stone circles around the edges for warmth, and the whole clan was bustling about, setting the tables and placing large platters of spiced roots, vegetables, truffles, and mushrooms, as well as berry tarts, and dried fruits.

As Kara made her way around the tables, placing the jars of honey for use in the teas, she could feel the random looks and apprehension of the villagers. A lot of them wouldn't have known her, so it was more about a stranger in their home, but she could sense that a few recognized her and were more than a little surprised. One in particular kept stealing glances, and Kara remembered him. Nir'lathin, one of the Healers and her father's best friend. Kara had been a bit of a wild youngling and had visited the healer on many occasions - broken bones, nettle removal, bandages, and tonics - he had also tended to her sister until the fever took her. His family was one of the original founders of the village along with hers, though that was a few generations before his time. Their eyes met, and though there was a hint of fear, seeing what she had become, there was also a sense of joy that she still lived. The final bell rang across the square, signaling for everyone to be seated. Each elf found a spot and settled in, as the Sovereign stood at the center to address the clan and lead the affirmations.

"Clan de Lyria," Elaria started, "as the sun sets on this day, we gather to share a meal and strengthen the bonds of community that hold this clan together. As I am sure many of you have noticed," she gestured with an open hand towards Kara, "we have a guest seated among us. Some of you may even recognize her." Every eye turned to her and Kara suddenly felt terribly exposed. "For those who do not, it pleases me to introduce you to Kara...also known as Amalthia de Lyria, *mi'filia*, who has returned home after thirty-six years." There was a collective gasp, and a cacophony of murmurs filled the square. Elaria gave it a few moments, then lifted her hands to silence the clan.

"She has come home to share news of the outside world and ask for our aid, which she will address once we have finished our meal." The whispers started again. She waited for them to die down, then commenced the affirmations.

"Clan de Lyria, first Wards of Cylendri, Keepers of the Sacred Harmony,

Protectors of the Great Forest and all who call it home, we gather to partake in the gifts Deavita provides and to strengthen both our bonds to the elements around us as well as the connections to our brethren within. We give thanks for this bountiful meal, and to all the hands that helped prepare it. We also give thanks for helping one of our kin find her way home and ask for guidance in the coming months. *Beni'Dea*."

"*Beni'Dea*," the whole clan said in unison and the meal began. Kara filled her plate as she looked around at all the families here, sharing laughs and stories, completely insulated from everything happening beyond this valley. She felt guilty that she had to tell them that this was all going to change...ever the bearer of unwelcome news. But she was helping, she was trying to fix her past mistakes and do real good in the Realms. And she had Lucian. She had finally torn down every last one of his defenses, and he was more beautiful beneath the layers than she had imagined. She smiled as she thought about the night before.

"I hope I get the chance to meet them," her mother whispered to her, catching the same dreamy smile she had seen on Kara's face earlier. Kara looked incredulously at Elaria, and her mother continued, "a mother knows."

Kara smiled, "I hope you get the chance to meet *him*, as well. I promise I'll bring him home as soon as I can." They finished their meal surrounded by laughter and joy, and Kara realized how much more she had that was worth fighting for. At the end, when the last berry tart was gone and the older elves were all sipping their tea or mead as the younglings played around the square, Elaria stood in the center again to address the clan.

"Clan de Lyria, thank you all for the wonderful meal. As I mentioned before, our visitor has some news for us, so please take a moment and listen carefully," and she gestured for Kara to come up. As Kara stood before the people, her people, she steeled herself and began.

"Thank you for allowing me to spend the evening and a wonderful meal among you and your families. I know you're all curious why I'm here. I bring news from beyond the valley, and a choice for each of you to make." She took a deep breath and continued, "Not long ago, I learned of a plot against Ess'Magis and the High Gods, a plot by their children, the Demigods," she paused as the whole square erupted in chatter and whispers. Taking a cue from her mother, she waited for it to die down, then continued, "I have assembled a team of warriors, healers, and strategists. We have been diligently working to unite the Factions, as well as notifying the independent clans and tribes to ensure that everyone has a choice. Should the Demigods succeed, all Cylendri will fall - they are trying to bring down the Mag'nicelo. Soon, we will have to face them head on, and we will need every bit of help possible. So, I ask the Wards and Healers among you, would any of you rise to the challenge, and help protect not only your homes and families here, but all of Cylendri and those who cannot fight for themselves?" She stood firm, her words hanging in the air as each elf considered what she had just asked of them. As she began to worry that she would be leaving here without good news, Nir'lathin stood and made his way to Kara, taking her left forearm in his hand.

"Mi'promit'ia," he said to her. I pledge myself. Then, one by one, each of the Mages in the square stood and made their way to her, *"Mi'promit'ia."* They all promised their magic; it filled her with such pride and gratitude. These were her people; this is where her heart had come from.

"I am so grateful for each of you, and proud to call this my clan," she smiled.

Elaria stood with her and said, "as am I. I know this is disturbing news, and we have much to discuss, but Kara will stay with us tonight. We will hold the council in the morning, and she will tell us everything we need to know. Take solace in the knowledge that the Great Forest will provide us with strength and abundance as long as we protect her." With that, the dinner ended, and the square bustled with the clearing of dishes and tables, until it finally grew quiet as the clan retired to their homes. Kara followed her mother back up the hill to sleep in a bed she hadn't seen in nearly four decades. But she was happy that she had come home.

Fourteen

Weapon of the Elves

Kara arrived back at the Citadel the next afternoon, after the council of Healers meeting and her hike back to the Travel Stone a few miles from her village. The team was inside, she could see them around the table having lunch through the windows as she made her way across the courtyard. Lucian looked up and met her eyes, a smile spreading on his face. She headed straight for the kitchen.

"Our fearless leader returns!" Gondyr exclaimed as she walked in.

"What's for lunch?" she asked, famished.

"Markus made the most mouthwatering Terastralis dish with black rice, peppers, mushrooms, onions, and zucchini. It's spicy and wonderful!" Dahlia said before shoving another spoonful in her mouth.

"It was one of my mother's favorites dishes," he smiled, though Kara saw a hint of sadness in his gilded eyes. She realized she knew little about the Gryphon.

158

"Well, it smells amazing, and I am starving," she replied as she set down her pack in a chair by the door and got herself a large helping before sitting at the open seat next to Lucian. He squeezed her leg under the table, and she smiled up at him before digging in, the warmth of the spices filling her up. She looked around the table at this new family she had cobbled together as they talked and laughed with each other, who were strangers not long ago, whose paths may have never crossed if not for her. She saw Markus and Dahlia, and the sweet, almost innocent way they showed their newfound affection for each other. Gondyr and his brother Nalor laughing with Sel'arin, a pair of dwarves unlike any she had ever known and an elf who had never left her home tree until now. Aleric and Lucian, deeply engrossed in a conversation about Spirit lore, each learning mysteries from the other. And she thought about her life...or her lives rather. So many years spent running, collecting broken shards of an existence that she could never fully live. And now they were converging, creating something new, something unbelievable. She never had more to fight for than she had at this moment, and realizing that, she knew she had to learn more about this power inside of her. She had to go back to the Library of Cylendri - surely the Gryphons had some information that could help her.

***

After lunch, Kara went to her room to change her clothes and take a moment to think about everything that they had in front of them. She sat on the edge of her bed, took off her boots, and laid back. They had the Solstice, and the mysterious contact. They had to finish informing the remaining independent clans, including sending Markus and Pytra to do the same with the tribes in the South. She had to try and figure out what this magic in her was, and if she could potentially wield it without destroying

159

herself or anyone she cared for. And they still had the Demigods next move ahead, with no idea how much time they had until then. As she pondered what lay ahead, there was a knock at her door...she could smell the coffee and lavender.

"Come in," she said and sat up, smiling as Lucian opened the door.

"I hope you weren't napping," he said hesitantly.

"No, just thinking. It's okay," she assured him. He sat on the bed next to her.

"I missed you last night."

"I went home...to Lyria," she told him, "I saw my mother."

"Oh?" he asked, holding her gaze. "That must have been...something. How did it go?"

"It went well actually. We had some wonderful conversations, and I had dinner with my whole clan. I did spend the night in my old bed, which was strange," she laughed.

"How long has it been?"

"Thirty-six years," she said with a sigh, "it's hardly changed, but it has grown even more lovely. There's at least three times as many elves there as when I left, many of them Wards and Healers. And we have their support, every single able elf volunteered. I couldn't believe it."

"That's amazing!" Lucian smiled. Kara thought she saw a hint of something else flash in his eyes...but she couldn't figure out what. She shook it off and didn't think about it again as she told him all about her village.

***

Lucian lay awake in his bed, contemplating a pot of coffee. He was stuck on his conversation with Kara that afternoon. Particularly the part where she hadn't been home in nearly four decades, basically since he was just a baby. She had been gone for twenty years, with the Vipers for sixteen years before that, and how many years had she actually lived in her village before she left? He was human, which meant he had a relatively short lifespan compared to most of his team here. And Kara was an elf...they can live for centuries; some are even said to be immortal. He had never considered it until that afternoon, but she would outlive him by several lifetimes. And she was still a vivacious young woman physically, for all her years and wisdom. But he would age, he would decay. His mind reeled with this information.

"Maybe you won't," Ira chimed in.

"What do you mean?" Lucian asked him.

"You have me," the Spirit replied.

"I don't think you can stop me from growing old."

"How do you know?"

"I don't. I just can't figure out how that would make sense." Ira was quiet after that, leaving Lucian to his thoughts.

The next morning, before the sunrise, Lucian made his way down to the kitchen and brewed a pot of coffee. He hadn't slept, the thoughts of his own mortality keeping him awake as he considered all that it meant for him and Kara. He would have to discuss it with her eventually, but he had no idea how to even begin that conversation. This was going to be tricky.

***

By the time Kara made it downstairs, most of the team was already in the kitchen, Sel'arin helping Dahlia prepare breakfast. Gondyr and Nalor were playing cards by the fireplace, and Lucian was brooding with his coffee, sitting in one of the windows. Markus and Aleric weren't around.

"Good morning," she said to her elven and nymph sisters as she poured a cup of tea, "what are you making?"

"Truffle potatoes and honey butter flat cakes," Sel'arin said cheerfully. Kara smiled and went to where Lucian was sitting, staring out into the courtyard.

"You look like you have a lot on your mind," she said to him, eyes narrow with concern, "is everything alright?"

He smiled. "Everything is fine. I just didn't get a lot of sleep." She sat in the chair next to the window and sipped her tea.

"You could have come to my room and crawled into bed with me," she smiled and winked. He took her hand in his, gripping it tightly, but didn't say anything. She could tell he had something simmering beneath the surface, but he clearly wasn't ready to talk about it, so she left it alone. They sat there together in silence, waiting for breakfast as Nalor groaned in frustration and Gondyr laughed having beaten his brother at another hand. Markus finally joined them in the kitchen. He smiled at Dahlia as he passed her, making his way over to where Kara and Lucian were sitting.

"We have much to discuss," he told Kara.

"That we do," she replied. "I have some questions for Carmine, and was hoping we could head back to the Fortress today."

"Let's speak in the library after breakfast, and we can figure that out," Markus said, an ominous tone in his voice. Kara nodded in agreement, feeling Lucian's curious eyes on her.

After breakfast Kara, Markus, and Lucian met in the library. There was tension in the room she couldn't place. Something didn't feel right.

"So, did you find out about this 'weapon' that the Historians discovered?" she asked Markus, getting right to the point.

"Yes, but the texts are incredibly old, and difficult to fully translate. They don't quite make sense, and the Lord Gryphon has asked if you could potentially help," Markus informed her.

"I can try..." she replied, "but what do the texts say with the current translation?"

"They speak of a power buried deep, an old magic that was 'hidden from the Gods' by the First Elves to ensure their survival in the event that the High Gods broke their word, and tried to enslave them again," Markus explained.

"Alright, well that's something. Does it say anything about where this power is hidden?"

"That's where it gets tricky. We don't know, we can't make sense of the translation. It's like a riddle created to keep the information from falling into the wrong hands. Whatever this power is, the First Elves both revered and feared it." His words hung heavily in the air as the three of them contemplated the implications. If the First Elves were afraid of this power, not just falling into the wrong hands, but actually feared the power itself, then they would need to tread very carefully.

Kara finally broke the silence, "we need to go speak with Carmine."

"Agreed. I'll get Sable and meet you at the Stone," Markus replied, and they all left the library. Lucian followed Kara silently up the stairs, both lost in thought. She reached for the handle of her door, but Lucian grabbed her hand and pulled her to face him, his eyes haunted.

"I don't like this," he said, the concern plain on his face. "If this power was buried so deep, and the First Elves feared it, then we might be better off leaving it be."

"We have to know more," she pressed, "and if what we learn once it's properly translated shows that we should leave it be, then we will. But we must figure something out, Luca. We don't have anything that could do real damage to Solaris and the others, we're flying blind here."

"I know..." he sighed, "I just don't like it."

She kissed his hand in hers and said, "I don't like it either, but that's never stopped us before. See you at the Stone."

They arrived at the base of the Path a short time later. Kara and Lucian climbed onto Sable, and all of them flew up to the Fortress. Pytra was waiting at the gate, smiling at the group as they approached.

"Good to see you all again," she greeted them as she opened the gate.

"You, as well Pytra," Kara replied, and they headed inside. They found Rowan and Carmine having a heated discussion in the main hall, though when he looked up and saw them entering the Fortress, Rowan held up his hand to cut the conversation short. Carmine was clearly frustrated, but he fell silent.

"Markus, back so soon?" Rowan bellowed, his voice echoing in the grand space, "and you brought your friends!"

"Yes, Lord Gryphon. Kara would like to speak with Carmine and take a look at those texts he found. She might be able to help him translate them further," Markus advised.

Carmine met Kara's eyes, and she could see a mix of apprehension, curiosity, and even a bit of fear. It unsettled her, but she had to know more about this weapon. Then he looked at Rowan, who nodded.

"Follow me," Carmine said with a heavy sigh. Kara and Lucian exchanged a furtive glance, then made their way through the Fortress behind him. After a few minutes of walking, Kara realized they weren't heading for the Library. They were in a part of the Fortress she hadn't visited last time. They eventually made their way down a long spiral staircase that seemed never-ending until they reached a small door at the bottom. Kara could see the shimmer of Ward magic covering it. Carmine turned and finally spoke, "this is The Sanctuary. Since the texts and relics here cannot be removed, the Lord Gryphon has granted you temporary access...against my better judgment," he scowled. "Please *do not* touch anything unless I tell you to. Very few eyes have seen what you are about to see, and I don't think I need to tell you how imperative it is that you don't speak a word of this once we leave. Understood?"

"Understood," Kara and Lucian replied in unison. Carmine stared at them both for a few moments, driving his point home, and then turned to the door. Kara didn't see a lock, but as Carmine brought his hand to the wood, a keyhole appeared in the very center. Carmine lifted a key unlike any Kara had ever seen and unlocked it, gesturing for Kara and Lucian to enter first. Her skin felt like it was being poked by thousands of needles as they passed through the door, and she realized Carmine hadn't taken the ward down, he had simply reworked it to allow her and Lucian to pass through.

They entered the dark room, and Carmine waved his hand over a small brazier just inside. A ball of light magic appeared in it, then a row of identical braziers lit down the left and right side of the room, illuminating everything. The space was a long hall, with tables and glass cases like the ones at the top of the Library down the center. As they walked slowly through the room, Kara saw strange items inside the cases. Some looked like weapons, others like trinkets and tools, but she could tell that they were ancient, and a lot of them sizzled with magic. There were also scrolls of parchment and large tomes laid out on the tables. They reached the back of the room where a desk sat, with an exceptionally large volume lay open on top.

"These are the passages," Carmine advised. "And this parchment here is our translations so far. You'll see that there are some words and phrases we have been unable to translate. If you can help with those, perhaps we can unravel the rest of this mystery," he told Kara.

"I'll get right to work," she said quietly, the gravity of this situation not lost on her. She could feel the whole weight of the world on her shoulders as she began to read. As she found the words and phrases the Gryphons had struggled with, elven words that hadn't been used in centuries, the dread grew in the pit of her stomach. She translated in silence, Lucian watching her work as Carmine thumbed through another book. It took the better part of the afternoon to get through all the text. When she was done, she looked at Lucian, and she knew he could see the distress in her eyes.

"I'm finished," she told Carmine. He looked up from his book, and upon seeing the look on her face, he took a deep breath.

"It is as I feared, then?" he asked.

"It is as we both feared," she replied, and looked again at Lucian, her heart pounding in her chest. "We need to speak with Rowan." She gave the parchment of the full translation to Carmine, and they left the Sanctuary, Kara lost in a sea of terrifying thoughts. She held Lucian's hand tightly as they weaved their way back through the Fortress and up to the Lord Gryphon's office. Carmine didn't knock, he simply opened the door, and they walked in. Rowan looked up from his desk, and upon seeing them enter, he smiled.

"Did you find what you needed?" he asked, the smile leaving his face as he studied the look on hers, and Carmine warded the room against prying ears.

"We did..." she began, unsure of how to explain this to him. She took a few moments to gather her thoughts and push through the anxiety. "This power, this weapon, was hidden in the blood of an elfling when she was barely a few days old. The First Elves knew that they couldn't simply lock up this power somewhere a dwarf could stumble across it while mining, or a mage could access it with a spell like the Mai'ngolo. So, when they struck the bargain with the High Gods allowing them a choice in their enslavement to the old magic, and they knew that they had to protect the future of this bargain at all costs, the Eldest among them gave their lives to combine their magic. They encoded it into the very life-force of this baby before the High Gods split the magics up between the races so as not to give one more power over the others. These were the four original Mages, one for each of the four Magics - Death, Spirit, Ward, and Elemental - all now held in the blood of a single child. And not just any child - Moira'nila, the last-born daughter of Alamira. She was the mother of all Elves, our *Esselda*." She took a deep breath and allowed them all a chance to process what she had

168

uncovered. Lucian had gone white, and Rowan's brow was so furrowed it looked like his head might implode.

"There's more," she continued, "the elfling was then taken from the First Tree to be raised by one of the independent clans that had chosen to renounce the old magic. Since she was too young to make the choice for herself, she was never disconnected from it. She lived with this power inside of her, never knowing that she possessed it, and passed it down to her children, and they to their children." She looked again at Lucian and held his gaze as she spoke her next words, "the last known location of her living descendants was the Village de Lyria, my village." Lucian's eyes exploded with icy blue fire as he worked out what exactly she was saying.

"No..." he whispered, the fury welling up inside of him.

"What?" Rowan asked angrily, clearly frustrated that he had missed something.

Kara looked at him, feeling the white-hot fire burning in her eyes, and finished, "I believe I am the descendant of Moria'nila." The silence in the room was excruciating. She could feel the fear behind Lucian's fury, and the disbelief that Carmine and Rowan shared at hearing this.

"It has to be wrong, you must have mistranslated the text," Lucian stated, pleading with his eyes for her to agree with him. She wished she could, but knew she was right.

"I didn't," she replied quietly, looking down at her hands as she fought against the tears.

169

"How do you know?" Rowan finally asked. "How do you know that you're the weapon?"

"It's a long story, but I technically died by a Death Magic spell many years ago, the day Gondyr and I met, and I was pulled back through the Spirit Realm by an opposing spell," she told him, "which unlocked something dormant inside of me that I have been fighting to keep caged ever since. I've never come up with an explanation for how I survived, or what this power is inside of me, until now."

"Fuck," Rowan sighed. "This is...a lot. I'm not even sure I fully understand what this means, or what we should do with this information."

"We need to keep this quiet," Carmine finally spoke. "If word gets out that an Elven Assassin is carrying ancient volatile magic in her blood, we could have a lot of very serious problems on our hands."

"You're right Carmine," Kara sighed, "I have to tell my team something, but I will keep it as vague as possible. Otherwise, this knowledge does not leave this room." Rowan nodded in agreement. "We need to get back to the Citadel. We have a meeting with an unknown contact tomorrow night that should give us the location of the Demigods' next move. We need to prepare," she told him.

Carmine removed his ward, and they all left the office, their moods heavy with uncertainty. They didn't speak again as they made their way down to the main hall, Kara and Lucian heading straight out into the courtyard where Markus was speaking with a few other Gryphons. When he saw them making their way to him, his face grew serious. He could see that something was wrong.

"What is it?" he asked as they approached.

"We'll talk after we get back," Kara told him, climbing on Sable without another word. Lucian mounted the Pegasus behind her, and they all headed back down to the Stone.

Fifteen

The Mysterious Contact

When they arrived in the courtyard of the Citadel, Gondyr was outside and waved at them cheerfully, but when they didn't return the greeting, his smile faded, and brow furrowed in concern. Kara didn't say a word, simply walked through the stables, and headed for the woods beyond. She needed some fresh air, and some time to think. She got to the spring, took off her boots, and stood in the water, eyes closed and heart pounding so hard she feared it might just leap from her chest. She stood there a long time, trying to untangle all the knots in her mind, but every time she worked through one, it seemed another had formed. After a while, the familiar scent of coffee and lavender washed over her.

"What can I do?" Lucian asked behind her. She turned and walked through the water to him, tears streaming down her face, and collapsed into his chest in a fit of emotions. He held her as she cried, allowing her to simply be, to simply feel everything she had been avoiding her whole life. She had always known she was somehow different, that she didn't quite belong anywhere in this world, and that knowledge only grew when this power unlocked within her. Now she had the answers she had so feverishly craved, but she no longer wanted them. She felt so fucking selfish. This magic in her could stop the Demigods, it could save everyone and everything she loved. But what would be the cost? What would she have to sacrifice? Her own life? After she finally found some semblance of peace, of love? And she was fuming. She didn't even have a choice; she was just born with something she had no knowledge of or control over and expected to save the world without considering herself for even a second. How could the First Elves have done this to an infant? How could they expect an elf millions of years in the future to just accept her fate and not prepare her for this? She was completely lost and had no idea how she was supposed to find her way back.

***

Lucian held her, doing his best to not let his fury and sadness destroy the strength he knew she needed from him. He felt so foolish and selfish, having spent the previous night concerned with his own mortality, and here she was, expected to use a power she knew nothing about, a power that could potentially kill her, to save the whole of existence. Feeling her sobbing in his arms splintered his heart in ways he didn't know was possible. He couldn't protect her from this. All he could do was support her, help her try to carry the weight of it, and hope against all the odds that they could find a way to save her.

They stood there until the sun dipped low behind the trees, and she had finally stopped crying. When she pulled away, he looked in her eyes and saw that iron resolve she somehow always found a way to wrap herself in, and his admiration for her grew infinitely. She wouldn't let this destroy her, and neither would he. They walked hand in hand back to the Citadel, no

173

longer caring who saw them together. They had so much more to worry about. As they entered the main hall, they found the whole team waiting on the chairs and sofas around the fireplace.

***

Kara knew she had to tell them something - they were all clearly worried, but she had to walk a fine line here, else she endanger them no matter which way she falls.

"We found something in the Histories," she started, straight to the point, "and while I cannot share any of this information with you, I will tell you this...we will stop Solaris and the Demigods. I promise that all your hard work and trust in me won't be for nothing, and I will fight for each of you as long as I breathe."

"I don't like how this sounds," Gondyr said forcefully, "why can't you tell us?"

"Because this information was buried and lost for an incredibly good reason, and one slip of the tongue, one misspoken word, could mean death for everyone and everything we all hold dear. Simply knowing this information would put each of you in unimaginable danger that I will not be responsible for. I need you to trust me now and know that I withhold this information for the good of all of you, and the future we are trying to save. I know that's a lot to ask, but if we are going to succeed, I need to know that you all understand what I'm asking, without question." She looked around the room, stopping on each face, waiting as each of them nodded that they understood. Gondyr was last, and they stared sharply at each other for a

174

long time before his face softened a bit, and he finally nodded.

"Thank you," she sighed, "now, we have a big night tomorrow, and we need to be at our best. I suggest you all enjoy the evening and get some good sleep. We'll gather in the morning to go over the plan one more time, make sure we're ready." Gondyr got up from his seat, pushed past Kara and Lucian, and went out the door with a huff. She knew he was simply scared for her, he could always see more than he let on. "I'm going to go talk to him," she told Lucian.

"Alright. Come find me in my room when you're done," he replied with a smile and squeeze of her hand before letting go. Gondyr was in the courtyard chopping firewood, more aggressively than usual. She stood there for a few minutes before she spoke.

"I know you're not really mad," she started, but he cut her off.

"I'm not mad, I'm fucking *furious*," he said. "Something big is happening, something I know has a lot to do with you, and you're not telling me...you've never *not* told me Kara, since the day we met."

"Gondyr, my dear friend, I would give anything to tell you. This is tearing me up...but I can't."

"Oh, but the Assassin knows?" he shot angrily at her.

"That's not fair...I didn't know what we'd be walking into when we left for the Fortress this morning."

"I know, I know," he growled, then sighed. "I'm sorry, I just don't like feeling helpless, especially when it comes to you. And I just feel so helpless right now."

"To be honest, so do I..." she trailed off.

He studied her face. "This has to do with your lightning, doesn't it? The power in you that you keep caged?" She just looked at him, knowing she couldn't confirm his suspicions. "Your silence speaks volumes," he said, and smiled softly. "Okay, you know I trust you with my life, with all our lives. If this really is the way it must be, at least I understand why. Just let me swing the axe for a bit, I'll be alright."

"Fair enough, I'll leave you to it," she smiled, "and thank you Gondyr, for everything. I wouldn't even be alive now if not for you. I have never forgotten that, and I never will." She kissed his cheek and let him get back to his chopping. She could see Dahlia and Markus through the kitchen windows as she headed back inside, Dahlia sitting on his lap, laughing together. She sighed - another thing they were all fighting for, a chance for this unlikely pair to try and create a life together. She went upstairs to Lucian's room, then knocked gently on the door.

"Come in," she heard from inside. She found him sitting up in his bed, with a cup of coffee in his hand. "Just so we're clear, you never have to knock, you are always welcome in here...you hear that magical room?" He smiled and pointed to a chest of drawers by the door, upon which sat a pot of tea. She poured herself a cup before sitting on the edge of the bed and had a long drink. It was warm, strong, spiced citrus, with a spoonful of honey...her favorite brew.

176

"Mmmmm," she sighed, "did you make this?"

"I did. How is it?" he asked shyly.

"It's perfect." She set the cup down on the nightstand, took off her boots, and snuggled up next to him. "Thank you."

"You're welcome. I just thought you could use a little warmth."

She looked up at him, deep into his enigmatic eyes. "No, I mean for being with me today, and all the days since we found our way back to each other. I don't know if I would have had the strength to make it this far on my own."

He brushed the back of his hand against her cheek, moving a strand of hair from her eyes, and smiled. "Yes, you would have. You have survived so much, lost everything, and you continue to stand up against the absolute worst this world has to offer with more strength and determination than I even thought was possible in a single spirit. You started this thing without me, and not one of us, especially me, would be here without you. Don't give any of that credit away to anyone," he asserted. "Even as a boy I admired your courage, your kindness, your ferocity...and your never-ending quest for justice." He kissed her forehead and held her to him, "As a man, I not only admire it, I'm in complete awe of it...I love you, Tia."

"I love you, Luca," she whispered, and nuzzled her face against his chest.

They awoke with the sun the next morning, and headed down to the kitchen to make breakfast, both feeling surprisingly well rested. Lucian got coffee going, and Kara started the tea before diving into prep work. She made her berry tarts, everyone's favorite, and he made mushroom and truffle omelets. They enjoyed working together in the kitchen, a brief moment of simplicity within the whirlwind of chaos around them. The team trickled in as they worked, and the kitchen filled with chatter. Kara smiled - this day would end rough, but they could still find beauty in the moment, something worth fighting for, and it would make them sharper. After breakfast, they gathered in the library to go over the plan one more time.

"Dahlia, how's the glimmer for Lucian?" Kara asked.

"Strong. We practiced all day, and it will move seamlessly with him. He won't be seen until he needs to be. Plus, I wove in an untraceable charm, so he won't be detected by even the strongest Mormagi if they show up," Dahlia replied.

"Nicely done," Kara smiled. "So, we all have our positions, and everybody knows not to move or be seen unless you see the signal from Lucian. Dahlia, you will come with us to Dellalun this afternoon so we can get everything set with the Vipers. The rest of you trickle into the city behind us, spacing it out, and keep a low profile until it's time to get into position. Gondyr and Nalor, you'll have to travel separately as the rest of the team needs your Stone Magic. Luckily, Dellalun is always full of different people from all over Cylendri, so none of you should stand out too much and raise any flags." She paused, and then added, "we've got this. We're as prepared

178

as we can be, and I trust all of you. Get your asses back here after we have what we need, don't extend the fight longer than necessary, got it?"

"Got it," the whole team proclaimed in unison.

"Nalor, do you have those new daggers ready for me and Lucian?" She asked as the rest of the group dispersed.

"Yes ma'am," he winked.

Lucian raised an eyebrow at her. "What daggers?"

"Let's go look," she smiled slyly, and they headed out to the forge. When they got across the courtyard, Nalor pulled two slips of rolled up leather from the workshop shelves and unrolled one of them on the bench in front of Kara and Lucian. It was lined with beautiful, sleek, darksteel daggers. Lucian picked one up, admiring the craftsmanship. Its edges were sharper than he had ever seen on a dagger, and it had a thin vine engraving that snaked down the middle of the blade on one side starting a few millimeters above the handle, tapering at the tip. The handle was wrapped with dark green leather strips, allowing for a solid grip, but it was still lightweight and perfectly balanced. As he held the dagger, it felt like it was made for his hand.

"The engraving allows for more poison on the blade, instead of just the tip. It can pool and settle there. And Nalor custom crafted the handles to fit our hands specifically. Do you like them?" Kara asked.

"They're perfect," Lucian smiled, "thank you both."

179

Nalor beamed with pride, "I don't usually get to craft such small, precise blades, or work with darksteel. I enjoyed making them! There's also a set of throwing daggers to match," he said as he handed each of them a second, smaller bundle. They both grabbed their bundles and headed to the training room to get in some practice. A few hours later, once they felt comfortable with the new daggers, they went to the alchemy room that had recently appeared where they added the poison and then let them rest while they had an early dinner. The first group left for Dellalun not long before sundown.

***

The city was in better shape after the Belua were run back out, you'd hardly know the streets were a battlefield not long ago. Unless of course, you had been there. Dahlia, Kara, and Lucian met Vivvain in the common room of The Den. She had five other Ammodytes with her.

"Good to see you, First Fang," Vivvain said. It was still strange for Lucian to be addressed as First Fang, but he didn't let his discomfort show.

"You as well, Viv, and the rest of you. We're grateful for your help this evening." Lucian tried to be diplomatic, like Marciela had always been.

"Of course," Vivvain replied, "shall we go over the plan? We have the map of the Gardens here." They gathered around one of the tables, Lucian looked at Kara and she nodded.

"The meeting is at nine, so be in position well before then - the contact will already be waiting for us. We'll have two sets of Vipers in each of these three locations," he pointed to three spots around the map, "and our team will be spread out here, here, and here. Dahlia will be up in the tower just outside the Gardens, controlling a glimmer on me. I'll be down on the ground here. She'll also provide updates telepathically as she has the best vantage point of the meeting place and each entrance. Kara will appear to be going in alone and will hopefully get the information we need without any bloodshed. But if it goes sideways, look for my wings. The glimmer will disappear, and I'll be in flight. The goal is the information...if we don't get it without a fight, then we take down the contact and hopefully get it off their body. Our team has been instructed to pull back as soon as we have it, and I suggest you do the same. We don't know what we're going up against out there, so be ready for anything, and then get the hell out of there when you can. Understood?" All the Vipers nodded. *"Flessial, Adatil, Ni'Riveael."*

The Vipers dispersed, and Lucian took a deep breath, not sure he was cut out for leadership. He much preferred the simplicity and anonymity of assassin work, without the politics of diplomacy.

"You did great," Kara said, pulling him from his thoughts. He squinted his eyes at her, and she raised an eyebrow, "true leaders don't crave leadership, so the power never goes to their head. It gets easier, but it should always make you a little uncomfortable. If you're ever getting too comfortable, I'll remind you."

"You two are so intense," Dahlia said playfully, "but you give me hope." Kara and Lucian smiled. "I've never actually spent any time in Dellalun...can we visit the market since we have some time?" she asked.

"That would be nice. And we'll be closer to the Gardens anyways," Kara replied. So, they left The Den and headed for the market. The stalls had just opened, and the City of Moonlight was coming to life.

***

After perusing the stalls for a while, they took Dahlia down to the docks in the Port District to see the bustle of commerce that took place there every night. Then, as nine o'clock drew closer, Dahlia headed off to her post in the tower, leaving Kara and Lucian near to the Gardens' main entrance.

"Stay close," she said, her heart racing. She always hated this part, the moments just before you get your mark, or start a fight, or have an uneasy meeting.

"I'm right behind you," he assured her, "no matter what." He leaned down and kissed her fiercely, then left to get into position so Dahlia could get the glimmer on him. Kara took a few breaths, steeled herself, and started moving. The clock tower chimed as she walked through the great floral arch of the Gardens, and weaved her way through the bushes, hedges, and trees to the center. She emerged into the space on the last chime, and she could feel Lucian not far behind, just to her right.

"Punctual...ever the assassin," a deep, guttural voice said from the other side of the large whitestone fountain that sat in the center. Kara's hackles went up...she knew that voice.

"Nero, you son of a bitch...*you're* our contact?" she said incredulously, eyes full of white fire. A giant beast of a man came around the fountain - eight feet tall, massive, curved horns at his temples, brown skin painted

182

with battle scars, and soulless, black eyes. His lower half was completely covered in thick, coarse black hair, and he stood on large black hooves. This monster had murdered countless innocents, destroyed part of the city she loved, and had taken Marciela hostage. She should jam every single one of her daggers in his fucking face. But she had to get the location if he had it. "You got me here; do you have the information I need?" She asked firmly.

He laughed, loud and sinister, "such ferocity for such a small thing. But you're no ordinary elf, are you?" he said with a sly look. "No, you're not. Or you would have become wolf shit for my pack the day you tried to kill me. You should be dead, and not by my hand."

"I don't know what you're talking about," she replied coolly, feeling Lucian move a bit closer.

"I'm no fool, elf. I know far more than you, or anyone else, gives me credit for. To be honest, I'm getting tired of the politics," he sighed, "of having to play nice with those filthy Death Mages. And now they're asking me to sacrifice my own fucking kind for a place at the table in Ess'Magis..."

Kara scowled, she knew he was ramping up to something. She had studied him for years before she got her chance to take him out, and he was nothing if not predictable. "So, you thought you'd just, what? Hand over some information and the Vipers would forget everything you've done?"

"Oh no, child, you deeply misunderstand. I'm not handing over anything, it's beneath me. The Demigods are quite persuasive, and the Mormagi have paid very well. But one way or another, we're all going to be

183

dead, so why delay the inevitable. Only one of us is leaving these gardens alive tonight." Suddenly, over two dozen Death Mages appeared out of thin air all around them, and Kara already had her daggers in her hands.

Sixteen

Nero's Sacrifice

A red light flashed, and a spell came hurtling at Kara. She jumped to her left onto the edge of a stone planter and pushed off towards the fountain in front of her. Lucian was in the air to her right as she landed on the rim of the fountain, then leapt for a Death Mage and rammed a dagger in its chest. Before it sent a spell at Lucian, she threw a dagger to her right straight into the head of another.

The gardens erupted in flashes of red, green, white, and blue. Arrows flew from Sel'arins bow, Gondyr and Nalor were shouting battle cries as they swung their axes and hammers, Markus went flying behind her with two Mormagi in his hands face down as he dragged them along the rough stone pathways, their inky blood staining the rocks. Not a moment later, Vipers were all around her, taking down Mormagi with lightning-fast precision. Aleric was strangling three of them in the air with icy blue spirit hands that extended from his chest, and Sel'arin ran towards her, using her magic to ensnare a few more in vines and branches from the plants around them.

185

"Where's Nero?!" Kara shouted as loud as she could.

"Heading for the south exit," Dahlia spoke inside her head. Kara turned and saw his horns just over some hedges. "Lucian! Nero!" she pointed and took off after the Belua as the battle raged behind her. He flew up at her back, lifted her off the ground, and launched her at Nero's back. She landed hard and stuck two daggers in each of his shoulders, then two more in his neck before he could react, enough poison on them to take out an entire village. He grabbed her with his massive hand and threw her across the gardens, against one of the outer stone walls, before he crashed into the tree to his right and went down. She crumpled to the ground, and Lucian was at her side in moments.

"Tia?!" he shouted, the panic clear in his voice. She moaned as she rolled over a bit, something was definitely broken. "Gods, how the fuck did you survive that?!"

"Dahlia...ward..." was all she said, then winced and moaned again as she tried to take a deep breath. "Nero?"

"He's down, the poison was quick." He looked up to the tower and could see Dahlia. *"Focus all your energy on her. I know you think you're not ready for broken bones, but you can heal her,"* he told her telepathically. After a few moments, a golden shimmer covered Kara - every strand of hair, every pore sparkled. She grunted and moaned as Dahlia's magic slowly healed her cuts and started mending her breaks.

"I've got her," Dahlia told him, *"the team needs you, go!"*

186

Lucian shot in the air and headed back into the fray, slicing through Mormagi with his Khyber as he flew. He and Ira were working in perfect tandem now, Lucian using the Wrath Spirit's unrestrained strength to land on and tear the arms off a Death Mage. He saw another sending spell after spell at the dwarves as they hid behind a large stone planter and launched two daggers straight into its spine. Another had Vivvain around her neck, hand up next to her head, and was pulling her life-force out in smokey red tendrils. He turned and slung his final dagger into its right eye, barely missing Vivvain's ear. She dropped to the ground.

"Aleric, Vivvain needs your attention!" he shouted, and Aleric was there in a blue flash. Markus had the last two Death Mages at least twenty feet in the air, and he slammed their heads together before dropping them. They were likely dead before they landed in the thorny bushes below. Then it was eerily quiet. Lucian took a couple of deep breaths as he looked around, and the air reeked of death. "Fucking walking corpses," he snarled in disgust. "Everyone alright?!"

Gondyr and Nalor groaned, Sel'arin waved lazily from the ground nearby, Markus looked unharmed, and Aleric was tending Vivvain as the other five Ammodytes made their way back to the fountain. They looked like they had taken a few hits. He needed to check on Kara and get Dahlia down here to help Aleric. He flew back over where she had been lying, but she was gone. He looked around and saw her with Nero's body.

"I see Dahlia finally graduated her healing magic...what are you looking for?" he asked her as he landed.

187

"The information, I know he has it..." she said as she frantically searched the pouches on his belt. "Fuck!" she exclaimed and fell back onto the ground, defeated. "There is nothing here...it doesn't make sense..."

"What doesn't?" Lucian asked.

"You heard the way he was talking... *'tired of the politics, filthy Death Mages, sacrifice my own kind'*...he wasn't talking like someone who was interested in continuing his dealings with the Mormagi, or the Demigods. His words were...riddled, and oddly sorrowful." She sat in thought, that crinkle in her nose as she focused on remembering the conversation. *"Only one of us is leaving...delay the inevitable...not handing over anything..."* her eyes shot up at him, "it's beneath him!" she exclaimed. Then she got up and ran over to where he had been standing next to the fountain, looking around at the stones in the ground.

"I don't understand, "Lucian told her, a puzzled look on his face.

"He said *'I'm not handing over anything, it's beneath me'*...why did he use those words? Handing something over is *'beneath me'*. That's a strange thing to say. I think," she said as she circled, "it's here, under one of these."

Lucian looked down at the stones now and noticed one near her foot looked like it was loose, sticking up just slightly at one corner. "There," he pointed, and she looked straight down, moving away from the spot. She knelt, wriggled the stone out a bit with a dagger, then yanked it all the way out. She stuck her hand inside the hole it left, and pulled out a piece of parchment, along with a glowing red crystal hanging on a thin piece of leather, like a necklace.

188

"What is that?" Lucian asked.

"I don't know...everybody head back to the Citadel," Kara ordered. Markus grabbed Dahlia and carried her off through the air to the Travel Stone across the city. Gondyr, Nalor, and Sel'arin headed in that direction on foot.

"Viv, are you good?" Lucian knelt next to her while Aleric finished tending to the other Vipers.

"Yeah, thanks," she muttered, still a little out of it, but she looked physically okay.

"Good. Get back to The Den and get some rest. You fought hard, we wouldn't have succeeded without your help," he said gently as he helped her up.

She smiled, brushed the dirt off, and said, "for Dellalun, for Cylendri."

Lucian nodded and sent them on their way as Aleric glided off towards the Stone. Then Lucian wrapped Kara in his arms without a word and lifted her into the sky.

***

Kara clung tightly to Lucian as they flew above the city, looking down over her shoulder at the dazzling lights below. Dellalun was safe, for now. They had a lead, and she had finally completed her mark on Nero. The Belua had no leader and would disperse. Not to mention, the whole team survived another nasty fight and were getting stronger. This was a win. They landed a short time later at the Stone where Aleric, Dahlia, and Markus were waiting.

"Sel'arin, Gondyr, and Nalor should be here any moment, we'll wait for them. I'm not leaving without all of us together," Kara insisted. After a few minutes, the whole team gathered around the Stone and were gone. They all arrived at the Citadel and made their way to the library.

"I don't know if it's the information we were promised," Kara started, "but I retrieved this stone and parchment." She set the necklace down on the table in front of her. Aleric picked it up with magic and spun it in the air slowly.

"What does the parchment say?" Sel'arin asked as she looked at the red stone with a mix of apprehension and curiosity. Kara untied and unrolled the parchment, then read it aloud.

"Faithful followers of the True Gods, the time grows near. While disruptions from the Subverters have proven to be more bothersome than expected, we will soon have the elf who leads this small rebellion in our custody, and it will crumble. Our plans will not be unraveled again. Est'alda will fall, the Mai'ngolo will be under our control, and Ess'Magis will belong to the Chosen!" Kara paused and looked around the room, fear and fury plain on every face. Then she continued, *"Bring your strongest warriors, your wisest mages, and your most insidious assassins to The First Tree on the next Full Moon, along with this Stone of Fealty, to gain access to the Well. A Sacri'Sanguis of the highest quality must be paid if we are to open the pathway. Rest assured, however, that we shall rebuild your great*

190

Factions and armies once the High Gods have been removed from their seat of power, and you shall have your place at our table!" She set the letter down and took a deep breath.

Aleric was the first to speak, "If I understand that, the Demigods are going to mass murder the Belua, Mormagi, and any other wayward followers to bring down Est'alda so they can access the Well, killing countless others."

"Yes," Kara whispered, eyes sizzling with fury.

"And this Stone of Fealty...it's magic is strange, unlike anything I've ever seen or studied, but it feels like it has protection spells woven into it," Aleric continued.

"Yes, I feel that, too," Dahlia agreed.

"Which means that those holding these stones will be immune to the Blood Sacrifice," Aleric finished, resting the necklace back down on the table.

"We will soon have the elf who leads this small rebellion in our custody, and it will crumble," Gondyr repeated the line, "clearly, they underestimated you, Kara."

"They always do," Lucian chimed in.

"This is what Nero meant by *'and now they're asking me to sacrifice my own kind for a place at the table in Ess'Magis'*. And why he was ready to give

191

me this information, knowing he would likely die. If the Belua leader is dead, they will scatter. Some may run to the Mormagi or the Demigods, but it won't be enough. He sacrificed himself for his people," she sighed - she had underestimated him. "And with control of the Vipers under Lucian instead of Cassius, they won't have the numbers there either. They will have to rely on other innocents, which means they will have the Mormagi spread thin attempting to gather slaves and prisoners. We will need to warn everyone and send help to as many corners of the map as we possibly can. Markus, the Gryphons will be instrumental in that."

"It's time my brethren did more than just break up petty squabbles. I will inform the Lord Gryphon in the morning," Markus replied.

"I will visit the Halls of the Undead, as well," Aleric offered, "the Spirits will be able to move quickly in spreading the word throughout the Clans, Tribes, and Factions."

"I need to get home and speak with Nae'lin. They need to fortify defenses around The First Tree and the Well," Sel'arin added.

"Alright," Kara addressed everyone, "we have less than twenty-eight days until the next Full Moon. Markus will focus his efforts on protecting the people from the Mormagi, and Aleric will get the word spread so the smaller clans and tribes have a chance to defend themselves until help arrives. Sel'arin, take Gondyr with you to Est'alda, he can aid with the defenses, and relay updates back to me frequently. Nalor, we need the Stone Faction, they cannot sit idly by any longer. They will help us move groups of citizens with the Travel Stones and build up fortifications. Dahlia, I will take you back to Aquanalis so you can update the High Priestess, and the Nymphs can be ready to travel and tend the wounded, then I will come straight back so Lucian and I can go speak with the Vipers. Dellalun will become ground zero for the displaced and wounded. We will need the largest group of healers there, where we will house every life we can throughout the city. The Vipers will coordinate, and record information on the state of things throughout Cylendri to ensure we're staying ahead of those assholes. Do not allow any city or village to go unprotected, be smart - make sure there are warriors and fighters left behind to defend their homes and try not to concentrate our assets in large numbers lest we draw the attention of the Demigods. I will focus all my efforts on a plan to end this at the next Full Moon. They will all have to be present, and that will be our only chance to take Solaris and the others down." Kara paused for a moment, then added, "you all did amazing out there, and I am so grateful each of you is on my side. Get some rest, we can't do anything more tonight. Tomorrow, the final battle will be in sight."

Seventeen

A Powerful Discovery

The group dispersed, save for Kara and Lucian. "How do you do that?" he asked as she sat down in the chair behind her.

"Do what?" she sighed.

"You almost died tonight...again. I know you're still in pain; you're exhausted. And yet, you found the information we needed, you made sure we all got here safely, then you laid out a plan with specific instructions within a few minutes of knowing what lies ahead of us, and they all listened to you without question. You wear the heavy crown of leadership with such grace...and such resilience. How?" he asked again.

She chuckled and rubbed her temples. "Hyper-focus? Gluttony for punishment? A debilitating need to control every little thing I possibly can? Take your pick."

He lifted her chin to meet her eyes, "you're remarkable. I hope I figure out how to be half as good at gaining loyalty and trust as you are," he said with that knowing smile and look that melted her resolve. "Come on, I think you need a swim." He took her hands in his and pulled her up from the chair, then led her out to the spring. They removed their daggers, boots, and leathers, and made their way to the center of the water, where Kara dipped below the surface for a moment, then came back up. The cool water felt so good on her aching muscles. Lucian looped his arm around her waist, pulled her to him and just looked at her, studying her face.

"What?" she asked shyly.

"Every time I think I've lost you again, I realize that my memories are such precious, fragile pieces of my past that were once moments so important to me. I don't want to forget ever again, I want you to be imprinted in my mind so deeply that nothing, and no one can ever take you from me, in this life or the next." He wrapped her in his arms, and held her body close to his, his face buried in her neck.

She stroked his hair and kissed his cheek, and they held each other in silence for a while as the wind rustled through the trees around them. When Lucian finally pulled away, he leaned in and kissed her with such passion, it almost broke her heart. It was filled with need and showed her just how much he feared losing her. He loved her, knowing that her spirit would carry her straight into the eye of every storm, and that any of those storms could be her last, but he loved her that much more for it.

***

They laid together in Lucian's bed, after making their way back in from the spring, Kara curled up on her right side asleep, the blankets barely covering her naked body. Lucian was awake on his left side, watching her, memorizing the way she moved with each breath. She looked so peaceful. He knew she didn't need him to protect her, but he wanted so badly to steal her away from all of this, so she could just be without all the obligation and responsibility, just live simply. He also knew she'd never really be happy without a cause, a mission, a life to save and a battle to win. So, he would embrace the time he had with her exactly as she is, however long it would be, and commit every moment to his memory - every smile, every tear, every last scar, every laugh and sigh, every single moment with her - etching her existence on his very soul.

***

The whole team was already in the kitchen when Kara finally made her way downstairs well after sun-up.

"Good morning, Kara," Sel'arin said cheerfully, and handed her a hot cup of tea.

"Good morning, thank you," Kara replied with a smile. "It smells wonderful in here." The table had an impressive spread of food on it, from flat cakes and omelets to hand pies and berry salad.

"We all made something we love," Dahlia chimed in, "you're just in time."

Kara sat down between Lucian and Gondyr, and the whole room filled with clanking, chatter, laughter, and the occasional grunt from Nalor. They filled up on delicious food and friendly conversation before everyone headed off to prepare for their assignments. The Citadel was buzzing with activity, everyone gathering equipment, tending to the Pegasi, suiting up, and slowly leaving via the Stone. As she was leaving the library after grabbing a few maps, Kara caught Markus and Dahlia saying goodbye in the main hall before he left, sharing a playful hug and a tender kiss. Markus nodded to Kara, smiled once more at Dahlia, and left.

"You guys are so mushy," Kara said with a wink, "and you give me hope."

Dahlia blushed, "I'll be ready to go in just a few minutes. Meet you at the Stone."

Kara headed out into the courtyard and found Lucian sitting by the fire pit, cup of coffee in hand. "I won't be gone long; I just need to make sure Dahlia gets to Aquanalis before I come back. The Stone isn't far, and we don't have to take the river like Gondyr and I did last time, so maybe an hour or two."

"I'll be right here when you get back," he smiled. Dahlia walked by, and Kara turned to follow her to the Stone. They arrived not far from Aquanalis a moment later.

"We have a hidden entrance this way, through the only part of the ward that touches the land," Dahlia told her, and started walking northeast. They walked in silence for a while, both lost in their own thoughts about the coming month. Then Dahlia broke the silence, "I'm happy I left home. You know? That I volunteered to go on this journey with you. It's been terrifying, and overwhelming, and...wonderful, too. The world is unbelievable. I never

197

thanked you for standing up for me when my mother asked if she should let me go but thank you. Whatever happens, I'm happy I left home with you."

"I'm happy you did, as well," Kara replied. "I see so much of myself in you. Always remember to stay true to yourself, to your worth. The Realms need souls like yours, Dahlia...souls who spread light wherever they go, who are full to bursting with a genuine thirst for life and knowledge. Don't let anyone - your family, your friends, your lovers, or yourself - take that from you, ever." She smiled, "and thank you, for saving my life last night. If you hadn't gotten that ward around me, I don't think I would have survived the hit to the wall."

"But...I didn't ward you, I only healed you after. If there was a ward around you when you hit the wall, either you've got a guardian spirit, which you know are increasingly rare, or you created it yourself," Dahlia said, puzzled.

Kara stopped and thought about that for a few moments. If she held the combined magics inside her, then it would make sense that she created the ward. How many times had she done that since it unlocked, she wondered. She had enough knowledge to help break a ward but not create one. How many times had she used a bit of magic without knowing it? And could she learn to manipulate each of them, or all of them?

"Kara?" Dahlia asked, pulling her from the spiral.

"Sorry...um, it's complicated," she stammered.

"Ah, the *secret information*," Dahlia winked, "got it. Let's go, we're almost there."

They finished the last leg of the walk surrounded only by the sound of the forest. As they approached the tree line, Kara could see the river where Aquanalis stood above the water, but it wasn't there. They hadn't passed through the ward yet, though Kara could feel it starting to sizzle ahead.

"The entrance is between those two trees there, the ones that are closer together," Dahlia told her telepathically. A countermeasure in case they were being watched, even though they would simply disappear through the ward, and couldn't be followed. Kara slipped between the two trees behind Dahlia, the buzzing of the ward louder than before, likely because it was even stronger here. They made it through, and there were the floating islands, looming before them. A long bridge of roots and vines extended from the mainland up to one of the lower-level islands that were a few feet above the water. Kara followed Dahlia across and met the High Priestess and Lilum on the other side.

"Kara, Dahlia, what a lovely surprise," Vitellina greeted them.

"Mother, we need to speak. Kara has obligations elsewhere," Dahlia advised, standing up straight and a bit defiant. She clearly had been taking cues from Kara on roguish diplomacy.

"A lot has happened, High Priestess. I trust Dahlia to fill you in and report back when she's ready," Kara explained. Vitellina nodded, Kara bowed her head, and she took her leave back down the bridge, disappearing in the trees at the edge of the ward. Once through, she headed straight for the Stone and back to the Citadel.

Lucian was still in the courtyard with his coffee in hand when she appeared. "How are the Nymphs?" he asked as she approached him.

"Fine," she replied sharply, and he gave her an inquisitive look, brow furrowed and onyx eyes narrow. "I'm sorry, I kind of figured something out while speaking with Dahlia, and I'm not sure what to do next."

"What did you figure out?" he asked, the concern rising in his voice.

"I think...I created the ward that saved me last night," she started, then took a breath, and continued, "Dahlia said it wasn't her. Aleric wasn't anywhere nearby, no one was except you, and unless Ira gave you some new powers you haven't told me about, that only leaves me."

"It wasn't us," Ira hissed.

"Think about it, I have all four magics in my blood, and there were situations even before the power manifested when I don't know how I survived. Is it possible I've warded myself before? Or manipulated other magics without realizing it? Do you think I could figure out how to focus and wield at least one of them? All of them?" Kara knew she was rambling, but she just had so many questions.

"Well, there's only one way to find out...when we're next here with Aleric, the two of you need to spend some time exploring it," Lucian said as he set his coffee down and stood up. "Right now, we have an appointment in Dellalun, and a city to prepare," he smiled, taking her hand and heading to the Stone.

Lucian had every Viper that was close enough to receive a raven quickly gathered at Dellalun Manor instead of The Den. It was less conspicuous for them to trickle in through the private docks, or the hidden cellar entrance in the gardens than to have them pouring in through the lower levels or busy docks of The Den. Besides, he didn't trust the eyes and ears around every corner in that place. The ballroom here was warded thanks to a deal Marciela made with a mage for a rather unique trinket many years ago. You couldn't step foot in the room if you weren't truly loyal to the Faction or the First Fang, and you couldn't hear anything even if you were right outside the door and everyone was yelling. No one except her and Lucian knew that. And now Kara, as she could feel ward magic.

Dozens of Vipers surrounded them on the main floor, up the grand staircase, and on the second level balconies. Once the last of them had filed into the space, and Viv gave the signal, Lucian put his hands up to quiet the crowd. He stood in the very center of the room, at the lowest and most vulnerable spot in the whole place. He hoped that he showed the humility and virtuous spirit he was asking all of them to possess now.

"Vipers, I stand here before you to humbly ask for your help. The Demigods have chosen to sacrifice thousands of innocent lives as they make their final play for the throne of Ess'Magis. They intend to unleash a Blood Sacrifice the scale of which would ripple across all Cylendri, and they believe that we should just accept our fate. But I tell you now, I will not accept that!" He waited as the room erupted in agreement, then continued, "We are the only city large enough to house the wounded and the displaced by Death Mages scouring the land for souls to sacrifice. We are the only place where all the races and Factions can roam freely and find a little piece of home in the markets and taverns or coming in at the docks. So, I ask you to help us persuade our citizens to aid in this cause, to open their homes to other families and clans who have likely lost everything, and to host a group of Healers to treat our guests, and Ward Mages to protect our people. If they choose not to help, that is their choice, and we cannot force this upon them. But it starts with us, this is our city!" Another round of cheers and applause. "Now go spread the word through the Dwelling District and then report back to your Pit Leaders. Ammodytes, you focus on the ports and markets, we're going to need to double our commerce, and make sensible deals with the merchants. We don't know exactly when they will start arriving but expect to see the number of people in the city increasing in the next few days."

"Flessial, Adatil, Ni'Riveael!" Every Viper declared the Creed in unison and then began to disperse. Lucian took a deep breath, held it for a moment, and let it out slowly.

"You will make a fine leader," Kara told him, taking his hand as Vivvain and Marciela made their way down the stairs towards them.

"Yes, I think he will," Marciela agreed, "he's clearly been paying attention to you, my dear."

Kara laughed, "and you all these years. I can't take all the credit."

"I'm standing right here," Lucian said tersely.

"Yes, we all know you've perfected the art of brooding," Marciela

202

quipped. "But that was very well addressed. I will manage the Manor here and the Mages, we have more than enough room and they will have access to anything they may need. Vivvain will run things from the Den and manage the incoming reports. You focus on Est'alda, we will have nothing left if the First Tree falls." Lucian nodded in agreement, and Vivvain left for The Den. "Tia, can I speak with you for a moment?"

Lucian kissed her cheek, "I'll meet you in the foyer," then left the ballroom.

"I see things have...progressed with you two," Marciela began. "It seems to have made him stronger, more focused, less emotionally imbalanced," she smiled. "I just wanted to congratulate you on taking Nero out. We can finally remove that mark from the wall. And I want to give you my blessing. I'm happy that you and Lucian have found your way back to each other. After you left, I knew he would struggle but believed it to be a silly boy's desire that he would outgrow. However, as the time went on, I realized he would never love another, not truly...his heart belonged to you long before yours belonged to him. We both mourned you, but he never quite let go." She took a deep breath, "when you showed back up in The Den a few months ago, I thought I had seen a ghost, so my concern for Lucian when he saw you was something I had to weigh heavily before asking you to rescue him. I'm glad I did, and I'm happy that you're home. I have missed you," Marciela finished with tears in her eyes.

Kara pulled her old friend into a firm hug, and whispered, "thank you. I promise to treasure him and repay the years that I owe him."

"Alright, enough blubbering," Marciela said as she pulled away. "I'm afraid I have one more thing to add to your plate. We received a handful of disturbing reports. It appears that a certain Death Mage is looking for Lucian...and you," Marciela informed her. "An open mark by the name Domi'dolori."

"Fucking bitch!" Kara exclaimed, dropping the diplomacy. "Has she hurt anyone?"

"Not mortally, nothing that can't be healed...yet. Her attacks are increasing however, and we cannot allow her to continue. She needs to be dealt with."

"Easier said than done. She captured Lucian, for fucks sake," Kara growled, "she's fast, and immensely powerful. We encountered her in Fini'via. She was Cassius' contact."

"That's how she knows about you Tia, and that Lucian is with you. Tread carefully with this one," Marciela warned, handing Kara a parchment, "she wields unrestrained Death Magic, she feeds on the pain she inflicts. That may be the only thing keeping her alive at this point. Here is her last location, and other details that should help you find her. We'll send regular reports on everything else, just keep us updated." Kara nodded and the old friends went their separate ways. She met Lucian in the foyer, then they headed for the streets of Dellalun, on their way back to the Citadel.

Eighteen

Death of a Madwoman

They were in the library after Kara had told Lucian about Domi'dolori. He was pacing, wings out, icy fire in his eyes.

"Marciela is right, we have to do something," Kara said, "but we have to have a solid plan."

"*We know!*" Ira barked.

"Hey! Don't snap at her!" Lucian shot back. Ira just growled.

"Given her last few locations, we know what direction she's heading, and we know where she should be tomorrow. Who do you think we should have with us?" Kara asked.

"Aleric...and Sel'arin," Lucian replied. "We need quick, efficient, and deadly."

"I agree. And how are we going to play it? We won't have a glimmer."

"It's me she wants, so why don't we give her what she wants?"

"I don't think that's a good idea…"

"Why not?"

"Because we have no idea what else she did to you…she could have planted more than Ira, she could still have a claw in you. If you go charging in there, you would just be making it infinitely easier for her to put you back in that hole," Kara asserted.

"That's…a valid point," Lucian grumbled. "What do you suggest?"

"The unexpected. We send Aleric in as a distraction, and the rest of us surround them, catching them off guard. Our best shot is the first one, she's too fast for us to waste the element of surprise, and we're not letting her get away again. We'll send a raven for Sel'arin now, and Aleric should return in the morning. There isn't anything else we can do tonight."

***

In the morning, Aleric was waiting in the kitchen when Kara and Lucian made their way downstairs.

"Just the Spirit we were hoping to see," Kara greeted him.

"Do we have news?" Aleric asked quizzically.

206

"Yes, but not related to the Demigods," she explained as she started her tea. "The Death Mage responsible for Lucian's capture and torture is on the war path...she's looking for him. We must end it, before she does any more damage. And we need your help."

"What's the plan?"

"We need Sel'arin, too. She should have received the raven already, so hopefully she'll return soon, and we can go over everything together. The Mormagi will reach a small elven village in the south of Cylendri Forest this afternoon, and that's where we will stop her." Sel'arin arrived as they were finishing breakfast, so they sat at the table in the kitchen and went over the details.

"Aleric, you will be our distraction. They won't expect you...you keep her attention so that Sel'arin and I can get close enough to take her guards out at once, and Lucian gets his mark before she even knows what hit her."

"How do you know we'll have a good line on them?" Sel'arin asked.

"She's been making quite a show of her power as she's been looking for a lead, so we suspect she'll be right out in the open. We need to minimize destruction here - fast and focused. She won't give us another chance."

"No pressure," Sel'arin quipped.

"We leave in a couple of hours, the nearest Stone to the village is a bit of a hike." Lucian said pointedly, raising an eyebrow at her.

"Got it. I'll be ready," she replied warily.

***

As the sun reached its peak, they arrived at the Stone near the village and started their trek through the forest. Kara could feel the anticipation in the air, this mark was as big as the one that took her life. Lucian had been eerily silent since the previous night, but Kara knew to let him have his space. She was here with him, that's what he needed, and they would do this together.

Within the hour, a village came into view through the thinning trees ahead. Kara decided to have Sel'arin lead, she would appear the least threatening and hopefully the clan would be easy to persuade. They needed these elves to get to safety before the Death Mages arrived. As they cleared the trees and approached the village, Kara noticed an elf leaning against the first building. He stood up straight when their eyes met, and she saw he had a bow in his hands and a quiver on his back. It wasn't common for Archers to be outside Est'alda, and the independent clans didn't have warriors or fighters, they only dealt in Ward Magic. Besides, this elf was taller and had shorter ears like Kara, so he had to be self-trained, not from the Faction.

"I think you might want to turn around and head back the way you came, friends," the archer advised as he pulled an arrow and knocked his bow.

"We need to speak with your Sovereign," Sel'arin said slowly, "we don't mean any harm."

208

"Why don't you tell me what brought you to our village, and I'll decide if the Sovereign needs to get involved."

"There's a small group of Mormagi headed straight for this village, looking for information no one will have, and they will destroy this place without provocation. We are here to stop them."

The archer stood there for an unnecessarily long time, looking at each of them until even Aleric appeared uncomfortable. Finally, he removed the arrow from the bow and walked over to the group. "Welcome to Clan de Mira'lyn. I am Kaisilus, the Sovereign." Kara was taken aback. This roguish elf didn't share any of the same regal or diplomatic qualities of most other clan leaders, especially considering that he carried a weapon.

"Please, follow me," he instructed, and headed into the village, the group in tow. Kara noticed that the other elves in this village shared the same ruggedness of Kaisilus, with dark eyes and hair, and tanned skin, their clan markings black ink instead of the traditional pale brown. How was it possible that there was an entire clan of elves in the forest that she didn't know about? She didn't see or feel any Ward magic here, which was also strange. They snaked through the dwellings as Kaisilus led them to a fire pit in the center of the village surrounded by tree stumps for seats, where he gestured for them to sit.

"Alright, you have my attention. Tell me, what are these Mormagi after?" he asked as they all settled in.

Kara spoke this time, "they're after us."

209

"And who are you?"

"I am Kara. This is Lucian, Aleric, and Sel'arin." She didn't want to reveal too much, she wasn't sure that she trusted Kaisilus.

"Two Vipers, a Necromancer, and a Tree Dweller...not a common sight to see a group like you traveling together. So, I'm going to ask again...who are you?" Kaisilus asked, eyes narrowed on Kara.

"It's...complicated. And we don't have time for the full version. The condensed version is, one of the Death Mages headed straight for this village is exceptionally vicious, and she wants two of us dead. Instead of allowing her to sweep through every village in the forest looking for us, we plan to stop her here. But that means you and your clan need to leave, we don't want any innocent blood spilled, and she won't think twice about decimating this entire place." Kara felt the fire rising, they didn't have time for this. He stared at her for a few moments, and she held his eyes.

"Alright Kara," he finally said, "I will have my clan evacuate, but I won't be leaving with them. This has been my home for an extraordinarily long time, and I will not stand idly by while you turn it into a battleground. I'll be right back, and I'd like to know your plan." He got up and headed off to one of the dwellings.

"What are you going to tell him?" Lucian asked.

"The plan," Kara replied. "If he's any good with that bow, we could use him. And we don't have the luxury of debating this any further." Lucian nodded.

A few minutes later, Kaisilus returned. Kara noticed the elves around them starting to gather themselves and head away from the village. "It won't take long for them to clear out. Now, how are you planning to deal with this Mage?"

"We keep them outside, using Aleric as a distraction. He'll hold her focus long enough for us to take out her guards and get to her. She's unbelievably fast, and powerful. We only get one shot...and we could use your bow," she told him.

He nodded. "I'll show you the best vantage points, and we can get set. How long before they arrive?"

"Not long," Kara replied, "we need to move." They worked quickly, and got everyone set, with Aleric in the center of the path through the village, waiting for the Mormagi. Before long, the group of flowing red and black robes made their way through the trees and straight for him.

"A Necromancer?" Domi'dolori exclaimed as they approached. "And what would you be doing all the way out in a little village like this?"

"Research," Aleric replied calmly. "What business do the Mormagi have here?"

"I'm looking for someone," she sneered, "and was hoping the good elves here could point me in the right direction." As they spoke, the rest of the team moved in closer, keeping themselves hidden.

"Well, I'm sorry to disappoint you, but there are no elves here. This is

211

an abandoned village."

"That is disappointing. However, you're here, and a Necromancer could be especially useful," she said with a wicked smile. "I think I'll add you to my collection." As she lifted her hands to attack, arrows flew in from both sides, hitting two of her guards, and Kara finished off the other two with her daggers as Lucian flew straight for Domi'dolori. Before he could touch her, a red spell shot from her right hand like a shock wave and knocked back the rest of the team as she grabbed him by the throat mid-air, his feet dangling. The witch turned, pulled his face close to hers, and hissed, "there's my favorite little pet. I knew you'd find your way back to me." A sharp black tongue slithered out from between her lips and licked his face while he struggled to escape her grasp, "I've missed the taste of your anguish."

A moment later, she howled and looked down at her leg where a dagger was buried deep in her thigh, then up to Kara with a twisted scowl. Kara just smiled and winked. The witches spell hadn't had the desired effect on Kara. While she was distracted and her grip loosened, Lucian plunged the two daggers he had in his hands right into her withered heart. A piercing wail escaped the Death Mages mouth as she dropped Lucian and crumpled to the ground in a pile of inky blood and rotting flesh. Lucian stood and spit on the pile, disgusted. "Fuck you. There's not a hole in Infernus deep enough for your wretched soul to rot in."

"Well, you are certainly a lively group," Kaisilus laughed. "And very well-coordinated. I get the feeling you've been working together for a while now."

"We have," Kara replied as she checked on Lucian, bruises from the witches fingertips already forming on his throat. "Now that we have a moment, you should know that the Demigods are making a play for the throne of Ess'Magis and staging a Blood Sacrifice at the Mai'ngolo on the next Full Moon. Your people aren't safe here - no wards, no protection - there will be more Death Mages, looking for souls to offer as tribute." Kaisilus stared at her, digesting everything she told him with a shadow of horror behind his calm, clear eyes.

"How can you be sure?" he asked.

"Because we're leading the rebellion to stop them. Do you have somewhere you can take your clan?"

"Not that would keep them safe for very long..." he trailed off, the gravity of the situation sinking in.

"You can take them to Dellalun, we will help escort everyone using the Travel Stones and provide protection there," Kara told him, "I'll send a Gryphon tomorrow to coordinate with you. Don't stay here alone, go be with your people and prepare them for what's ahead."

"You have been quite busy. I'll be back here in the morning, awaiting your Gryphon. And when my clan is safe, I would very much like to speak with you again." She bowed her head slightly before the group turned and headed back towards the Stone.

Once back at the Citadel, Sel'arin headed to the spring to wash up before she returned to Est'alda, while Kara and Lucian headed to the library

213

to prepare a letter for Marciela. Aleric had already left for Atri'anima to check in and see if there were any updates.

Nineteen

Return to Lyria

Lucian and Kara had an uncommonly slow evening - a workout in the training room trying some new things with the daggers, a swim in the spring, dinner by candlelight as the sun set, coffee and tea out at the fire pit under the stars. It was strange to have the Citadel to themselves, and to have no plans to discuss or orders to give. Simply living. As they sat in the cool air, she thought about the next few days, and how much was going to change. She had one last thing she needed to do before she could focus on trying to control her magic, and a plan for destroying the Demigods.

"I need to go to Lyria, I need to warn them," she said suddenly, cutting through the silence.

"Alright, I can wait here for some of the others to return if you want to do that tomorrow," Lucian replied.

"I want you to go with me," she said firmly. "I don't know what's going to happen as the Full Moon approaches. I want to show you my village, and I want my mother to meet you," she smiled. He got up from his seat and

215

knelt in front of her, taking her hands in his.

"I would be honored," he kissed her hands, "we'll leave right after breakfast. Let's go get some sleep," he said and stood up, pulling her with him.

The next morning, Markus was the first to return. Kara and Lucian found him in the kitchen, preparing breakfast.

"Good morning, Markus. How did it go with Rowan?" Kara asked as she poured a cup of spring water and sat at the table.

"Good morning. The Gryphons are mobilizing - they started heading out already and will be stationed across Cylendri. Within the next few days, every city and village will be protected," he told them. "Also, I have this for you," he handed her a piece of parchment, "thanks to your translations, Carmine was able to decipher more information from the old texts that he believes will help in the coming weeks."

Kara opened the parchment and looked it over. "This is...very helpful," she replied, and handed the parchment to Lucian so he could read it. "Aleric and I have some work to do once he returns." Markus nodded.

"Dahlia made it into Aquanalis," she told him, knowing he was thinking of her, even if he didn't show it. "I'll go back to get her tomorrow."

"That won't be necessary," Markus replied, pulling a small, triangular pebble hanging on a thin piece of leather from a pouch on his belt. The stone glowed faintly with a golden light.

216

"Where did you get a Travel Charm?" Lucian asked incredulously.

"The Castellum holds many secrets, many relics from generations past," he replied with a sly smile, "and the Lord Gryphon wanted me to be able to travel quickly, as he has named me *Legati Pri'mas*."

"First Lieutenant? That's excellent Markus!" Kara exclaimed.

He simply nodded, and then continued, "so I will go to Aquanalis. I would like to speak with the High Priestess. I need her permission to station a few Gryphons there."

"One less thing I need to do, then," she smiled. "Before you do that, can you please go to a small village in the southwest, Mira'lyn? The Sovereign is expecting you - he needs to coordinate travel with his clan to Dellalun."

"The Blended clan?" Markus asked nonchalantly.

"Blended?" Kara looked at Lucian, who shrugged.

"Yes, that clan is only half Elven. They're also Terastralis," he told them, "did you not know?"

"I did not, but I feel like I should have put that together. I had no idea there were any Blended families left."

"I'm sorry, this was common at one point?" Lucian asked.

217

Kara laughed, "yes, back before the last war between the Factions, a few thousand years ago. There was a lot more unity between the races, and blended bloodlines were a normal thing. But most didn't survive the conflict, and I thought the rest had died out since."

"All but the Mira'lyn clan. Strong bloodlines on both sides," he said with a wink. "I'll head there first, and we'll work on getting them to Dellalun after I return from Aquanalis."

They ate in silence, enjoying the warm dryroot and vegetable hand pies Markus had made, another Terastralis recipe - dryroot came from a beautiful desert plant that bloomed with delicately sweet flowers, and had deep root systems. The plant was integral to Terastralis life as it was versatile, and completely edible. She had lived on a lot of these recipes during her years in the South. She loved their use of spices - complex and full of heat but perfectly balanced, unlike some of the mouth-burning Dwarven meals she had suffered through.

After breakfast, Kara and Lucian packed for their visit to Lyria Village, and Markus prepped Sable for travel. They would take the Pegasus with them, cutting down the time it would take them to get from the nearest Travel Stone to the waterfall entrance. Before they left, Aleric arrived back at the Citadel. He and Kara spoke in the library.

"We had an impressive response to our call for aid," Aleric told her, "Spirits are already spreading the word throughout Cylendri and reporting back. Some of them have even seen the Gryphons arriving in villages."

"We're very lucky to have you and your help, Aleric," she smiled, "we couldn't possibly have this level of communication across the divides without it."

Aleric smiled back, still a strange thing for Kara to see - most of the spirits she had come across were quite unpleasant and very moody. "Happy to be of service," he said proudly.

"Lucian and I are heading to my village after we're done here, and we'll be gone for most of the day, but when we return, I'll need your help again. I've learned some things about my...caged anomaly that could be impactful if I explore them further, and I think you would be the best guide for that journey. Partly because you already knew more about it than I did when it unlocked, but mostly because I trust you," she told him.

"How intriguing. Of course I will help, in any way I can."

"Thank you, Aleric. I'll see you tonight!" And with that, she left for the Stone where Lucian was already waiting with Sable.

***

Once they arrived, a few miles from the waterfall, they both mounted Sable and she flew there in a matter of minutes. They landed gently on the edge of the pond, and the Pegasus started munching on some of the plants around the banks. "Good girl, you stay here and stay out of trouble. We'll be back in a few hours," she told the beast, giving her a nuzzle.

"Alright Lucian, this is the tricky part," she told him as they removed their boots. "You need to step *exactly* where I step. When my foot moves, you place yours in the exact same place it was, got it?"

"Got it," he said hesitantly.

"There's a specific path, and traps on all sides of it, so just follow my lead, you'll be fine," she assured him.

"I'm right behind you," he replied, more confidently, and they began the walk across the water, slow and steady. It took longer than it would take just her because she knew this path by heart, but she remained patient and allowed Lucian to be set in each step before taking another. When they reached the waterfall, she spoke the words and the rock split, allowing them to squeeze through. Once on the other side, they put their boots back on and stood overlooking the village.

"Beautiful," Lucian said with a sigh as he marveled at the village below them, spreading across the small valley, surrounded on all sides by sharp, treacherous mountains that kept this place generally insulated from the outside world. The waterfall was one of only two entrances unless you had wings and inhumanly strong lungs, as the air at the crest of the mountains was very thin and frigid. Even if you could survive that, you wouldn't see the village due to the ward over the whole valley. They occasionally got a winged beast, or an injured Gryphon who landed in the valley, but even that was a rare occurrence. Kara explained all of this to Lucian while they made their way down the hill along the stream. As the got closer, a Patroni'usi appeared out of thin air and let out a sharp grunt, startling Lucian.

"Oh, so there is *one* thing that can sneak up on the deadliest assassin who ever lived!" Kara laughed, petting the magical Elk-like creatures' cream-colored and speckled fur.

"I've never been this close to one," he marveled at its great antlers akin to moss-covered tree branches. The beast shook its head and turned a large, forest green eye on Lucian as he approached it.

"She won't bite, they're quite docile when not being hunted for their blending pelts, and very intelligent. This is the only full herd left in all Cylendri that I know of, they were nearing extinction before the clan brought them here." Three more came up the hill to inspect the newcomers, ensuring that the village was not in danger, and Kara watched with adoration as Lucian, completely awestruck by the elusive animals, giggled and fed one of them a handful of reeds from the banks of the stream. She had never seen him so unguarded, so full of wonder.

"Is it true they're all females, and new ones are born from their antlers?" he asked curiously.

"It is. Pieces of their antlers fall off naturally from time to time and if it falls in fertile soil on a New Moon, a Patroni'usi takes root and grows, emerging from the dirt two full moon cycles later when it is fully formed. All of the soil in this valley is fertile and rich with the nutrients they need to mature, so they have flourished," Kara educated him.

When they crossed the small wooden bridge that served as the entrance to the village, a youngling ran up and shouted, "Kara is back!" as she jumped into Kara's arms. She carried the young elf through the main square, stopping to sample fruits and vegetables, introducing Lucian to her clan, and laughing as the girl braided Kara's long hair down one side. As

221

they neared the square, the girl's mother called for her, and Kara sent her on the way.

"Doesn't look like she's down here. She must be at home." Kara turned and they headed up the hill to her old dwelling.

***

Lucian enjoyed watching Kara among her people, her first people, and seeing a light in her eyes that wasn't white hot fire, but more shimmering snow, delicate and filled with wonder. Not only was she a natural leader, but she also had such a gentle heart...not something you'd commonly find in an assassin. He always thought she didn't quite fit the Viper mold, and now he understood why. He took a few deep breaths as they approached her childhood home. He had never *'met the parents'* of any of his lovers, likely because they never lasted long or meant much to him, so this was all unfamiliar territory, and he was more anxious than he had expected. But he would do anything for Kara, and he could see how important this was to her.

A beautiful elf who shared the same sharp, but somehow soft features as Kara, the high cheekbones and commanding brow in particular, was tending a garden in front of the dwelling. Long, wavy white hair sparkled in the sun and cascaded down her back. When she turned and looked Lucian dead in the eyes, it was the dagger-like stare that Kara had, but the eyes were the same he had fallen in love with as a boy, just filled with more wisdom. This was clearly her mother, and it was a bit eerie.

"Amalthia," her mother said, surprised, "I wasn't expecting to see you

222

again so soon. Has something happened?"

"It has," she replied, "can we speak inside."

"Of course." and she set down her pruning shears before heading for the door. She let Kara and Lucian in, closing the door behind them. "Would you like some tea?"

"Yes, that would be lovely," Kara replied.

"I am assuming this is him then?" Elaria asked from the kitchen as she prepared the kettle.

"Yes, this is Lucian," she answered, a blush in her cheeks that melted him. "Lucian, this is my mother Elaria de Lyria, Sovereign of the Clan."

"It's lovely to meet you Lucian," her mother smiled as she came back into the room carrying a tray of tea and biscuits to the table in front of the fireplace and gesturing for them to sit.

"And you, Elaria. Tia speaks very highly of you, and your beautiful village," Lucian smiled, pouring a cup for each of them before himself, ever the gentleman. While it wasn't his favorite, he wouldn't dare turn down Elaria's tea.

"She has spoken very little of you," Elaria replied, a hint of playfulness in her steely demeanor, "but the way you make her smile is unmistakable." Kara blushed again, and Lucian grinned shyly. She reminded him of Marciela, and now he understood how Kara had been so close to his grandmother all those years ago. "Now, what news do you have for us?" she asked after taking a sip of tea.

"We have a location, and a plan," Kara started, "but the next month is going to be crucial. The Demigods will attempt a large-scale Sacri'Sanguis on this next Full Moon to gain access to the Realm of The Divine by way of the Mai'ngolo. We have taken the Belua out of the equation, and the Vipers are being led by Lucian now, so we have the numbers. However, that means the Mormagi will be hunting for prisoners and slaves to offer as tribute, lest they find themselves on the serving platter. We are stationing Gryphons throughout the villages and cities, the Spirits are spreading word to warn everyone, and each other Faction is aiding in some way." She paused to let Elaira process the information.

"Even a hidden village like Lyria will not be safe," Elaira finally said, "we are unprotected if the ward comes down."

"Yes, which is why I want to place a few Gryphons here...and a Stone Dwarf," Kara said slowly.

Elaira looked at her hotly, and the air was tense. "We will not have one of those sour little hoarders in this village," she spat.

Kara took a deep breath, and Lucian knew he needed to hold his tongue. "Sovereign, your clan needs protection, and our cause needs your healers. Only a united front across all Cylendri will bring down the Demigods, who threaten the very existence of our entire world - every race, every creature, every plant, every child. We cannot squabble over our differences, not now. The Stone Faction has a unique magic that would be a

224

great advantage for this valley, you cannot turn your nose up at it." Kara's resolve was something to behold. Lucian watched her as she stood firm in it, challenging her mother, the leader of the clan, and an elder who was likely a few centuries old. He felt Elaria's eyes on him and met them. She was searching for something, though Lucian couldn't tell you what, but he held her gaze until she looked back at Kara.

Before Elaria could respond, they heard shouting in the village. Kara gave Lucian a concerned look and they all rushed outside. In the middle of the square was Sable, wings flapping and clearly distressed, elves frantically trying to get out of her way. Kara ran down the hill, Lucian closely behind.

"Hey girl, calm down, *shhhh*," Kara moved slowly towards the beast, inching closer as she tried to settle her, "I'm right here, you're safe," she assured Sable as she got close enough to pet the bridge of her nose. Sable calmed but was still huffing. *'Pegasi must be able to see through wards,'* Kara thought. As she stroked Sable and moved down her side, Kara noticed a small gash on her hind quarter. She had been attacked. Then they heard it, a crashing sound, up by the waterfall entrance, like something was trying to break through.

"Is she yours?" Elaria asked, coming up behind them.

"She's under our care," Kara replied. "Can you stay with her please? We must get up there now Lucian, they're trying to break through!" Without waiting for Elaria to answer, Lucian spread the Spirit wings, picked up Kara, and flew off towards the waterfall.

225

Lucian dropped them down just before the entrance, and they could see the rock behind it had a massive, unnatural crack. Something was hitting it with great force from the other side. Suddenly, a spark of red magic came flying through the crack, narrowly missing Kara. "They're going to break through, we have to hold them off here!"

"These bastards won't touch the village," Lucian and Ira growled in unison, rising in the air.

A moment later the rock exploded, sending shards of stone and death magic everywhere, and Mormagi poured through the hole. Kara tore the first few open at the belly with her daggers, then Lucian flew into the group, slicing throats before picking one up, taking it at least forty feet in the air and letting go. It fell into the crowd with a loud crack, taking three more out with the force. They already had more than half of the small horde down. Kara jumped on the back of one, jamming a dagger in its spine, riding it down to the ground before leaping for another as it landed. She missed it as a spell flew in from her right, then another from her left. As the second came at her, she threw her hands up and focused, and the spell bounced off a small, relatively weak ward that she produced. Then a much bigger ward appeared around her, and she looked up to find a few of the village Mages had made their way up the hill, including Nir'lathin. They were protecting Kara, protecting their home. Kara smiled and threw two daggers, one at each of the Death Mages in front of her, hitting them both in the heart simultaneously. Lucian had the last one in the air, legs wrapped around its chest and ripped off its head.

"They broke the stone, we need a strong ward here until we can figure out a solution," Kara told the Mages. They all went up to the hole under the waterfall, and wove a tight, multilayered protection ward into the space that was left. It glowed bright and golden as they worked the magic, then faded and disappeared.

"That will hold it for now. If anyone attempts to come through, that will burn them from the inside," Nir'lathin told her.

"Good. Thank you," she replied.

He lifted an eyebrow, and said, "looks like you might have some magic of your own. It's clearly new, you don't know how to use it, but it's powerful. A ward that weak, it would not normally stop a death spell at that range." He looked down his nose at her.

"A story for another time perhaps," Kara said, avoiding his gaze, "we have to deal with this wall, and I need to finish speaking with my mother."

"I'll help here; we'll find something. You go back to the village," Lucian told her as he landed next to her. The Mages all looked at him warily. They knew what he had in him, and even if he had just protected the village, Ira scared them. She lifted up on her tiptoes and kissed him tenderly, hoping it might help settle their nerves at least a bit, to see his gentleness.

"I'll be back shortly," she told him, and he smiled down at her. Then she smiled at the Mages and headed down the hill.

Twenty

Seed of Magic

Elaria was still in the square with Sable, having retrieved a brush from the stables, lovingly running it through her mane while speaking sweetly to her. "She's quite something, isn't she?" Kara asked as she approached them.

"She is. I haven't seen one in ages, I thought they might have disappeared," Elaria replied. "Wherever did you find her?"

"The Gryphons, they have the last few mated pairs that remain, and care for them at the Castellum In'Caelo," Kara told her.

Elaira looked at Kara now, regret in her eyes, "I am sorry, *mi'filia*. I should not have been so quick to dismiss you earlier. We have lived here so long, hidden from the rest of the Realm, keeping ourselves insulated from the evil and darkness that lurks out there. But the fury of the Demigods seeps through everything, and I cannot protect my people without accepting that we all must work together, that every life is precious, even the ones who have harmed our kind in the past. Thank you for helping me see that," she smiled.

"Thank you," Kara sighed, "we'll help patch the wall up before we go. I want to get the Gryphons here as soon as possible. Though I'm not entirely sure how we'll get out of here now."

"That I can surely help with. There is another way through," Elaria started, but Kara cut her off.

"We can't go through the other side of the forest and risk being seen. The Death Mages could be looking for another way in."

"Not the other forest entrance," Elaria said and raised an eyebrow at her, "there is a mountain pass, just low enough for survival, but still impossible to reach from the outside. Sable would be able to fly you right through it. In the Southwest, at the lowest point between the two smallest peaks there," she finished, pointing in the distance.

"Well, I'm just learning all sorts of new things lately," Kara scoffed, "let's add that to the list."

"We are both learning quite a bit, like your chosen mate has a Spirit bound inside of him, and that you have magic, powerful magic...ancestral magic." Kara looked at her curiously. "A mother knows."

"I can't speak on it," Kara sighed, "but I am figuring it out. And don't judge Lucian on what was done to him. He didn't ask for Ira, he spent five years in the Crypta being tortured, experimented on by one of the worst Death Mages I have ever seen. The fact that he's alive is a testament to his

229

will, and he has saved my life on numerous occasions. He's...remarkable."

"I wouldn't be anything if she hadn't saved me from that nightmare," Lucian walked up behind them, making Kara jump. "Worst assassin ever," he said playfully. "But she has made me a better man, Elaria, and I love your daughter, with all that I am."

Elaria looked at him for a long time, making Kara rather uncomfortable. Then she got up, walked over to him, and hugged him. Now Lucian was visibly uncomfortable, but he hugged her back. She pulled away and said, "I see you now. And I see why she loves you." Then she went and hugged Kara. "You have a rebellion to get back to. We will be alright here until the Gryphons and Stone Dwarf arrive. Is there anything else?"

"We could use a few Mages of Light in Dellalun, Wards and Healers. We'll be housing the wounded and displaced there and will need all the hands we can get. I can come back in a day or two for them."

"I shall get a group ready and prepare space for our guests."

"The hole is patched for now, but we'll instruct the Gryphons to help you work out a better solution. They're strong, and quite resourceful." Lucian added, then he helped Kara onto Sable before climbing up himself, and they flew into the sky, heading for the pass.

***

They arrived back at the Citadel just after sundown, and found Aleric and Nalor in the library, a small pile of letters on the table in front of them.

"Ah, excellent timing, the first reports have started coming in," Aleric told Kara as they walked into the room. "How was Lyria?"

"The Mormagi attacked, but we were able to take care of them. Is Markus here?" Kara asked.

"Right behind you," Markus announced. "Kaisilus and the rest of clan Mira'lyn have all been relocated to Dellalun."

"Thank you for handling that. Now, we need some Gryphons to go to my village in the southeast of the forest. Grab me a map and I'll show you. Nalor, please tell me we have the Stones' support?"

"We do. Rhygan has agreed to help. The Stones began traveling this morning. They will provide aid wherever there is a need as they travel, making their way to the villages. I sent a small group to help Gondyr in Est'alda." Nalor replied.

"That's a relief. I also need a Stone in my village. There's a high concentration of Mages of Light, and it's one of the largest clans in the forest. They need extra protection, and some of them will need to travel to Dellalun."

Markus rolled out a large map of Cylendri Forest on the table. "Lyria is right here," she showed them, pointing to a spot in the southeast of the map, "in the valley of this mountain range. The nearest Travel Stone is here. The village is warded, so it's not visible to most from the air, and

231

exceedingly difficult to access. The Death Mages attacked the easiest entrance, it's now a weak point that needs to be patched. You can't use the other entrance on the ground, as they could be watching the area. There's a pass, here in the southwest, at the lowest point between the two smallest peaks. You'll have to fly - they're expecting you, so you should have no problem passing through the ward. I'd like you to go with them, Markus, ensure everyone makes it and report back before you go to Aquanalis. Please?" She knew she didn't have to say it, but this was her clan, and she was worried.

"Not a problem, Kara," he assured her, "should I go tonight?"

"No, they'll be fine for the night. Thank you."

"I'll go in the morning to get a Stone, and meet you there," Nalor told Markus, and he nodded.

"Lucian and I can go through the reports, none of you have to stay if you don't want to," Kara told them.

"I would like to stay," Aleric advised. "In case there is information I need to pass along to the Spirits." Markus and Nalor left, and they started going through the letters.

"This one is from Est'alda," Lucian said, "Gondyr says the fortifications are underway, and they have an evacuation plan in place if it comes to that. A handful of Gryphons have arrived, and a few Necromancers from the Undead Faction are helping strengthen the wards at the Mai'ngolo."

232

"I didn't know the Undead agreed to leave Atri'anima..." she said, puzzled.

"Oh, yes, some of them decided they wanted to be more hands on with their help, so we agreed Est'alda was the place they would be needed most," he smiled.

"Alright, that's good news," Kara replied, "this one is from Dellalun, Viv. The Manor is ready for the Mages, the merchants have begun to arrive with extra supplies, and a lot of the citizens are willing to open their homes. They haven't seen anyone new arrive other than a few Gryphons, but the city is ready."

"This one is from Dahlia," Aleric started, "The Nymphs will be ready to leave for Dellalun by tomorrow. Their scouts at the perimeter of the ward are reporting activity from the Mormagi in a few places, so they have strengthened it. That makes it much more difficult to pass through, even with an invitation. She wants you to warn Markus but tell him he does have the invitation."

"Hmmm, how did she know Markus was heading to Aquanalis? He didn't have the charm until after he got back this morning and she was already gone..." Kara thought for a moment, "I wonder if she can reach him telepathically still, even at that range?"

"Well, we are at the crossroads of Realms here, the junction of everything, maybe he's not actually that far," Lucian offered.

"That...makes a lot of sense," Kara laughed. "And that should be all the reports. Lots of good news. But things are about to get rough, we've got to hold together. United is the only way we win. Aleric, thank you. I am ready for some rest, so I'll see you in the morning and we'll speak further."

"I'll be right up," Lucian told her as she headed out of the library. "Aleric, please just be careful with her," he said quietly once she was out of ear shot, "you know how she pushes herself, I don't want her taking chances with this power. Anything she learns will be helpful; it doesn't have to be grand to be impactful. Do you understand?"

"I understand. I will pull her back if she gets close to the edge, I promise," Aleric assured him.

Lucian nodded in gratitude and headed up to bed after her.

***

When Kara got up to her room to drop a few things there before heading to Lucian's, she was surprised to find that the wall between their rooms had dissolved, making it one large space with a door on either side. The bed was larger and the whole room was reorganized. She loved the Citadel, how it grew with them, changed as they changed. She would miss this place when they no longer had need of it. She took off her boots and leathers, got into a nightshirt, and crawled into bed to wait for Lucian. A few minutes later, one of the doors creaked open.

"*Oh,*" she heard Lucian whisper.

"The Citadel made some adjustments," she laughed.

234

"I can see that," he replied as he sat on the edge of the bed to take off his boots. She turned and watched as he removed his leathers, peeling off each layer until he stood bare in the glow of the candlelight, admiring every inch of his exquisite physique. He pulled on a pair of lounge pants, blew out the candles, and slid under the covers behind her, his chest against her back, wrapping his arm around her waist and kissing her neck. She took a deep breath, feeling perfectly safe and somehow stronger in his embrace, as his beating heart lulled her to sleep.

The next morning, Kara awoke before Lucian and made her way down to the kitchen. She made coffee, and a kettle of lavender tea, then poured herself a cup before taking a seat on the cushioned sill in one of the windows, As she looked out into the forest, watching the sun rise, she ruminated on all they had accomplished. Not long ago, everything looked hopeless; she felt lost and helpless, the task ahead of her impossibly daunting. She had believed Gondyr's faith in her was misplaced. How could she have known that this junction was exactly where she was meant to be, this is who she was meant to become? It had all been so overwhelming. And yet, here she was, here they were - the impossible had become possible, the unbelievable had become achievable. Her lives had collided, and she had survived it. Even though she was proud of how far they had come, she tempered that with stark humility. So much hung in the balance, so much at stake, and if she lost her grip for even a moment...well, she simply couldn't. There were too many lives depending on her.

Aleric joined her in the kitchen. "Would you mind if I had a cup of tea?" he asked her.

"Not at all," Kara smiled. He poured himself a cup, then joined her by the window, sitting in one of the chairs.

"You were deep in thought," he said simply, "anything you would care to discuss?"

"I was just thinking about the last few months, about how massive the task had been as it loomed before me then," she told him.

"And now?"

"I have more faith in this team and our cause than I could've imagined, and it doesn't seem as impossible as it once did."

"We have all come a long way. Without you, this team would not be, and Cylendri would not have a chance in this fight. You are the cornerstone, and it has been inspiring to watch your growth. I have never known a corporeal being with so much strength and sheer will," he said to her, and smiled. "We all believe in you, and it is good to see you finally believing in yourself."

"Thank you, Aleric, for joining me on this journey," she paused, "and for saving my life knowing what the cost could have been."

"A decision I will never regret," he assured her. They sat in silence for a while, until Markus, Nalor, and Lucian joined them in the kitchen.

"Did you make coffee?" Lucian asked, surprised.

Kara smiled, "I did." Lucian and Nalor each went for the coffee, Markus opting for the tea. They sat around the table, snacking on leftover meat pies and vegetable-potato-stuffed biscuits from the night before.

"Markus, we received a letter from Dahlia," Kara remembered, "she wanted me to let you know that you have an invitation from the High Priestess and should be able to pass through the ward in Aquanalis, but she also warned that it is stronger now, so be prepared."

"How did she know?" Markus asked.

"We think that she was able to pick up on your thoughts as this place sits at the center of the Realms," Kara advised, "though it would seem she cannot actually communicate with you telepathically or she would have told you her herself."

"Fascinating," Aleric chimed in.

After they finished breakfast, Kara wandered out into the courtyard to find that not just their rooms, but the whole Citadel had changed, grown. The stables had doubled. The forge was bigger, three times as many shelves and tools had appeared overnight. And there was a second tower now, between the walls where the kitchen and the forge once met. The whole space was larger, as if the walls had spread further apart, like the ripples of water when a stone disrupts its stillness. Lucian walked out behind her and looked around.

"It's like the Citadel is preparing itself for what comes next," Kara said, astonished. "I guess this means we'll have a lot more activity here soon," she laughed.

"This is probably the safest place in all the Realms," Lucian said matter-of-factly, "otherwise, don't you think the Demigods would've already attacked us here?"

"I agree, though I'm still not sure how the magic works. I'm not sure how a lot of things work right now, in fact. It's a bit unsettling," she admitted.

"Then it's time you and Aleric get to work," he told her. "I'm going to check on Dellalun while you do that." He kissed her forehead before heading back inside to get ready. Kara waited in the cool morning air and finished her tea. Nalor was the first to depart for Lapidis, then Markus for Lyria Village. After she made sure Lucian arrived in Dellalun, she returned and made her way to the training room where Aleric was waiting for her.

"Alright," she began, "I must explain this carefully. I swore an oath to keep certain information secret, but I believe I can give you enough so you can then fill in the gaps yourself and be prepared for the work ahead." Aleric nodded in agreement, so Kara continued carefully, "I have learned that I may be able to manipulate the magics, due to an anomaly in my blood passed down through many generations. An anomaly that, as you're aware, is volatile and dangerous if not controlled, focused. So, I would like for you to teach me some basic ward spellcasting to start and see how that goes." She paused, watching him as he pieced the rest of the puzzle together.

"I understand," he finally replied. "We will approach this simply and start small. For me to do this, I need you to follow my lead, to listen for understanding, not for responding, and when I say we need to stop, then we stop." He held her gaze as she looked at him defiantly. "I am no fool,

238

Amalthia de Lyria. I know what lies within you, whether you tell me or not. I know the histories, the old tales. And I know exactly what it is capable of. I will not have you rushing off a cliff with this power and risking everything we have all worked so diligently to accomplish, or the fate of what lies ahead. If we are to succeed, you cannot do this through sheer will, you need patience and discipline. If you cannot agree to that, then I cannot help you...and rest assured, that cage will break, and what is inside it will kill more than just you."

After a few moments, her face softened in understanding. "Alright Aleric, I trust you, and I will follow your lead," she finally agreed.

"Good. We will begin with meditation. You need to see the power, how it moves, how it responds to your manipulations. Once I feel confident that you can direct it, then we will move to spellcasting." They sat on the ground, a circle of white pillar candles surrounding them, and a gold candelabra holding four candles of distinct colors burning between them. "The circle of white light will protect us as we travel between Realms, both inside and out. The candles before us represent each of the four magics, and the gold serves as a conduit for the power between them and you. Close your eyes, breathe deep and steady, clear your mind of desire, distraction, and obligation, creating space for knowledge," he instructed.

Their breathing began to sync, and Kara could smell the candles, a mix of complex scents both earthy and sweet, smokey and light. She focused on visualizing the power that each represented - pale yellow for the Ward Magic, icy blue for the Spirit Magic, emerald green for the Elemental Magic, and blood red for the Death Magic. That last one scared her, but she heard Aleric from somewhere in the distance, "do not fear death or the magic it

239

holds. It is a part of the whole, a necessary step in the cycle of all life, and can be quite powerful if used correctly. The Mormagi corrupt it, use it with selfish and reckless abandon, they do not respect it. The sacrifice must be weighted, balanced, and absolutely necessary. Do this, and the power can have a profound impact with the sacrifice of only a blade of grass."

Kara pushed the fear from her mind, focusing on the balance of power, the intricacies of each magic as they stood alone. "Good," Aleric said, "now, begin to weave them together, slowly, one strand at a time." For the next few hours they sat in the middle of the room as Kara painstakingly pulled and directed the strands of magic, Aleric intervening from time to time offering wisdom and guidance but allowing her the space to do this on her own. "Careful, feel the magic before you place it, ensure it is the right one, that it does not resist," he told her. Once, as she went for a strand of Spirit Magic, her mind began to wander to Lucian. "No," he warned, "stay focused only on you and the magic. Do not weave him into the power, or it could damage you both." She pushed Lucian from her mind, not an easy feat, and regained her center before plucking the strand.

By the time she finished, the four magics were one, a complex seed glowing pure white with power, and she slowly took the seed in her hands. "Now plant it, deep and secured, where you are sure you can contain it," Aleric directed her. She walked for a while in the darkness, the only light coming from the seed, letting her intuition lead, and then stopped suddenly. She knelt down, pushed aside what felt like earth below her, and placed the seed gently in the hole she had dug out, then covered it until no light was visible. As she did so, she could feel the power in the center of her chest, and tiny tendrils of magic began to branch out of it, like a seedling sprouting its roots.

Aleric appeared with her in the darkness. "Well done. Follow me." And he led her out of the meditation. Kara opened her eyes, the candles around and between them burned down to practically nothing. The room brightened with light magic, and Aleric was smiling across from her.

"That was most excellent," he advised, "I expected it to take us a few tries to get through that part of the process, but you handled it beautifully."

"I feel more connected to the power," she told him, "less afraid or unsure of it. It's amazing."

"The most important part is over. It will take some time for that to root fully inside of you. You must nurture it, hold it lovingly, allow it to spread throughout and become part of your very essence, your spirit. Meditation will help. When you are ready, we will take the next step together." They stood, Kara feeling more steady and sure of her place in the world than she had in almost a hundred and forty years of life. They left the training room, Aleric heading to the library, Kara to the kitchen for a cup of spring water before going outside and starting a fire to combat the chilly, overcast weather. She sat, staring into the flames, watching them dance as if witnessing it for the first time. She could almost see the magic inside of it, magic that she could learn to manipulate. Then she heard the faintest footsteps, Lucian clearly trying to catch her off guard again. But her senses were sharper now.

"You won't get me again," she said playfully, and he laughed.

"There's the assassin," he said before sitting down next to her. "How did it go with Aleric?"

241

"Really well actually. We just finished." She explained to him what they accomplished, and what the next step would be. "I just feel so much steadier. I'm no longer exhausting half of my energy to keep this thing caged inside me that was constantly fighting to be released," she told him.

"That's unbelievable...but also not surprising," he winked, "I never doubted you for a moment."

Twenty-One

Home of the Rebellion

After dinner, Kara decided to take a walk through the new areas in the Citadel while Lucian bathed out in the spring. The kitchen now had two large brick ovens, and three small cooking fires, as well as a small greenhouse and garden off the outer wall. She walked through them and found fruits and vegetables, flowers, and spices growing throughout. The kitchen also had another door that led to the new tower, with stairs that went up and to the left from there, but there wasn't an open space like the main hall. Instead, there was a door to her right that led outside, and a door in front of her. She went through that one to find a beautiful space with a floor-to-ceiling window looking out through the trees - it had flowering plants on the walls, a small pond with its own little waterfall to the left, and a raised stone column filled with candles and incense on the right. The center was lower in the ground, down a couple of small steps, and had pillows scattered around. The Citadel had given her a meditation room, and it was perfect.

She left the room, telling herself she would visit it once a day, and went back out to the courtyard. The fire pit was larger, with long wooden benches

243

adding ample seating around it. As she was passing the forge, she noticed an archway to another room off the outer wall there and made her way over. The room was quite spacious, with shorter walls and no roof, instead a large tree sat in the center that reached up to the sky, its branches creating a canopy over the space. It reminded her of Est'alda.

She then worked her way around the stables as Lucian was coming back from the spring. He came through the opening at the back of the stalls, still wet and wearing only his lounge pants. He always ran hot, like a smoldering fire just as the last flame was dying out, so the cool air and water made his skin steam. He saw her and flashed that irresistible smile, the one that radiated through his dark eyes, stirring the thirst of her desires. It was hard to believe that just a couple of months ago he thought her dead, and she never could have imagined that she would see him again.

"The spring is bigger; there's two pools now..." he told her.

"Sounds about right - there's a greenhouse and garden off the kitchen, a meditation room in the new tower along with more bedrooms, and a smaller version of Est'alda on the other side of the forge, too. I think we're going to be hosting guests," she told him. They headed inside and up to bed.

**

In the morning, when Kara and Lucian went downstairs, the Citadel hummed with activity. Pytra and a few other Gryphons including Calisto and Doramyr were in the kitchen eating, and Nalor was showing a couple of dwarves around the forge. There were Nymphs fawning over Sable, and some Tree Dwellers practicing with the archery targets at the other end of the courtyard. Aleric and another Necromancer were in the library, discussing a thick tome that he held.

"What is going on Aleric?" Kara asked as they entered the library.

"Ah, good morning! Markus and Nalor brought a few friends back with them last night, and Gondyr arrived with Sel'arin and some elves early this morning. This is Chrysanthem, my apprentice," he told them.

"Blessings Kara, Lucian," She greeted them.

"Nice to meet you," Kara said, and Lucian simply nodded. She was slight and ethereal, even for a spirit. "Are you...were you a Nymph?" she asked quizzically.

"I was," Chrysanthem replied with a gentle smile. "Not common, I know. My fascination with the Spirit Realm did not fit my upbringing, so I left Aquanalis to join the Undead. Aleric has been my mentor for nearly two hundred years now." Kara wanted to know everything. Not only had she never considered a Nymph to become a Necromancer, but she also knew little about what Aleric did outside of his adventures with her and Gondyr. *"I'm intrigued by you, as well,"* she said to Kara telepathically, *"and I would love the chance to learn more about the direct descendant of Moira'nila."* Kara tensed at hearing that. *"I can see much, but I promise to keep your secret."* Lucian and Aleric exchanged a puzzled look as the two women shared a silent moment.

"Well, this is not at all what I expected to wake up to," Kara laughed, breaking the tension. "I'd better go check in with Markus and Gondyr, then we'll gather the team here in the library," she said to Aleric. "We'll speak soon, Chrysanthem." With that, Kara and Lucian headed out to the stables where Markus was tending the Pegasi.

"Good morning, Markus."

"Kara, Lucian...good morning," Markus replied with a smile.

"I see you've brought some friends back from Aquanalis."

"Yes. We decided it would be good to gather the Mages of Light here first, that way getting them all to Dellalun would be an easier feat." The Nymphs stared at Kara with bright jeweled eyes of pink, purple, and green, clearly intimidated. "This is Rosalyn, Tulipa, and Jasmine."

"Nice to meet you all. I'm Kara, and this is Lucian. Welcome to the Citadel. Please make yourselves at home." They all blushed as Kara and Lucian smiled at them, then nodded and went back to helping Markus with the Pegasi.

"They're quite shy," Markus advised, "but they'll come around."

"We're grateful to have their help. We should give them a little time here to adjust a bit to the outside world before we throw them into the fray," Kara thought aloud. "We will take them to Dellalun in a couple of days. When you're finished here, I'd like to gather the team for a full update. Meet us in the library?" Markus nodded, and they left to find Gondyr. It gave Kara so much hope to see all these races, this melting pot of vastly diverse cultures, working together and learning from one another. And it filled her with pride - she rarely enjoyed taking credit, but she knew that without her, Cylendri would have remained fractured, and the Demigods would have easily destroyed the fragments. They were stronger together, like her magics, and she now genuinely believed they could win this fight. They passed through the forge, greeting Nalor and the Dwarves there, then found Gondyr with Sel'arin at the great tree.

"There's my favorite Elven Assassin!" Gondyr exclaimed. "I've missed you my friend, we have much to discuss!"

"That we do," Kara smiled, "it's good to see you both. The team will gather in the library shortly, meet us there?"

"Of course," Sel'arin said, "we are just ensuring the other elves get settled, and we'll be right over."

"Perfect," Kara replied, and they left to head back inside.

***

Lucian and Kara waited in the library, looking over a map on the table, and he watched her as she silently worked through whatever plan she was forming next. She was so much more self-assured than she had been yesterday. He hadn't realized how fiercely she had been battling her own nature within, and for so long. *'Exhausting half my energy'* she had said. While that had only been after it fully unlocked, knowing what he now knew, he was sure she had been fighting it on some level her entire life. A weight he couldn't begin to understand had been lifted from her, and her power

247

was so much more evident, she almost glowed with it. He also knew they still had to talk about his...mortality. While he had pushed it from his mind, they couldn't avoid it forever, and this new information about her told him that she could very likely be an immortal. She needed to be prepared, and he needed her to understand that it didn't matter how long he had with her, he would cherish every second.

Gondyr, Nalor, and Sel'arin walked into the library, joining them at the table. Then Markus and Dahlia, followed by Aleric. It had been almost five days since the whole team was together like this. Much had been uncovered and even more had been done in that time. Lucian never thought he'd see such cooperation between the factions and races.

"The last few days have been so productive, "Kara began, "we are making great progress. I know that inevitably the dam will break, and we'll have new problems to combat, but to see how ready Cylendri has become in the face of the approaching storm...it's humbling. You have all been instrumental and should be truly proud of how much we have accomplished. Let's go around the team, everyone provides an update so we can ensure we aren't leaving anything on the table, starting with Est'alda."

"The Mormagi have increased their presence around the First Tree and the Well, but with the help of the Gryphons, Necromancers, and Stone Dwarves, they have not advanced," Gondyr advised.

"There's a handful of Mages of Light from the smaller clans around Est'alda who volunteered for Dellalun, so we brought them here. We have a few more to go back and get before you take them all to the city. There's another group of Archers who want to help the clans and villages throughout the forest, so we will disperse them wherever you see fit," Sel'arin added.

Nalor spoke next, "Lyria is protected, and will have Mages of Light for Dellalun ready to go tomorrow. I brought two more blacksmiths from Lapidis with me to help make more weapons in preparation. The Stone Dwarves should have started arriving throughout villages. A few interrupted some Mormagi attacks and have already taken refugees to Dellalun."

"The Vipers have the city ready," Lucian advised. "They are helping manage correspondence throughout Cylendri, keeping some marks running so as not to draw suspicion and using that as a means to receive updates."

Then Markus chimed in, "the Gryphons are stationed throughout the cities and villages, including the tribes across Terastra. Some of those tribes have offered additional warriors, so I will coordinate getting them up to the North as soon as possible."

"Aquanalis is fortified and the Mormagi around the outskirts have not breached the ward thanks to the Gryphons, Stones, and Archers that are patrolling the area," Dahlia told them. "We have Mages of Light here, ready to head to Dellalun, and an evacuation plan in place if necessary."

Aleric spoke last. "The Spirits have spread word across Cylendri. They have reported back on areas where support is needed, and we are working with the Gryphons to provide that. We have a few Necromancers stationed in Est'alda, and a few more who can go wherever needed. We have the full support of the Undead Faction."

Lucian watched as Kara took in all the information, weighing each update carefully to decide what the next move would be. They all waited silently as she processed.

She finally spoke, "that is all excellent news, but we can't get complacent. The next few weeks will become increasingly more difficult and demand more of everyone. Lives will inevitably be lost, and not everything will go our way. But if we keep the pressure on, if we remain vigilant and focused, the damage will be minimal, and our enemies will fall. I am not leading this rebellion; we are leading it together." She paused, making sure everyone understood. "That being said, we now need to focus our efforts on maintaining communication and resources, ensuring supplies, rations, and weapons are available wherever needed, and minimizing losses." She stopped again as Pytra came into the library, a letter in hand.

"Sorry to interrupt. We received a raven from the Lord Gryphon," she said, handing the letter to Kara.

"Thank you, Pytra," Kara replied, and the Gryphon left. Kara read it, then gave it to Lucian. "Rowan wants to speak with us, he has some field reports that he said we need to see. We'll head out after we finish here," she advised, and then she got that look Lucian had come to know very well...she had the next phase figured out.

"Markus, with the ravens being an issue, I want to ensure no communications are missed. I would like you to stay on top of that as you will be traveling regularly, which means you also need to visit Dellalun to receive their field reports from Vivvain. Make sure that any requests for supplies are given to Gondyr." He nodded and she turned to the Dwarf, "I'd like for you to coordinate that. Find a place here in the Citadel where rations and weapons can be stored and establish a tracking system for what's coming in and what's going out. Everyone needs to be clear on where they are traveling next so that we can make drops as needed. This should include healing supplies, perishables, linens, and weapons. Nalor, your focus is the forge, keep it running and turn out whatever is needed."

"I'll get on it right away," Gondyr assured her.

"I already have my two apprentices working on bows and arrows, crossbow arrows for the Vipers, and armor pieces for the dwarves. Just let me know what else we need," Nalor offered, and Kara nodded.

"Next, we have to keep this place from being overrun, we won't do anyone any good if we're tripping over each other. Dahlia, can you please manage the flow of visitors? Ensure everyone gets a place to rest, knows where everything is, helps with the chores while they are here, and coordinate the travels for Wards & Healers out to their posts. Make sure to work with Gondyr so they always have a supply run with them when they leave."

"Not a problem," Dahlia replied.

"Sel'arin, we have a lot of warriors, bruisers, necromancers, and archers who want to help. Can you focus on them? They need orders, a post, and travel. As they come through the Citadel, ensure they have

251

everything they need, and coordinate mixed teams to head out wherever needed. Work closely with Dahlia, send a Healer or Ward with the teams if necessary. If we don't have enough at first, we can have them running shifts, except for anyone going to Dellalun. They have a place for the Mages and need to keep them close."

"On it," Sel'arin said tersely.

"Aleric, you are our only connection to the Spirit Realm. Not only are their reports lucrative, but I am hoping they can...expand their radius. The High Gods have not intervened, why? How could they be allowing their children to even consider destroying all of Cylendri and bringing down the Mag'nicelo? They must know what's happening, and they have been silent. Can we ask the Spirits to get a report on Ess'Magis?" She asked, the hesitation plain in her voice.

"I will ask, though that is a very large ask," Aleric replied, "the Realm of The Divine is difficult to access, even for Spirits, and I assure you if the High Gods catch one snooping around, they can still very much hurt us. It will be tricky."

"I understand, and I don't want them to think we're pushing. Assure them we will respect their decision, and we are grateful for their help regardless." Then she turned that determined, piercing look on Lucian. "You and I are going to the Castellum. When we return, we are going to pour over the maps and strategize. A battle plan is necessary, and we'll need time to adjust, get input, and set things in motion in the days before." She looked around the group, "I trust Lucian to make decisions in my stead if you can't find me. This is a massive undertaking - work together, don't overdo it. Get rest when you need it, and lean on each other, lean on me. We'll be back soon, and you'll find us right here."

Everyone left, except Sel'arin and Lucian. "Do you need something more Sel'arin?" Kara asked.

"Nae'lin has also requested an audience with you. He did not give me a letter, and only said *'tell her I know about the seed,'* whatever that means," Sel'arin told her. Lucian and Kara locked eyes, a flash of incredulity crossing hers.

"Thank you, Sel'arin. We'll get to Est'alda as soon as possible," Kara replied, and the Archer headed out.

"That can't be good," Lucian said once she was gone.

"Could be the first crack in the dam, or it could help us, who knows at this point. But we have other matters to attend to first. Let's go."

***

They arrived to find a half empty Castellum as a lot of Gryphons were out in Cylendri. Most of those still here were the Wingless and the Historians. They headed into the main hall and were escorted to Rowan's office. They found the Lord Gryphon behind his desk, a pile of parchments in front of him.

"Ah. Kara, Lucian, thank you for coming so quickly," Rowan said, clearly frazzled. "We've been receiving an influx of ravens, and some of the

253

letters are weeks old, so it's been a struggle to weed through for the newest ones. I think whatever is going on out there has tempered our ward, so they're all finally able to pass through." He got up and came around the desk, three pieces of parchment in his hand, "these I think you should see."

Kara opened one and handed another to Lucian. She read through it, looked at Lucian and Rowan, and opened the remaining parchment.

"Well, there's the fucking crack in the dam," Kara said with a sigh. "The Demigods are responding to our disruptions. And they're getting bold, coming out from their hiding place. Terranis was spotted near the City of Stone, and she's causing earthquakes in the mines. Aeranis is in the deserts of the south, plaguing them with massive dust storms. And Aquanis has been seen stirring up the waters around the Nymphs. Luckily, with all the Gryphons out there, wards are either going up, or being strengthened, but they won't hold forever. We need to figure out a solution - Dellalun won't hold all of Cylendri."

"Oblitori..." Rowan said quietly.

"I'm sorry...what?" Lucian asked.

"It's a long shot..." It was almost as if Rowan was talking to himself.

"Lord Gryphon?" Kara asked sharply. Rowan looked up suddenly and realized where he was.

"Oh. I...need to...check on something," he replied, and went to pull a book from one of the shelves.

254

"Alright. Well, we will head back to the Citadel. Let us know if you come up with something..." Kara said slowly. "And thank you for the updates." Kara looked at Lucian, and they turned to leave.

"Be careful, Kara. If they're fighting back already, the timeline could accelerate...they might risk doing the Blood Sacrifice without the Full Moon, which could be even more catastrophic," Rowan said as they left.

Twenty-Two

The Great Tree

B ack in the library at the Citadel, Kara was pacing. Nae'lin knew about her ancestral magic, the Demigods were wreaking havoc already, and Rowan had acted very strangely. As soon as they figured out one set of problems, a whole new set arose. They needed a plan if things got out of control...they had to get the people of Cylendri to safety.

"How many more, realistically, could Dellalun hold?" Kara asked Lucian as he watched her walk back and forth.

"Maybe a couple thousand...it's already a pretty well-populated city," Lucian replied.

"That's not nearly enough. The rest of Cylendri holds at least four times that." She paused and thought for a moment. "What did Rowan say?"

"Oblitori...I've never heard of it."

"It's...familiar, but I can't put my finger on it. Ira, what about you?"

"I don't know it," Ira hissed.

"Damn. I wonder if Aleric would know, or if there's a book here somewhere that references it."

"It's possible, but where would we start?"

"What if I could use the Citadel's magic? Ask for it...see what happens?" Kara shrugged.

Lucian considered it, and said, "it couldn't hurt." Kara put her hand on one of the bookshelves, closed her eyes, and quietly asked the Citadel for a book referencing the word *Oblitori*. She waited a few moments and then opened her eyes.

"Anything?" Lucian asked.

"Nothing," she replied with a sigh.

"Well," he said, taking her hand in his, "we can ask Aleric after he returns. In the meantime, we also need to go to Est'alda. If Nae'lin knows, maybe he can help." She smiled at him, growing ever more grateful that he was fighting this battle at her side.

"You're right. I haven't eaten yet today, and I'm famished. Let's have an early lunch and then we'll go," she said and led him to the kitchen. They made a root and vegetable salad with lemon juice, oil, and breadcrumbs. Shortly after Nalor, Gondyr, and Dahlia came in to start lunch for the rest of them and their visitors. Kara and Lucian moved to the chairs by the window to be out of the way as they ate. Watching the three of them in the kitchen together was amusing. The dwarves were still enamored with the Nymph and got distracted by her often. But she had really opened up, and you could see she was beginning to enjoy their company. They finished their salads and headed out, letting Gondyr know where they were going as they left the kitchen.

When they arrived in Est'alda, things had clearly escalated. The air was hot and weighty, which was not common here even in the warmer months. They made their way up the tree sluggishly...leathers were not ideal for this climate. The Tree Dwellers were struggling, too. As they approached the top, it only got warmer, and Kara was feeling lightheaded. Nae'lin was just outside his dwelling when they came up, both practically crawling.

"Hurry inside, before you pass out!" he instructed, and they moved as quickly as their bodies would allow. Once inside, they instantly felt cooler. Kara noticed that there was a light dusting of snow on everything.

"I am regulating the temperature inside of here," Nae'lin advised, "all the dwellings are, but there are not enough of us to do this inside the ward."

"What's causing it?" Kara asked.

"Solaris. We just received reports that he has been spotted in the forest. However, I am not sure how he is doing it."

"Of course. Could he be affecting the ward itself?"

"That is...quite possible. He could be heating the ward, weaving it with

258

elemental magic."

"How many Elemental Mages would it take to counteract it? And how many do you have here?"

Nae'lin thought for a moment. "Enough that we could surround the ward. Maybe forty or fifty - we only have about twenty still at the Tree, the rest are out near the Mai'ngolo or protecting the other villages. We would also need a few Wards to help weave the magic in and strengthen it."

"Alright, we'll call back enough to help and have a few Gryphons and Necromancers in place. When we get through this, we need to talk."

"That we do, *Esseld'iel*." He looked pointedly at Kara with that deep, swirling wisdom in his eyes.

"Lucian, do you think you can get us back down to the Stone quickly?" He nodded, wrapped her in his arms, and flew through the opening of the dwelling, straight down the tree. They went back to the Citadel to look for Dahlia. They would need her telepathy to coordinate the Mages. Once they found her, they informed her of the situation, and she went to collect a few more Nymphs to help. Then they found Markus and asked him to call some of the Tree Dwellers back to Est'alda. Lastly, they spoke with Sel'arin and had her collect the Elemental Mages that were here awaiting orders. Within a few hours, some of the Mages out in the field were arriving back at the First Tree, and the group from the Citadel was ready to go. They stood around the Stone, and Kara addressed everyone.

"We need to move quickly and be perfectly coordinated. I have no doubt this is both a distraction, and an attempt to damage our Mages. Solaris is trying to thin out numbers in the field, so we must get this done before anyone is burned by his magic and then get everyone immediately back out to their posts. The goal is to weave enough magic into the ward to prevent Solaris from burning Est'alda down and then strengthen the ward so he can't try this again. Nymphs, your job is to direct the orders, follow Dahlia's lead. Everyone ready?" They all nodded, and joined hands before Kara touched the Stone and they were gone.

The large group arrived at the base of the First Tree and immediately headed out to position themselves around the interior of the ward. There were already Elemental Mages, Gryphons, and Necromancers positioned around the exterior, a balance to ensure the weave would be tight and effective. The four Nymphs stood around the base of the tree facing north, south, east, and west so they could direct the flow of information without having to see their targets. Kara and Lucian stood with Dahlia awaiting the signal that everyone was in place. The mood was tense, the heat adding a heavy layer of weight to the air. Kara took Lucian's hand and held it tight, feeling a boost of strength and focus, almost as if Ira was sharing his power with her. She began to see the golden shimmer of the ward in the distance. Then, she saw the red heat of Solaris' magic snaking through, violent and volatile, as if the ward was trying to fight it.

"Ready," Dahlia announced.

"Okay, everyone needs to touch the ward at the exact same moment. Tell them to start weaving in their magic immediately, and don't pull away until it's finished. On the count of three..." Kara instructed and took a deep breath. "One...two...three!" Kara saw dozens of hands around the base of

260

the ward, blue magic flowing from them and slowly veining upwards, weaving through the golden glow, and forcing back the red. "Keep pushing!" Kara yelled as the air sizzled and popped with the massive amount of battling energies around them. "It's working! Solaris' magic is retreating!" Dahlia passed on the information, and Kara could see her struggling against the force of magic. But she stood firm and started to glow as she connected with the ward through the roots of the tree, adding her own strength to the weave. Kara was in awe - this Nymph had barely left the only world she had known for her whole life and had come so far. Her determination to prove herself was palpable.

Kara watched as the icy blue and gold intertwined about halfway up the ward, where a battle for dominance began. The magics pushed and pulled against each other. "The Mages are struggling; Solaris' power might be too strong!" Dahlia shouted. Kara would not allow him to win this fight. She took Dahlia's hand, and pushed the bit of ward magic she had control over through the Nymph, strengthening her connection. Kara marveled as white-hot threads of her magic streaked through the ward like lightning. A moment later, the blue and gold began pushing the red magic up again, and kept pushing until it reached the very top of the ward, where it exploded from the pressure, sending all of the Mages and Gryphons who had been holding the ward flying, and a rain of blue magic came down like droplets of water. The place instantly cooled, and Kara could see the ward like a beautiful tapestry of electric blue, white, and gold shimmering in the sky.

"Dahlia, is everyone alright? Is anyone hurt?" Kara asked frantically. Dahlia was silent for a few moments as she and the other Nymphs checked in.

"No fatal injuries, though a few of the Mages are hurt," Dahlia advised.

"Get the Gryphons to those Mages first so we can get them back here to the Stone immediately. The rest of them need to get back to their posts as soon as possible - have the Gryphons coordinate travel in groups."

"On it," Dahlia said tersely. Within a few minutes, Gryphons began flying in with the injured Mages in their arms, then headed back out to assist those needing to travel elsewhere. Once Dahlia confirmed that they were all accounted for and the other Nymphs joined them at the Stone, they left. Back at the Citadel, Kara instructed the Nymphs to get to work healing the Mages, then she and Lucian returned to Est'alda. He flew her up to the top, and they headed into the dwelling to speak with Nae'lin.

"As always, we are grateful for your assistance," he began, "that would have turned into an absolute disaster."

"Let's just hope we did it fast enough," Kara sighed.

"So, *Essald'iel*? When did you learn of your ancestral ties to the First Elf?" he asked, right to the point.

"In recent days," Kara replied, "thanks to the Gryphons and the Library of Cylendri. I was able to help them translate some incredibly old texts, which revealed the truth of my blood."

"And your powerful magic."

"How did *you* know?" Kara asked him pointedly.

"Dear child, I am over a thousand years old, I am tied to the old magic, and I can feel it wherever an elfling manifests their magic. I felt it when that power unlocked within you all those years ago, though I could not pinpoint the elf or the location. It was unlike any manifestation I had ever experienced. I searched for you, but was unable to trace your power, until a few days ago. I had suspected it from the moment we met, but that cage you kept it in was quite effective." He narrowed his eyes on her, "that seed you are rooting is dangerous."

"I am aware," Kara said forcefully, "I have been battling this my whole life. I did not choose this and have been walking blindly with it inside of me. Do not presume to lecture me, I am taking whatever steps I can to contain and control it."

"And to use it?" Nae'lin snapped, the first time he had allowed his calm demeanor to slip. Kara could see that this frightened him.

"If necessary, yes. Is that not what it was created for? Was that not the intention of the First Elves when they imbued an infant with this great power, without providing any sort of guidance or instructions? Are you telling me I should not have aided those Mages out there? Should I have let them die?" She challenged him. She was aware this was not very diplomatic, but he had sat up in this tree, not getting his hands dirty, and now he was judging her. He stared sharply at her, and she hoped he chose his next words carefully. She did not want to damage the progress they had made, but she didn't have time for this.

"I suppose you are correct," he finally said. "I imagine it has been quite difficult for you. And the fact that you contained such a volatile magic for as

263

long as you have is...impressive. But this power? It could destroy you. It could destroy all of us."

"Which is why I am working with a Spirit guide - to understand it, shape it, manipulate it. This is the great weapon of the First Elves, and I will not squander it. If you know something that could help, I would be grateful."

"I know little, likely not much more than you. What I do know is this - if you unleash that power on the Demigods, it has a very real chance of tearing you apart. The amount of power that it will take to destroy them will destroy you."

"That is a sacrifice I am willing to make," Kara admitted, "without question. If we are finished here, I have a rebellion to get back to."

"Of course," Nae'lin replied, his cool demeanor returned. "Keep me apprised of your progress, on all fronts." Kara bowed her head, then her and Lucian took their leave.

Twenty-Three

A Problem for Every Solution

At the Citadel, the noise had settled down as everyone was turning in for the night. Kara and Lucian headed up to their room after checking on the injured Mages, who were already recovering. Kara removed her boots and leathers the minute the door closed, feeling suffocated, and threw on a thin nightshirt before sitting cross-legged in the center of the bed as Lucian undressed and got into his sleeping trousers. He climbed onto the bed and sat in front of her, taking her hands in his.

"Talk to me," was all he said.

"Where do I even begin?" she asked, sighing and looking down at their hands. "We're barely a week into this thing and it's already cracking under the pressure. How can I hold it all together? And what happens if Solaris finds a way to move up the timeline? How can I protect the people? And how am I supposed to find time to understand and control this power inside of me?" She looked up at him sharply. "Speaking of which, something happened out there today, and it's added a whole new set of questions to my ever-growing list. Why did it feel like you were feeding me some sort of extra strength? You didn't see it, but with that added strength I weaved my own magic into the ward when I took Dahlia's hand, and I have no idea how. I just don't know where to begin..." she trailed off.

"First of all, I was...or rather Ira was sharing his Spirit with you. That's where the boost of power came from."

"I didn't know he could do that," Kara whispered.

"Nor did I, but we've been growing in strength the longer we work together, so maybe this is something new."

"It is..." Ira chimed in. *"I did not...try. I simply did."*

"As for your magic and the ward, as that seed roots within you, I imagine you will find there's a lot you can do with it. The first thing you've been able to tap into is the Ward Magic, so it's not surprising that you would connect to one steeped in old magic."

"That's very true," Kara replied, her mood brightening.

"I will do my best to remind you about your meditations. In fact, I think you should do that now, it will help you clear up the chaos and refocus on the controllables. I'll be here when you're finished," he smiled and kissed her softly.

"Alright, I'll be back in a bit," she said, then pulled on a pair of loose trousers, and headed to the Meditation room. As she entered, five colored candles lit on the stone column - white, pale yellow, light blue, emerald

266

green, and blood red. She chose a sage incense to burn, then settled on a pillow in the center of the room. She closed her eyes, taking deep and even breaths as she cleared the clutter in her mind, pushing piles aside to the left and the right making her way to where the seed was buried. It had sprouted a single vine with four leaves sticking out of it, which began to glow as she approached. She touched the leaves gently, feeling the power on her fingertips, and then sat in the center of her being with it, nurturing it. A single, small piece of parchment floated down and landed next to her. She opened it and found a drawing - a great castle she had never seen before, beset on one side by mountains, waves of sand on the other. She tucked it away for later. Then another fell on the opposite side of her. She opened that one, a simple list of names - her team - and she held that tightly in her hand as another piece fell in front of her, on top of the sprouting magic. She picked it up and opened it slowly. She knew it was The First Tree, but as a seedling barely sprouted from the ground and it looked exactly like her sprouted magic. She was connected to everything, to the very birth of Cylendri, and she understood.

Her eyes fluttered open; the candles were almost halfway burned down. Feeling centered, she blew them out, and headed back to her room. She crept in, trying not to wake Lucian as she was sure he was asleep by now, then crawled into bed next to him.

"Better?" he asked, wrapping his arms around her as she snuggled against his warmth.

"Much," she sighed. "Thank you."

"I may not always know what to say or how to help, but I'm always going to try," he told her, and kissed the top of her head. "You're not alone in this." The scent of coffee & lavender filled her lungs as she breathed him in deep and soon fell asleep.

***

The next morning, after helping Markus make a hearty breakfast for the whole Citadel, Kara and Lucian headed to the library to get to work on the next phase of the plan. As they rounded the large table where the map of Cylendri was laid out, Kara noticed a chestnut brown book with a golden sun sigil on its cover sitting on top that had not been there yesterday. She picked it up and inspected it. *"The Protectors of Cylendri: A History of the Gryphons,"* she read the title aloud. "I wonder if Markus was reading this." She opened it and flipped through the pages, then something urged her to stop on one. As she looked it over, one word caught her eye. "Lucian, look...*Oblitori*!" She sat down and kept reading as Lucian leaned over her. *"Of the Forgotten*. This great castle stood as the home of the Gryphons in the First and Second Ages, though no record of its true name has ever been found. When the massive fortress was overrun by the largest demon horde Cylendri has ever seen, and a portion of the great structure was set ablaze, the Gryphons left and founded Castellum In'Caelo high up in the mountains to prevent an invasion of that magnitude happening again."

"Looks like the Citadel just needed a little time to find the right book," Lucian laughed.

"This is amazing! I wonder if the castle still stands...must be what Rowan was looking into. That could be just what we need for a mass evacuation."

"Good, now that we have a potential solution for that, let's talk about the cracks. You knew this was going to be a battle up until we face the Demigods, it was only a matter of time. And yet, we have done so much in those few days, and we are ahead of the problems as they're coming. We are doing this together; you can't hold yourself wholly accountable for anything." He furrowed his brow and narrowed his eyes at her. "Understood?"

She sighed. "You're right. I'll be better about remembering that," she said as she wrinkled her nose at him. That look melted him, but he steeled himself. It was not the time to be distracted, he knew it was lucrative to keep her focused right now.

"Okay. Onto the battle plan. I assume you already have some thoughts on that?" he asked.

"Yes," she said and stood over the map. "We know that the Blood Sacrifice requires the Full Moon. If Solaris tries to accelerate the attack, he risks a lot of uncertainty and volatility with the spells necessary to complete the ritual. I'm still not convinced he would take that risk, no matter how much we impede him. So, we keep the pressure on. We stop the Mormagi from collecting sacrifices, which means the Demigods are going to have to convince the Death Mages to use more of their ranks instead. That could cause a lot of tension between our enemies. While they fight amongst themselves, we'll be preparing."

"And we know they will have to show themselves fully near the entrance of the Mai'ngolo to complete the ritual. So that's still our focus - how are we going to approach the attack?"

269

"We'll have teams - a mix of Archers, Gryphons, Stone Dwarves, and Necromancers - placed here," she pointed to the map, "here, here, and here. Each team will have an untraceable glimmer provided by the Nymphs, we'll likely need a few of them per team to do that. We should have Dahlia start working with them to ensure the glimmers are strong. That way, Solaris and the others won't see our back up. Markus, Nalor, Aleric, and Sel'arin will lead those teams. We'll see if Sel'arin can get the aid of the Aqui'noctura, and we'll bring the Pegasi for air support."

"Where will we be?"

"Walking headfirst into enemy territory," she smiled, "where else? We have the crystal; I need to learn more about it and see if we can increase its coverage area. Either way, we will be taking a small team straight to the fight - me, you, Gondyr, and Dahlia. We need a ward and healer with us, and a warrior with Stone Magic. You and I have the rest covered, and no one is faster than we are at taking down those assholes," she winked. "Besides, if I'm the weapon, I need to be as close to them as possible."

"I'm still not onboard with you sacrificing yourself," he frowned. "You better prioritize your meditations and work with Aleric so that is no longer on the table."

"I promise I will," she told him. "My magic is growing, it's rooting well. Last night, the seed sprouted. I need to nurture it regularly."

"Then we have a plan. Let's go check in around the Citadel, and then we have some Mages to collect from your mother," he laughed.

After they made the rounds, they stopped back in at the library to see if there had been any ravens before getting ready to leave, and Kara saw a letter on the table closest to the door.

"It's from Kaisilus," Kara told Lucian, "he's in Dellalun and wants to speak."

"Well, good thing we're headed that way."

***

They were in Dellalun after stopping in Lyira to pick up the Mages of Light, ensuring they were settled in at the Manor before making their way across the city. Per the letter from Kaisilus, he and his clan were staying in one of the abandoned buildings just outside the Burned District, so they had headed that way after speaking with Marciela. They found him outside the warehouse with a few other elves and a Gryphon.

"Kara and Lucian, thank you for coming," he said as he saw them approaching.

"Hello Kaisilus," Kara replied, "how is everyone?"

"We're all just fine, thanks to you," he smiled. The other elves headed off with the Gryphon towards the markets. "I never thought I'd be in the city, making friends with Gryphons and Vipers...what a strange few days it has been."

"Tell me about it," Kara laughed. "So, what did you want to speak with us about?"

"I would like to help," he started. "Our clan has been relatively insulated from the world for many years, and this has all been a bit of a shock, but we belong to Cylendri the same as you. We may not have magic, but we have a few archers who could be of use. What can we do?"

"That's a very generous offer. I think the best place for your archers is here - with us having to spread the protection out, we need to ensure that Dellalun has capable warriors and fighters if it comes to that," Kara told him. "However, I think we could use your wisdom, experience, and tactical mind. I realize you may not want to leave your clan, but if you really want to help, we will need you with us at our base of operations."

"As long as I have the ability to check in with my people regularly, I have no problem leaving them here. They are well protected and have everything they need."

"That won't be an issue. Gather what you need, and we'll be on our way." He nodded and went inside.

"Are you sure you trust him?" Lucian asked.

"I still don't know," Kara admitted, "he's unlike any elf I've ever met. But I want to keep him close, and he could be particularly useful."

"Then we keep an eye on him, and hope for the best," Lucian smiled.

"Exactly."

Over the last couple of weeks, Kara did her best not to get too lost in the chaos. The Citadel was practically running by itself. Supply runs with the Mages were on a regular routine as they came and went in shifts, the forge had a good rhythm turning out the arrows and weapons that were needed, the communications and reports ran though on a predictable schedule so much so that one missed report was enough to send a check in. Most of the time, it was a raven that never arrived, but a couple of them were particularly nasty Mormagi attacks with Risen hordes, and members of the team had to get involved. But Kara didn't have to do this alone, and the team had proven that in spades. She had stayed diligent in her meditations, allowing the seed to flourish, and had begun training in her magic with Aleric. She was able to produce fully formed wards, manipulate the elements in small bursts, and create wisps. As she improved on those, Aleric told her it was time to introduce Death Magic. Not something she was excited about, though she knew it was necessary.

Lucian had been in Dellalun since yesterday, checking on things with Viv and Marciela, but Rowan had requested an audience with Kara, so she headed to the Castellum with Markus. This likely had to do with the Castle Oblitori, and she didn't want to wait. They were six days from the Full Moon, and that was the last piece of unfinished business, she needed to know if it was a viable solution for a mass evacuation.

Rowan was in the courtyard when they arrived and seemed to be back to his normal self. "Kara, Markus, good to see you both!" He exclaimed.

"Lord Gryphon," Markus replied with a bow of his head.

"You seem to be in good spirits," Kara said with a smile.

"I am. And I apologize for my behavior on the last visit."

"No need, I understand. Though I imagine this has something to do with that last conversation," Kara asserted.

"It does. Let's get inside."

Carmine waited in the main hall and joined them as they headed for Rowan's office. He nodded at Kara but said nothing. Once inside the office, Carmine again warded the room.

"The last time you were here, we discussed the possibility of needing a mass evacuation plan," Rowan jumped right in, "and how Dellalun was not a viable option." He looked at Carmine, and Kara could tell the Historian was again not onboard with what Rowan was about to propose. "We know of a place, though there is an obstacle standing in our way."

"The Castle Oblitori," Kara said, and Rowan's brow furrowed.

"How did you know that?" He asked.

"You mentioned it before, but I don't think you realized that you said it aloud. Then, we found a book in our library at the Citadel which told us a bit more," Kara advised.

"Well, if you know about it, then you know why we abandoned it."

"Yes, the horde."

"There lies the obstacle...the Risen never left. Demons have overrun it, and the still active Summoning Crystal is deep with the Castle."

"That does pose quite a problem," Kara replied, frustration in her voice. "And we don't have a lot of time or resources to spare for something like that."

"That's where this gets interesting," Rowan said ominously. "There is a way to take out the whole horde by destroying the Crystal...but it's dangerous, and we're not even sure it would work."

Kara narrowed her eyes and simply asked, "how?"

"Spirit Magic. It would take an enormously powerful Necromancer, likely two. But it's not a common spell...in fact, it's almost unheard of. And they would need protection as they work through it, the horde won't just let you walk in and destroy their gateway. We do know exactly where the Crystal is, and it's relatively easy to access from the air."

"So, two strong Necromancers, a team to protect them, and wings...that's what we need?" She looked at Markus, "we can do that."

"Really?" Rowan and Carmine asked simultaneously, both wearing a look of bewilderment.

"Yes," Markus replied. "We just need to make sure the Citadel can run in our absence."

Rowan looked at Carmine, and the Historian pulled a piece of parchment from his robes, handing it to Kara. "That's the map. You'll find the Castle where the mountains meet the desert in the Southwest of Cylendri. The map has the location of the Crystal...there's a room down the hall from it with part of the roof missing, that's your access point." He looked at Kara, "but be careful. The demons have been there a long time, who knows what kind of monsters they have guarding that Crystal."

"We'll let you know if we're successful," Kara told Rowan as she and Markus got up to leave.

"Please do," Rowan replied.

Twenty-Four

Death Magic

Once they arrived back at the Citadel, Kara sent Markus to speak with Sel'arin, while she went to look for Aleric. She found him and Chrysanthem in the training room practicing some new spells.

"Hello Kara," Aleric greeted her warmly.

"I'm glad I found you together," Kara began, "we have a potential solution to the evacuation problem, but it comes with its own problem, and we'll need you both if we even have a fighting chance. When you're done here, please meet me in the library."

"We were just finishing up and will head there in a few moments," Aleric replied, a hint of concern in his voice.

"Have you seen Lucian?"

"Yes, he returned not long ago. He should still be in the greenhouse."

"Great, I'll see you both shortly," Kara smiled and left. She headed straight for the kitchen and indeed found Lucian in the greenhouse picking tomatoes. She leaned against the doorway and just watched him for a few moments, taking in the absurd beauty of a deadly assassin gingerly plucking fruit from a vine and placing it into a basket, taking care not to bruise or damage it. He was such a walking contradiction, and it was probably her favorite thing about him. She had seen him rip the head off a Death Mage with his bare hands, and yet he had such a tenderness to him.

"I can smell the jasmine on you," he said, "that's why you can never sneak up on me." He looked back at her and winked.

"How's Dellalun?" she inquired as she walked over to him and knelt to grab a tomato. She bit into it, savoring the fresh, earthy flavor as the juices dripped down her chin.

"It's...it's fine," Lucian stammered as he watched her, then went back to picking tomatoes. "They've had less wounded than expected, which is great news. Viv received a few reports of Death Mages trying to kidnap younglings from the smaller villages but luckily have not successfully taken any. The Vipers are helping with night patrols across Cylendri."

"Glad to hear it," she replied, "I also have some news."

"Rowan?" Lucian asked as he picked the last one and stood.

"As per usual. We need to speak with Aleric in the library. Are you all done here?"

"Yes. I'll just drop these in the kitchen on our way." He followed her out, and she could feel the heat of his eyes on her body. If it were anyone else, it would make her uncomfortable, but she loved the way he looked at her. They headed for the library where Markus and Sel'arin were already waiting. Aleric and Chrysanthem joined them a moment later.

"Markus and I spoke with the Lord Gryphon, and there is a place in Cylendri that could handle a mass evacuation. The Castle Oblitori, in the deep southwest."

"I thought that was a myth," Sel'arin stated.

"Not a myth, just long forgotten," Markus replied.

"I thought that place was filled with demons?" Chrysanthem chimed in.

"It is." Kara said plainly, "which is the problem."

"Wait, are you saying the demon horde that invaded it...*is still there*?" Lucian asked incredulously.

"Again, yes. There's a Summoning Crystal in the heart of the ruin that's still active. We can access it, and we could potentially take it and the horde out at once."

"How?"

"That's where the tricky part comes in," Kara started, but Aleric cut her off, his voice more haunting than usual.

"That is why you need both of us...*Dis'cutia*. The Shatter spell."

"That doesn't sound good," Sel'arin said warily.

"It is an incredibly sophisticated and lengthy spell," he replied, "one that I do not believe Chrysanthem could learn in time, talented as she is."

"Is there another Necromancer who could help us? Since the Spirits refused our request to infiltrate Ess'Magis, we need to have a backup plan here. Even if we don't need it now, we have no idea what will happen after we deal with the Demigods," Kara pressed.

"Possibly. I will go to Atri'anima and speak with the Faction."

"Thank you. If we can find another Necromancer, we have a map, an entry point, and a plan. The four of us will hold off the horde while they work. This is going to be a nasty fight - there could be demons we've never faced, ones that have mutated. We also need to make sure this place manages in our absence, so we'll have to pass off any responsibilities for the day. How much time do you need Aleric?"

"I should be back tonight."

"Good. Let's plan to leave tomorrow morning after we shuffle assignments around, assuming you return with good news."

Everyone dispersed, and as they left the library Lucian pulled Kara up the stairs into the shadows. He lifted her with one arm around her waist and held her against the stone wall as she wrapped her legs around him, his other hand gripping her thigh, then ravaged her mouth with his. The bristles of his beard scratched against her chin as she gripped his head firmly, and their tongues danced with unbridled hunger. He pulled away, both of them breathless, and looked deep into her eyes. "I can't live without you," he whispered, "my life is yours, however short it may be. I would leave all of this behind - the Vipers, Dellalun, this rebellion - if that's what you needed. I would burn the Realms to ashes if that's what you asked of me."

She ran her fingers through his hair and smiled, "all I want, or need is you." He buried his face in her neck, holding her tightly to him as if he feared at any moment she would simply disappear, like a perfect dream one desperately tries to cling to as it slowly slips away with the dawn.

"What's wrong?" She asked, "where did this come from?"

He pulled back again and put her down. She could see tears forming in his eyes as she looked up at him. "I know you're going to outlive me," he sighed, and looked away from her. "No matter what happens in a few days, I'm going to grow old and die long before you, and I can't do anything to change it. It feels selfish, but I can't stop thinking that my time with you is so finite. And one day, you'll have just...forgotten me, it will be as if I never existed."

Her heart ripped as the tears escaped his dark eyes, running down his cheeks. She had not even considered that...they had been so wrapped up in all the chaos surrounding them since the moment she rescued him, she didn't even have a moment to think about their future. He was right, and she didn't have any words of comfort or any idea how she could fix this.

"I really tried to push it from my mind, at least until after...but in all her grandmotherly wisdom, Marciela brought it up last night. We can't ignore it, I just didn't want to add another problem onto the pile, especially one we can't do anything about." He finally looked back at her, and she still didn't know what to say. She had always had a plan; there was never a problem she couldn't find a way fix or an obstacle she couldn't overcome. But this...

"*No*," she said willfully, and he furrowed his brow, looking at her quizzically. "No. I don't accept that. I *can't* accept that. I have seen the improbable, the impossible, and the utterly unbelievable that this world has to offer. I don't believe that there isn't a way to solve this problem. I will find it. I always do."

His eyes softened, and his look changed to one of adoration. He laughed slightly, and bit his lower lip, then picked her up and tossed her over his shoulder without a word.

"*Lucian?!*" She exclaimed with a laugh. He carried her up to their room, and they spent the next few hours entwined with each other, sharing and locking away another precious memory to carry them through the darkness.

***

Lucian knew they had to get out of bed, but he couldn't bring himself to let her go as she lay curled up in his arms.

She sighed, "we can't lay here forever."

282

"I know," he replied, and begrudgingly lifted his arm off her so she could get up. She rolled over and sat up, her violet hair cascading across her bare shoulders, and looked back at him.

"I'll find a way, no matter what," she declared matter-of-factly, white fire in her eyes.

He sat up behind her, kissed the Vipers Insignia brand on her right shoulder, and whispered, "I know you will." They got dressed and headed downstairs to the kitchen as the sun dipped behind the tree line to help Sel'arin and Gondyr prepare dinner, then sat out around the fire pit under the stars with some of the other elves, nymphs, and Gryphons while they ate. Lucian observed Kara as she laughed and swapped battle stories with Pytra, knowing that if anyone could find a way to save him from his mortality, it was her. As they were finishing up, Aleric made his way over to them, another Necromancer in tow. He was tall and slender for a Spirit, with a more smokey slate color than the brighter icy blue of most of the Spirits he had met. Something about him unnerved Lucian.

"Good evening, everyone," Aleric greeted the group, "this is Octavius. Kara, Lucian...a word please?" They got up and headed back inside, dropping their plates in the kitchen before making their way to the library.

"Octavius has agreed to help us," Aleric began, "on one condition."

"Which is?" Kara asked hesitantly.

"That I be permitted to explore the Castle Oblitori once it has been cleared." Octavius replied, his voice raw and slightly scratchy, as if his vocal cords had been damaged before he became incorporeal. His energy was dark, and Lucian got the sense he had been a dangerous creature in his previous life. He couldn't quite place the spirit's original race, which made him all the more disconcerting.

Kara narrowed her eyes at him. "Why?"

"It is one of the oldest structures in Cylendri, and many secrets of the past were left behind, forgotten when it was abandoned, hence its name. The Gryphons will prevent anyone having access until they have swept it clean. I simply desire the opportunity to observe it as it was left." Kara looked at Lucian, and he held her gaze as she decided.

She finally looked back at Octavius and said, "I can't stop you from staying behind and exploring, but I also can't stop the Gryphons from reclaiming their property. You will have as much time as it takes for us to let them know we cleared the horde, and they make it to the Castle."

"Then we have a deal," he nodded, "when will we leave?"

"In the morning," Kara advised, "make yourself at home while you're here."

"Thank you. I think I will stay here in the library - it is quite a lovely collection." A smirk spread across his ghostly face, and something about it was unnatural, even for a Spirit.

"Aleric, we have training to attend to when you're ready," Kara remarked with an uneasy smile.

284

"Yes, I will be just a moment, go on ahead," he said, so Lucian followed Kara out of the room. When they were out of earshot on their way to the training room, Kara asked him quietly, "did that seem strange to you?"

"Very. I'm not entirely sure I trust that Spirit, but we need him," Lucian told her.

"Agreed. We need to keep an eye on him and move quickly to let the Gryphons know the Castle is cleared, give him as little time as possible to *'explore'* it."

"I'm going to help clean up in the kitchen and then go out to the spring." He kissed her forehead, "come find me when you're finished." She smiled, then headed into the training room.

***

After a few minutes, Aleric drifted through the door of the training room. Kara found it amusing that he could go through any wall he wanted, but he always used the hallways and walked through doors. Maybe it was a habit from his days of corporeal life.

"I know Octavius is...a bit much. But he is a strong Spirit, and one of an exceedingly small few who know *Dis'cutia* well enough to aid me. I think you handled his request very diplomatically. I also know you are not going to let him roam those halls very long," Aleric told her. "Now, we have a very important lesson to complete - the last one, Death Magic."

As he said it, the back half of the room sprouted vines, plants, and trees. "As you know, this magic is the only one of the four that requires a sacrifice to be able to learn and use each spell. This is why the Mormagi look as if they have had their life sucked out of them - every sacrifice is different, those of the flesh and soul are worth far more than, say, a whole grove of trees, and the more complex the spell, the greater the cost. Yet, the longer you wield it, the lesser the sacrifices will become. It would take them much more time, and more life in other forms to train so extensively in Death Magic than they have patience or resources for. So, when they don't have access to any sort of life to take, they sacrifice a small piece of themselves instead. We will not be utilizing the shortcut and corrupting the magic, by extension corrupting the wielder. Understood?"

"Understood," Kara replied, steeling herself in her resolve.

"Good, let us begin," he said. "One of the simplest is *scali'perius*, the Slicing spell - inflicts minimal damage, and requires a relatively minor sacrifice. Go pick a good handful of flowers." Kara walked over to the edge of the plants and grabbed as many flowers as she could gather in one hand, then yanked them out. As she stood across from Aleric, she closed her eyes and reached for her magic. When she had a firm grasp on it, she opened them and in front of her a few feet away stood a dummy target. "Focus. Picture a sword slicing through your enemy, and speak the word sharply, *scali'perius*."

She took a deep breath, released it, and gripped the flowers tightly. "*Scali'perius*." The flowers in her hand wilted all at once as a red light slashed across the target, slicing into its chest.

"Excellent!" Aleric exclaimed. "Very clear and focused for your first time, and effective. Had you left the flowers in the ground, the life within them not already wilting from being removed, it would have been even stronger. The more vibrant the life, the more powerful the spell. Keep this in mind as you wield the magic. Try again, this time, grab two handfuls."

***

A couple of hours later, Aleric and Kara finished the lesson. Kara was feeling much better about the Death Magic now that she understood the balance of it. She grabbed a linen towel from a set of shelves in the main hall and headed out to the spring. As she approached, she saw Lucian swimming in the center. Keeping herself to the shadows, she watched him glide along the surface, his strong arms pulling him effortlessly through to water before he stopped and went under, coming back up a few moments later, hair slicked back. She walked to the edge, into the light of the moon, then stripped down and stepped into the cool water as he turned those piercing eyes on her. She would never tire of the way he looked at her - a mix of awe, gratitude, and ravenous desire – and prayed he would never stop. He swam over as she made her way through the water, pulling her to him when she got close enough.

"How was the lesson?" he asked as she put her arms around his neck.

"It was good. I'm learning faster now that I've been at it for a few weeks, and the Death Magic is less intense than I had anticipated. Aleric is impressed with how far I've come in a short time."

"That's my Tia," he smiled.

Twenty-Five

The Castle Oblitori

The Citadel was abuzz the next morning. They were five days from the Full Moon, and half of the team was preparing to head out to the Castle, so assignments were being passed off and last-minute checks were being done. Once everyone was ready, they gathered at the Stone.

"Alright, the Travel Stone is right outside the Castle, so as soon as we arrive, we need to get in the air...the horde may not be limited to the inside of the ruin. We'll follow Markus, he knows the map and will be able to spot our entry point quickly. Then we get our asses to the Crystal and hold off the demons while Aleric and Octavius work. Ready?" Kara asked, and they all nodded. In a moment, they were gone.

They all landed on their feet or floated above the ground. A massive castle stood before them, set back into the mountains. Kara had never seen a single stone structure this large; it was practically a small city. She turned, and nothing was behind them but waves of sand as far as you could see. As she turned back around, demons came pouring out of the castle gate towards them. Markus picked up Sel'arin and carried her into the air,

288

Aleric and Octavius followed, and Lucian grabbed Kara, flying up last before the horde even got close.

They flew up over the rampart and could see demons in the courtyard, as well as throughout the bridges, walkways, and inside the castle in places where the walls or roof were missing. There were easily thousands of them. Kara wondered what kept them here, why they didn't venture out into Cylendri. She knew they were stuck, Summoning Crystals only worked one way. But it was strange that the horde stayed tied to this place. Once they got up above the third floor of the main structure in the center, Markus suddenly shot down; he had spotted their entrance. The rest of the group followed and landed in a small room with half the roof piled on the floor. Luckily, there weren't any Risen in the space, so they could collect themselves before heading out and down the hall.

"Out, left," Markus whispered, then led the way slowly. They could see the horde in the hall before they even exited the room. Aleric and Octavius went through the walls on either side of the door and swept through the demons with a blue shock wave to give the rest of the team a chance to get through the door and move down the corridor. They made it almost halfway to the room at the end, the room where the Crystal stood, before the fight began. Sel'arin shot three arrows in a row as she leapt through the air and landed on one of the giant stone braziers along the wall, then shot three more in succession, taking six demons out in seconds. Markus flew past Kara on her right as she sliced through a group of demons, her daggers moving at an imperceptible speed. He cleared a path as he flew, hitting and throwing demons with inhuman strength. Kara followed, Sel'arin running behind her and creating a strong gust to help carry Markus even faster. Aleric and Octavius were further ahead, still helping with the horde, but

focusing on getting to the Crystal.

Lucian flew in on their left, picked up two demons, and tossed them into the stone wall, then landed on the shoulders of a large horned demon and stuck two daggers in the top of its head. He jumped back in the air as the demon dropped to the ground and disappeared. They got to the large door at the end of the hall, and Markus smashed through it. A great crimson light poured out of the room, and the largest Summoning Crystal Kara had ever seen stood in the center. Aleric and Octavius went straight to it, while the rest of them spread out. There were Risen everywhere, and some of them were enormous with spikes jutting out of their backs and huge, razor-sharp claws. It was the biggest horde she had ever fought, they just kept coming. Arrows flew past her, and Kara quickly warded Sel'arin as she was jumping across the backs of a group of large demons before a colossal claw came swiping in from behind her, knocking her from the air. The nimble archer landed on her feet and shot two arrows at the beast demon, one in each eye.

Lucian glided up behind Kara and lifted her in the air. She threw two explosive potions to her left and right, straight into a mass of demons on either side, and the room shook as pieces of demon flew everywhere, disappearing midair. That thinned the hoard a bit. Lucian dropped her back on the ground, and Kara looked to see how Aleric and Octavius were doing. They each had both hands on either side of the crystal, staring intensely at each other and chanting the spell repeatedly. She could see their magic snaking through the red glow, as if they were slowly cracking it. Markus was on her left, using his bare hands to crack demon skulls together, and throwing them across the room. Sel'arin was on the other side of the room, perched on a brazier and taking out the biggest demons with her bow.

Lucian was on her right, leaping from demon to demon, jamming daggers in chests, necks, and eyes.

Then she noticed two nasty little monsters on all fours with long tails, wide eyes, and a full mouth of sharp teeth, sprinting for the Necromancers. She burst into a run, and just before one of them got their hand around Aleric's arm, she jumped and threw a dagger into its hand. It let out a piercing shriek as Kara landed on its back, jamming a dagger in the middle of its neck. The other demon whipped its tail around her waist, throwing her across the room. She slowed herself down using the air around her and landed on her feet before sprinting back towards the center. An arrow came from the left and went right through the demon's chest before Kara got to it. A moment later, the Crystal exploded in a shock wave of purple light that flew out of the room in all directions, and the demons evaporated. Kara dropped to the ground from the impact of magic, she was the only one on the ground when it happened. Lucian flew in and landed next to her.

"I'm fine. Is everyone else alright?" She asked and looked around the room. Sel'arin jumped down from the brazier and headed their way, Markus landed next to them, Aleric and Octavius were floating over. She stood up and brushed herself off.

"I should have warned you about that," Aleric said, "I apologize."

"It's okay, Aleric. I'm fine, really. It was just the force that knocked me over. That was...impressive."

"I almost lost my grip for a moment there. Thank you, Kara and Sel'arin. I would have been dragged to Infernus if not for you two." They both looked at him quizzically. "If a demon gets its hand on a Spirit, it has a one-way ticket back home, and the Spirit becomes a demon...permanently."

"I...was not aware of that," Kara admitted.

"Nor was I," Lucian and Sel'arin said in unison, then laughed.

"I was," Markus said flatly, "that's why you don't often find the Undead battling the Risen."

"Alright well, we need to get going. I see Octavius has left to explore already. Markus, get Sel'arin back to the Citadel, then go let Rowan know we were successful." He nodded, picked up the Archer, and they took off. "Are you two ready to go?" She asked. Lucian grabbed her around the waist, and flew out of the room, Aleric close behind.

***

It was the evening before the Full Moon, and everyone was anxious. The Gryphons had swept the Castle Oblitori and as a precaution, Est'alda as well as all surrounding villages had started evacuating, including Lyria. Kara didn't want to wait until it was too late, so she had convinced Nae'lin and the other Sovereigns to take their people to safety instead of clinging to the First Tree. Cylendri Forest was almost completely emptied of elves, leaving only those that chose to stay and fight. The Citadel was full as all of the mages and warriors they needed were gathered and ready. Kara had gone over the plan a few times, and everyone had their assignments.

Kara and the rest of the team worked together in the kitchen, making a grand feast so they could all enjoy one big meal before the potential end of the world. They had put out tables throughout the courtyard, which were being set with platters of hand pies, root and vegetable salads, potato rolls, spiced Terastra soup, tomato and zucchini pasta, teas, spring water, and Honeymead that Kara had brought from Lyria. As everyone gathered around the tables, and the cacophony of voices and clanking dishes filled the night, Kara gazed across the harmonious scene before her. It reminded her of home, but it was also something completely new and wonderful. Nymphs, Gryphons, Elves, Dwarves, Humans, and even Undead - all sitting here together, laughing, sharing stories over a meal, ready to fight for each other, ready to defend every life in Cylendri. This is what it was all for. Everything she had been through, every obstacle the team had overcome, every fight over the last few months, had all been for this. She wouldn't let any of them down - the Demigods and the Mormagi would burn for what they had done, and what they planned to do. She found her seat between Gondyr and Lucian, who put his arm around her waist and squeezed, tenderly kissing her cheek before he started filling up his plate.

"I'm very proud of you," Gondyr whispered to her, "and it warms my old heart to see you so centered, so confident...and so in love."

"Thank you seems so grossly inadequate..." she choked on the words for a moment, "but I'm eternally grateful for all of the ways you've saved my life over the years, for your unwavering faith in me, and for being at my side through all of this. I love you, dear friend."

Gondyr's eyes misted, "and I you, no matter what." She smiled, and they both went about filling their plates.

The conversations and stories ran well into the night, slowly tapering off when the nearly full moon reached its highest point in the sky as individuals and groups started turning in. The last ones around the fire pit were the core team - Kara and Lucian, Gondyr, Nalor, Sel'arin, Aleric, Markus, and Dahlia.

"I want to say what a treasure it has been to live and work among all of you over the last few months," Aleric suddenly broke the silence. "Your acceptance of me and my kind has been nothing short of extraordinary, and I have learned so much from each of you."

"This experience has been unimaginable," Dahlia added as she took Markus' hand in hers, "I will never regret leaving home and joining in this journey with all of you." Markus kissed her forehead and smiled.

"Without this team, I would still be locked in that black hole of despair, with no hope of ever leaving," Lucian offered. "You are the best group of souls I have ever known."

"It has been quite an unforgettable journey," Nalor chimed in, "and I would like to raise a toast to Kara, whose strength, tenacity, and generous heart have carried us to this point. Thank you for bringing my brother home, and for leading this family of misfits to the threshold."

"To Kara!" they exclaimed in unison, and Kara felt the heat rise in her cheeks.

"You all humble me. I know I've said it already, but it always bears repeating; I could never have done this alone. Your faith, trust, and resolve have carried us this far." She stood up and held out her mug of Honeymead. "Tomorrow, we take back Cylendri! We take back our lives and our power from those that would enslave and destroy us, no matter what!" They all stood and slammed their mugs together, then exclaimed, "for Cylendri!"

A brief time later, they all headed to bed and would hopefully get enough rest to be ready for the monolith that lay ahead.

Twenty-Six

The Blood Sacrifice

Kara was up before the sun, lying awake in bed watching over Lucian as he slept beside her. His chest rose and fell with steady breaths, and he looked so peaceful, so content. She considered all the roads that had led them here, how she had gone from a fractured existence simply fighting for those who couldn't fight for themselves with no regard for herself, to having a whole life of her own worth fighting for, a future she didn't want to miss a moment of. And so had he. Their stories were intrinsically woven, as if their souls had once resided in a single body and were ripped apart, only to find each other again centuries later. She sighed, then climbed out of bed slowly and started to get into her leathers.

"Already?" Lucian groaned listlessly.

"If I don't get moving now, I'd let you and the bed hold me hostage the rest of the day. No matter how appealing that sounds, we have the world to save," she replied with a shrug and a half-smile. He and Ira growled in unison, then got out of bed.

"Fine, but if we make it through this, I promise I'll be taking you up on that tomorrow," he said with a wink.

"Please, please do," she laughed. They finished dressing and headed downstairs. More than half the Citadel was already awake and bustling around. Archers were getting in last-minute target practice, Dwarves were sharpening blades and tightening handles, Nymphs & Gryphons were tending to the Pegasi, Gondyr was in the library pouring over the map with Markus and Kaisilus, Sel'arin was in the kitchen with a group of elves preparing breakfast. Kara and Lucian made the rounds, speaking to everyone and making sure everything was ready. The next few hours passed in a blur of coordination, and once the sun had reached its peak in the sky, it was time for the first groups to head to Est'alda. Kara gave the same speech to every group at the Stone before they left.

"Follow your team leaders, stay quiet and sharp, keep your eyes up and minds focused. Timing will be everything, so as soon as you see the signal, Nymphs will remove the glimmers, replacing them with wards on any prisoners that the Mormagi have gathered and pulling them out of the fray, then you show those fucking Death Mages what happens when you threaten the full power of Cylendri! Keep them scattered, keep them under constant fire, and don't let up. You do that, and I'll bring down the Demigods before they can destroy anything!" She exclaimed with firm resolve.

The Citadel emptied, and it was just Kara, Lucian, Gondyr, and Dahlia left. They gathered at the Stone with Sable, and Gondyr said, "you led us here Kara. Now let's finish it, no matter what." She gave him a firm nod, took a deep breath, and put her hand on the Stone.

They arrived in Est'alda, and it was deafeningly quiet. The great tree and land around it were usually teeming with life, but today it was empty. Sel'arin and Gondyr climbed on Sable, heading into the sky. Lucian grabbed Kara around the waist and asked, "are you ready?"

"Let's go kill some gods," she replied, eyes burning with electric fire, and he gave her a wicked smile before lifting them into the air. They flew up next to Sable, making their way to the trees just south of where the Mai'ngolo was hidden. Groups of Mormagi were heading for the Well below them with terrified prisoners bringing up the rear. The sun hung low in the sky, which meant they only had a short time to get there. Dahlia got the glimmer up as soon as they landed in a small empty clearing just behind the Death Mages, and the group moved as swiftly and quietly through the trees as possible. The closer they got, the more Death Mages they saw, collected in small groups themselves, all heading in the same direction with the tributes for the Sacrifice that they managed to capture. It made Kara's blood boil to see these fuckers had still gotten their vile hands on so many innocents. They stopped at the tree line of the clearing and waited as the Mormagi filed into the open space. There were hundreds of them, more than Kara had ever seen gathered in one place. Her heart pounded in her chest and her ears buzzed from the massive flow of magic. Then Lucian put his hand on the small of her back, and it calmed some of the noise. They stood there awhile, the red stone in her pouch vibrating softly with the power growing around them, as the sun set, and the sky turned shades of orange and purple.

A few moments later, the ground shook beneath them, the air sizzled, and in a flurry of earth, wind, water, and fire, the four Demigods appeared in the center of the clearing with a loud crack that rang out across the forest.

298

Kara had only ever seen Solaris with his blackened scarred skin, and eyes filled with red-orange rage, but now they all stood before her. Aeranis a tower of wispy, swirling blueish smoke, likened to a Spirit of Despair. Terranis was a great tree with bright meadow-green eyes, covered in vines and leaves, wearing a crown of poisonous flowers. And Aquanis stood like a waterfall in a small pool of crystal blue collected below her feet, glistening and constantly cascading. They were beautiful, ethereal, and terrifying.

Then Solaris spoke, his guttural and gritty voice booming over them, "welcome Followers of the True Gods! We have beaten our adversaries, squashed the rebellion, and will purify this great land of the filth which dared defy us! As the moon rises, we will complete the ritual, and Ess'Magis will be ours! Where is that pestering fucking elf now?!" The crowd of Death Mages roared with cheers and approval, most of them completely ignorant to the fact that they would soon lay dead, either by the rebellion's hand, or the Gods they revered.

The sky darkened, and the full moon began to change color from illuminating white to crimson red as the Demigods lifted their arms in front of them, palms up. The forest filled with their ominous voices as they chanted the incantations, low at first and growing with intensity. The fealty stone heated against her hip, the vibrations increasing. Suddenly, the helpless prisoners mingled in with the Death Mages cried out and dropped to their knees in agonizing pain. Solaris sneered as he watched them, a look of sinister pleasure twisting his features, and the crushing weight of the old magic in the air nearly took the wind out of Kara, but she held her ground. She looked at Lucian who nodded, then to Gondyr, and finally Dahlia. They were with her until the end. She stepped forward, moving away from the group as the glimmer faded around her, and stood tall and seemingly alone in visible defiance before the Demigods.

Solaris' eyes turned on her and narrowed in utter contempt. "You little *bitch*," he snarled. "How dare you show your face, as if you have any power here. Your meager attempt at insurrection is dead, just as you will be. Kill her!" he shouted, and the Mormagi started to advance.

"NOW!" She yelled as she warded herself, and Lucian tossed a large potion bottle full of poison high into the sky, followed by a small stone thrown by Gondyr, and upon impact the bottle exploded in a massive spray of glowing green liquid that rained down. As it hit the Death Mages, they sizzled and burned, screams crying out across the space. The prisoners who found themselves under the spray looked around wildly, wondering why they were unaffected, not yet able to see the Mages who were warding them. Once it had settled, the rest of the rebellion came charging in through the trees on all sides, and a great battle ensued. Arrows and daggers flew in all directions. Streaks of red and blue magic crisscrossed the air. Roots lifted from the ground, grabbing Mormagi and pulling them into the earth. Large stones rolled past, crushing anything in their path. Gryphons barreled through their enemies and dragged them along the dirt. Aqui'noctura came out of nowhere, grabbing Death Mages in their massive talons, and dropping them from high above. Mages of Light weaved within the throes of battle, grabbing the intended sacrifices and getting them to safety before returning to the chaos to retrieve others.

Kara ran through the fray, slicing at Death Mages as she made her way towards the Demigods, their inky blood splattering all over the ground. Lucian flew on her left, ripping off limbs and jamming daggers into eyes. Dahlia and other Nymphs were up in the trees all around them, keeping

300

wards up, protecting the rebels. Kaisilus was on Sable, shooting arrows with deadly accuracy as the Pegasus swooped through the air above her. She lost sight of the rest of the team as she closed in on Solaris - she wanted to spill his blood more than the others. He saw her coming, and she felt the air around her heating fast, making it harder to breathe. She steeled herself and wove in an ice spell to her ward as she ran, narrowly avoiding a flash of red magic as she leapt over a group of Mormagi that put themselves between her and the Demigods. She threw a few daggers, hitting three of them in between the eyes, and dropped an exploding potion that sent the rest of them flying in pieces. She landed only a few feet from Solaris, and he glared menacingly at her.

"A nuisance!" He yelled, "you are nothing more than a child playing at things you do not understand! You shall witness the old magic and crumble before it!" Two flames of fiery orange magic shot from his hands right at her. She grabbed her power fiercely, strengthening her ward threefold before the fire hit her, pushing her back, but doing no damage. The other Demigods exchanged tense glances as this small elf defied Solaris' awesome power, then unleashed their own magic on Kara. The ground shook and broke in great cracks around the clearing, the wind whipped and raged in all directions, and a wave of water came rushing down from the hill to her right, crashing through the battle. Just before the wave crashed into her, Lucian lifted Kara into the sky and flew in a circle away from the Demigods, then picked up speed as he headed back for them. He dropped her in the same spot, water rushing around her feet, and flew off to help Gondyr prevent a group of Mormagi from activating a Summoning Crystal.

She broke into a run, jumping on rocks as they rolled by and the bodies of Death Mages to avoid the water, and threw three daggers into Solaris as she got close, hitting him in the chest with two, the stomach with the other. He howled, and a root came out of the ground, slamming into her. She flew off to the left, landing hard. As she got up, a gust of wind knocked her back into a small tree, the branches of which started to wrap around her. As the panic welled up inside her, a Tree Dweller appeared, and they used their combined magic to tear the branches away enough that Kara could get free, then the archer took off into the trees shooting arrows as they went.

Kara wiped blood from her lip and again sprinted towards the Demigods. The ground split beneath her feet as Terranis focused her magic on Kara, but Pytra came flying in from out of nowhere and grabbed her mid-air before the earth could swallow her up. Another gust of wind tossed them into a spiral and Kara crashed into the ground after Pytra lost her grip, flying off in the opposite direction. As Kara got up and surveyed the battlefield, she feared that the rebellion might lose this fight watching lifeless bodies of elves and dwarves roll past her in the shallow water. Above her, Kaisilus was hit by a spell and knocked off Sable, plummeting to the forest floor. Her ward enveloped him just before he hit a few feet from her. Luckily, she could see that he was still moving but was in no shape to continue fighting.

"Dahlia, get Kaisilus out of here!" she shouted telepathically. Within moments a Gryphon landed next to his body, picked him up, and flew away from the fight. Sable, clearly furious, barreled at full speed through the group of Death Mages that the spell had come from, trampling a few of them before taking to the skies again. Then, before Kara could move, a wave of water took her down and she was swept off to the tree line far from the Demigods, the bodies of Death Mages and her fallen brethren crashing into her as she rolled, finally stopping as she smashed into the trunk of a

large tree. She groaned and lifted herself off the ground, blood pouring from a large gash in her side. Rosalyn jumped down from a nearby branch and put her hands on Kara's wound, closing it to stop the blood loss.

"Thank you," Kara winced, and the Nymph smiled before heading back up into the trees as Lucian dropped in from the sky next to her.

"Are you alright?" He asked as he nervously inspected her side.

"Yes, thanks to Rosalyn. Get me back in there!" She exclaimed, the fire in her eyes brighter than he'd ever seen it, a raging storm of opalescent lighting and fury. They lifted into the air and flew to the center of the battlefield, where he dropped her back into the melee just as Doramyr was desperately fighting off half a dozen Death Mages that converged on him. She ran towards the fight, throwing two daggers that hit one in the gut and another in the eye, then she leapt onto the shoulders of a large Mormagi from behind. Wrapping her legs around its neck, she spun her body and pulled it down, then stuck a dagger in the top of its head before they crashed into the dirt. The dwarven Gryphon winked at her, then flew into a Death Mage at full speed, slamming into its chest and it went flying backwards. Out of nowhere, two small crossbow arrows whipped past Kara into the remaining Mormagi and Kara turned to see a Terastralis Viper she had not met running towards her. He jumped over her and headed into another fight.

She spun around and sprinted back towards the Demigods, determined not to get knocked back this time. She battled through more Death Mages as she made her way, doing her best to help take them down while not losing sight of her main targets. Another root lifted from the ground and swung around wildly, barely missing Kara. Instead, it hit Lucian as he flew past her, entangled with a demon, and sent them both hurtling in opposite directions. That meant a Summoning Crystal had been successfully activated.

"Fuck!" Kara was furious. As if they didn't have enough problems at this point, but she couldn't worry about that, the team would have to deal with it. She looked in the direction Lucian had been hit, then saw him burst into the air carrying two Death Mages with him, so she turned and continued to close the gap between herself and the Demigods. Solaris was shooting fire at her, but she deftly avoided each flame as she ran, now anticipating the old magic before it ever got near her, then flipped into the air and landed on a massive rock a few feet in front of the massive beings. She heard Aleric from somewhere behind her yell, *"now Kara!"*

Without a second thought, she reached within herself, grabbed her power with firm resolve, and unleashed it on the Demigods. Four white streaks of deadly lightning flew from her chest and straight at each of them as a wall of fire went up and blocked her magic. Her eyes exploded with sizzling light as she glared at Solaris. She pushed hard, trying to force it through, but Solaris' magic was stronger. She could see his twisted grin through the flames, his fire connecting with her lightning and slowly working its way towards her. As she fought against him, she feared that this was it. He had beaten her, they had lost, and her magic began to falter. In that moment as she was losing her grip, she noticed Gondyr standing atop an enormous pile of rocks behind Solaris to his right, just out of view. He smiled and winked at her, and in a flash the pile came tumbling down, Gondyr lost within the great slide. Her blood-curdling scream rang out across the battlefield as the fighting stopped, and every soul turned in her direction.

Lucian didn't hesitate. He flew directly for her and grabbed her outstretched hand, increasing her power with Ira's strength. He wasn't sure if it would help, but if she was going to die for this rebellion, then he was damn sure going out with her. Her magic filled him, sharp and searing, yet he held on through the pain, yelling in agony as Ira fought to double his strength. The rocks tumbled into Solaris, distracting him just long enough for his wall of fire to dissipate. Kara's entire body glowed white with her wrath, and she lifted slowly off the rock, Lucian losing his grip on her hand as she hit all four Demigods with her magic. Their screams and cries of anguish pierced the air and could be heard across all Clyendri. Her magic covered them in electricity as they violently thrashed against the pain and eventually fell one at a time to the ground, reduced to piles of black ash. Solaris was the last one standing, and he was fighting back with everything he had, gritting his teeth as her magic broke through his tough skin. She locked eyes with him and focused all her power on the center of his chest. He threw his head back, yowling as the lightning spread through his veins, slowly destroying him from the inside before he finally exploded in a shower of white and red sparks.

Kara dropped to the ground in a heap, bawling and wailing hysterically. Lucian was immediately at her side, summoning every bit of strength he had left, and pulled her up into his arms. "*Gondyr!*" She screamed over and over, her grief floating out across the open space. As the Mormagi that were left scattered, the rest of the team came running to the center of the clearing. They stood around Kara and Lucian, some crying with her, others stoic and somber. Nalor knelt next to her, placing his hand on her shoulder, tears streaming down his dirt and blood covered cheeks. One by one, the

305

rest of the team put their hands on her and Lucian, supporting her, feeling the pain with her as her magic touched each of them.

They waited there for a while until her cries died down, then Lucian looked up. "Get back to the Citadel and start sending word out. The Demigods are dead, Cylendri is safe."

"We can't...we can't just leave him here," Kara said quietly between sobs. "Someone find him...please...please take him back." Lucian looked at Markus, who nodded and went to find Gondyr's body.

The team dispersed, Gryphons and Pegasi carrying as many wingless as possible. "We have to go," Lucian told her softly. She nodded into his chest, and he held her tightly to him as he lifted into the air.

***

It was raining when they arrived back at the Citadel. Lucian carried Kara to the fire pit, setting her down on one of the benches before sitting next to her. The sky was dark and gray, fitting the mood. It was as if the Citadel felt their pain and mourned the loss of a dear friend with them. She leaned into him, still crying, and they stayed there until Markus returned carrying a small, bloody, lifeless body in his arms. They took Gondyr out to the forest of trees around the structure, to his favorite spot where he would sit and read, soaking in the rays of sun on a large rock. Everyone in the Citadel followed to honor the kindest, friendliest Dwarf any of them had ever met. The team helped dig a hole by hand, then Aleric lowered his friend into it. As the rain came down, each soul walked over, grabbed a handful of wet earth, and paid their respects as they dropped it in the grave.

Kara waited until everyone else had gone before she stood over him, tears mixed with the drops falling from the sky, and said a final goodbye. "You were my best friend, my mentor, my guiding light, and the most generous heart I have ever known. You saved my life in more ways than I could have ever repaid, and you gave yours in place of every soul in Cylendri. You will always be my hero, and your name will never be forgotten. I swear it."

She dropped to her knees and sobbed there as Markus, Nalor, and Lucian refilled the hole. Sel'arin and Dahlia sat with her then, putting their hands over hers on the earth, and used their combined magic to grow a beautiful bush of white flowers laced with golden magic over the grave.

"It will remain here forever bloomed, never wilt or die - it will serve as a monument to the Dwarf who saved the Realms," Sel'arin said softly. The crowd slowly thinned, heading back to their rooms, or out to spread the word in Cylendri. Kara finally stood, and Lucian walked with her back to their room in the tower, where she stripped everything off before climbing into the bed. Lucian followed suit, and crawled in behind her, sliding one arm under her neck, the other around her waist, and pulled her as close to him as she could possibly get. He held her as she cried herself to sleep, and exhausted, finally drifted off, as well.

***

The sun rose in the morning, but Kara couldn't bring herself to leave the bed. A part of her died yesterday, a loss she would mourn for the rest of her long life. She had a hole in her heart which would never be filled, and the only thing holding her together was the blankets she had wrapped herself in. She had felt Lucian get up, but she didn't move or utter a word, she had little strength left for anything more than breathing. He came back a little while later and set a tray of tea and biscuits on the table next to her, then sat on the edge of the bed, resting his hand on her side.

"You have to eat something," he gently told her, "you expended a tremendous amount of energy yesterday, and took quite a few nasty hits." She slowly looked up and could see the heartbreak in his eyes. He was only trying to help in any small way he could, so she took a deep breath, sat up and leaned against the wall at the head of the bed, then picked up a biscuit and bit into it.

"Lavender," she said with a slight smile.

"Sel'arin helped me make them," he replied, then poured them each a cup of tea before climbing up next to her and taking a sip. "You know, this tea isn't half bad."

She grabbed hers and took a long drink, letting the spice warm her weary bones, then positioned herself against his shoulder. "Can we just stay in here today?" she asked quietly.

"Of course. I promised, didn't I?" He whispered.

Twenty-Seven

A Bittersweet Goodbye

Days had passed and Kara had finally gotten some of her strength back, enough to wander the Citadel, speaking with those who remained. She thanked each Elf, Dwarf, Nymph, and Gryphon who had fought beside her, wishing them each safe travels when they headed back to their homes. Nalor had been keeping his distance from her, fearing that seeing him would strip her of the stability she was regaining, but she went looking for him. She found him out at the grave, talking to his brother. When he saw her coming, he averted his eyes and looked as if he was ready to dart away.

"Nalor, please," she pleaded as she approached, "I want to speak with you." He looked up at her, his grief stealing the golden glint of his eyes, and nodded. "Please forgive me...I know you just got your brother back, and now..." she trailed off as the icy fingers of guilt dug into her chest.

He took her hand in his, surprisingly gentle for his gruff and gritty demeanor. "Please don't blame yourself, Kara. He understood the risks. I always knew my brother would die in a great battle saving lives, it was his way." He squeezed her hand and looked down at the grave, "and he loved you fiercely. I never saw him look at anyone with such pride and adoration as when he beamed at you. I'm grateful he had you to look after him all those years, and that you brought him home."

She knelt and hugged him, "thank you, Nalor. I'll carry him with me and tell his story to all who will hear it." Nalor grunted and sniffled, before pulling away.

"A great stone statue will reside in Lapidis in his honor," he stated firmly, and they stood in silence for a time before she headed to the kitchen to help Markus and Dahlia make lunch, getting lost in the work and filling her cup with the love those two exuded. Lucian wasn't far behind her.

"Marciela would like to speak with us," he told her, then kissed her cheek. "Are you up for a visit to Dellalun?"

"It would be good for me to get out of here for a bit," she replied as she filled and pinched vegetable dumplings. "We can go after lunch."

***

They arrived in the city, and Kara had never seen it so busy during the day. The streets were full, there were parades and lines at the market stalls and children playing throughout the gardens. It was wonderful to see so much light and happiness in one place.

"They've been celebrating for days," Lucian laughed, "I don't think anyone has slept."

310

"It's…magical," Kara replied with a sigh.

They arrived at the Manor and the guards bowed before one opened the door. Kara looked up at Lucian, and he just shrugged as they entered the foyer. Maricela was at the top of the stairs, speaking with Viv. When she saw them, she rushed down and wrapped them both in a tight hug.

"I was so worried," she said, pulling away and looking at them both. Her eyes lingered longer on Kara. "Who did you lose?"

Kara could swear she was a mind reader. "Gondyr," she said quietly, choking back the tears.

Marciela wrapped Kara in her arms again, "oh, my dear friend, I'm so very sorry."

"Thank you. We couldn't have done it without his sacrifice."

"Then Dellalun will know his name, and will never let it be forgotten," Marciela replied as she pulled away. "Come, let us speak in my office." Lucian took Kara's hand, and they followed her through the Manor to her office, Viv not far behind. Once they reached the room, Viv closed the door behind the three of them and stood guard outside.

"What you and your team accomplished is nothing short of remarkable," Marciela told them, "and all of Cylendri owes you a great debt. I understand that you have some things to wrap up and I can give you a bit more time for that," she looked at Lucian, "but the Vipers need their First Fang, and I would like to hand the scales over soon."

311

"Of course," Kara replied, "Lucian has obligations. We should only be another day or two before he can return."

"You have obligations here, as well," Marciela said, eyes narrowed at Kara.

"What do you mean?"

"Vivvain? Come in please." Viv entered the room and stood behind Marciela. "Tell them."

"I need to return home to my Clan," she said decidedly. "My father is ill, and after everything that has happened, I just think it's time."

"This means the position of Second Fang is vacant, and Vivvain has proposed that Kara should fill it." Kara shot a bewildered look at Viv, who smiled.

"I don't know if that's...the best idea," Kara stammered, "I mean, I barely just came back, and I don't think the rest of the Vipers would agree that a deserter should be Second Fang."

"Nonsense. You have proven yourself worthy of your redemption three times over," Marciela said dismissively. "Of course, Lucian would have to agree," she raised an eyebrow at him.

"There's no one more deserving," he replied and looked at Kara, "but this must be your decision. I will support your choice, no matter what."

312

Kara held his eyes for a few moments, and finally said, "I have to decline."

Lucian smirked knowingly, but Marciela was clearly taken aback. "You have always been one of the very few who can surprise me. Can I ask why?"

"I have been out of this game for a long time, and while I am happy to be home, I think it's important for the Faction to see Lucian as the Leader without inserting myself as a distraction. Besides, you know as well as I do that Cylendri might be safe now, but we don't yet know if our actions will have consequences...we killed the Demigods. If something happens, I will have to go, and I can't stop him from going with me. Having someone else in the role of Second Fang to manage the Faction will be necessary."

"Always three steps ahead," Lucian said with a wink.

"Yes, I suppose you are right," Marciela agreed, "however, that means we need to appoint someone else. I did not come prepared with alternatives."

"I can put those together for you, First Fang," Vivvain offered. "I'll have a list of recommendations in a couple of days."

"That settles it. When the list is ready, you will return to Dellalun, we'll hold the Ceremony of Scales and you will choose your Second Fang," Marciela said cheerily.

"I'll get started on the preparations," Viv offered, then left the room. Kara got up without a word and followed, catching her in the hall. She pulled Vivvain into her arms.

"I'm sorry about your father," she said as she hugged her, "and thank you for everything."

Viv squeezed tightly, then pulled away and smiled. "I've never seen Lucian look at anyone the way he looks at you. I'll admit there was a time when I wanted nothing more than to be where you stand at his side, but that has always been and will always be your place. Treat him well and take care of the Vipers." Kara nodded, and they parted ways.

***

Back at the Citadel, things were changing. After the last of the visitors left, it had shrunk back down and was so much quieter than Kara had been prepared for. She could tell that the team found the taste of this being over as bittersweet as she did. Sel'arin would be going back to Est'alda but made them promise to visit. Same as Nalor in Lapidis. Markus had requested a post in Dellalun, so he and Dahlia would be joining Kara and Lucian there. Aleric could come and go where and when he pleased, so they were sure they'd be seeing him again soon.

Now she walked around through the rooms and halls, running her hand along the table in the library where they had met so many times, looking out her favorite window in the kitchen that overlooked the forest, strolling through the courtyard where everyone had first entered this special place. This was their home for months, and Kara was struggling with leaving. As she stood staring into the fire pit, she suddenly smelled coffee and lavender and smiled.

314

"Come on," Lucian said quietly, taking her hand from behind her. She turned and they headed through the stables, out to the spring. She would miss this place most. It was quiet, constant, and held some of their favorite new memories. They undressed and walked into the water together, swimming along the surface to the center. Lucian stood, pulling her to him, one arm firmly around her waist, and brushed her cheek with the back of his hand.

"Don't think we aren't talking about you risking your life a few days ago by grabbing me and my magic," she teased.

He laughed, and replied, "I told you, no matter what. I meant it. I saw you slipping, and I wasn't going to let them take you from me. Besides, it worked, so you can't be mad at me for it." He raised an eyebrow and gave her a devilish look. "You know, it's really not fair how much I love you."

She kissed him, deep and sensual, her magic flowing through her lips into his. He moaned and kissed her harder, then she pulled away slowly. "Did you feel that?" she whispered. He nodded, looking at her hungrily. "I think you have a bit of my magic in your veins." He kissed her again, and they could feel the flow of power between them. It was electrifying and filled them both with ravenous need. She wrapped her legs around him, and their passion exploded in white light rippling through the water all around them. He held her close as she shook from the pleasure and kissed her shoulder softly. "*Me'amata*," he whispered in her ear. They eventually headed back inside to spend their last night in the Citadel.

Sel'arin and Nalor left first after breakfast. He would take her back to Est'alda before going home. Next, Markus and Dahlia left for Aquanalis to tell her mother that she wouldn't be returning. Finally, Aleric made his way to the Stone. "What an adventure," he said to Kara with a soft smile, "thank you for sharing all of it with me."

"Same to you, Aleric. You know where to find us. I hope to see you again soon." He nodded slightly, placed his ghostly hand on the Stone, and disappeared. She turned to Lucian, "are you ready?"

He grabbed her hand, flashed that charming smile, and a moment later they left the Citadel for the last time.

Epilogue

Consequences

Kara and Lucian had settled into the Manor, though having Marciela around all the time was rather frustrating. It wasn't easy for a woman who had run things for the last few decades to just step back and allow someone else to lead. She had a terrible habit of making you feel like every decision you made was wrong. They found themselves spending more time at The Den to avoid her. The marks had begun to increase again, so there was always something that needed their attention.

"We have a letter from Dahlia," Lucian said as he entered the office where Kara was helping assign new marks, "She wants us to meet her outside the city."

"That's strange, why wouldn't they just come here?" Kara frowned. "Let's head out."

They made their way through the north gate past the gardens and docks to the large grove of fruit trees where Dahlia paced feverishly. A heaviness hit Kara in the gut as they locked eyes – the Nymph's panic was palpable.

"Finally," she said frantically, "we have a problem."

"What happened?" Kara asked cautiously.

"Aquanalis is falling!" She shouted. Kara looked at Markus, who nodded solemnly, then she looked at Lucian, his brow furrowed in concern.

"What do you mean?" Kara inquired further, trying to understand.

"I mean, the City on the Water is falling out of the damn sky! Something is wrong...I don't know what exactly. But I can feel it. We must go now!" Dahlia insisted, and Markus looked helplessly at Kara.

"Okay, okay. We'll go now. Lucian, go let Marciela know, then meet us at the Stone." He kissed her before flying off into the night sky as they headed back into the city. When they got to the Stone near Aquanalis, the ground shook, and they could hear crashes in the river nearby. Markus picked up Dahlia, Lucian grabbing Kara, and they flew straight for the ward. Kara was through first, and what she saw was unimaginable. The great islands, which had stood strong for millennia, were slowly crumbling into the river. Small pieces of earth broke off them and crashed against the surface of the turbulent water, Nymphs running everywhere, trying to get to safety. It was pure chaos.

"What have we done?" Dahlia whispered behind her.

Glossary of Terms & Pronunciations

Characters

The Team:

Aleric (Al-Er-Ick): Necromancer, Undead Faction, Ex-Human now Spirit (Spirit & Ward Magic)

Dahlia (Doll-Ee-Uh): Nymph, Mages of Light Faction, Healing and Protection (Ward Magic)

Gondyr (Gone-Deer): Kara's friend and mentor, Dwarven warrior, Ex-Stones Faction/Ex-Wingless Gryphon (Stone Magic)

Kara (Car-Uh): Elven, Assassin/Rogue and Strategist, Ex-Viper Faction/Ex-Second Fang (other names: Tia, Amalthia de Lyria)

Lucian (Loo-Shin): Luca, Human, Assassin/Rogue, Ira (Spirit of Wrath), Viper Faction, Current 2nd Fang

Markus (Mark-Us): Human Warrior (Terastralis), Gryphon Faction, Intelligence & Strategist (Ward Magic)

Nalor (Nay-Lore): Dwarf, Bruiser, Stones Faction, Blacksmith and Weapons Specialist (Stone Magic)

Sel'arin (Cell-Are-In): Elven, Archer, Tree Dweller Faction, Acrobatics (Elemental Magic)

Others:

Alamira (Al-Uh-Meer-Uh): the Esselda, the very first elf

Calisto (Cal-Is-Toe): Elven Gryphon

Carmine (Car-Mine): Human Gryphon Historian

Cassius (Cass-Ee-Us): Ammodytes Viper, Betrayer

Chrysanthem (Chris-An-Thum): Necromancer, Nymph Spirit

Domi'dolori (Dom-Ee-Doe-Lore-Ee): Mistress of Pain, Death Mage

319

Doramyr (Door-Uh-Meer): Dwarven Gryphon

Elaria (El-Are-Ee-Uh): Elf, Kara's mother and Sovereign of Clan de Lyria

Ev'lina (Ev-Lee-Nuh) & Balin (Bay-Lin): Tree Dwellers, Archers, Elemental Mages

Gymmlor (Geem-Lore): Stone Dwarf, Rhygan's son, thug

Kaisilus (Kai-Sil-Us): Mira'lyn Sovereign - descendant of the first Independent Clan, Non-faction Archer, last of the Blended (Elven and Terastralis)

Lilum (Lil-Um): Advisor to Vitellina

Lord Rowan (Row-An): Human/Belua Hybrid, Head Gryphon

Marciela (Mar-Cee-El-Uh): Human, Assassin, Viper Faction, current 1st Fang, Lucian's Grandmother

Moira'nila (Moy-Ra-Nil-Uh): Alamira's last born daughter (Esseld'iel - Daughter of the First Elf)

Nae'lin (Neigh-Lin): Sovereign of the Tree Dwellers

Nero (Near-Oh): Belua Leader

Nir'lathin (Near-La-Thin): Clan de Lyria Healer

Pytra (Peet-Ra) & Kratus (Crate-Us): Terastralis Gryphons

Rhygan (Ree-Gan): Stone Sovereign

Rosalyn (Rose-Uh-Lin), Tulipa (Two-Lip-Uh), Jasmine (Jazz-Meen): Nymphs, Mages of Light

Vitellina (Vit-El-Een-Uh): High Priestess of the Nymphs, Dahlia's mother

Vivvain (Vi-Vain): Ammodytes Viper

Antagonists:

Hordes/Demons: summoned from Infernus by Mormagi using Summoning Crystals

Mormagi (More-Maj-Eye): Death Mages

Nero & The Belua (Bell-Uu-Uh): Large horned anthropomorphic creatures

320

The Demigods: Divine Elementals, Children of the High Gods

Solaris (Soul-Air-Us) – Demigod of Furious Fire

Aeranis (Air-An-Us) – Demigod of Wind & Smoke

Aquanis (Ah-Quan-Iss) – Demigoddess of the Rains & Rivers

Terranis (Tair-An-Us) – Demigoddess of the Wild Forest

Creatures:

Aqui'noctua (Aqui-Knock-Two-Uh): Great eagle-owl

Leporidae (Lep-Iree-Day): Hares & Rabbits

Onyx Pegasi/Pegasus: Mounts of the Gryphons

Verris (Vair-Ess): Wild Boar

Patroni'usi (Pah-Trow-Nee-Uu-See): Magical Elk-like creatures with a chameleon ability (blending pelts), changing their fur to blend with their surroundings

Factions

Gryphons: Warriors & Historians, Ward Magic (all races, except Nymphs - write & keep the histories, provide intelligence across the region - new recruits are scribes throughout their training, then they have their fighting years, then they're historians who keep the Library of Cylendri)

Mages of Light: Wards & Healing Magic (Nymphs and Clan Elves)

Mormagi: Death Mages (all races - must use a killing spell on an innocent, and sacrifice a piece of their soul to cast the spell in order to join this Faction)

Stones: Bruisers & Stone Magic (Dwarves only - special magic, calls and manipulates stone, activates/prevents location tracing when using Travel Stones)

Tree Dwellers: Archers & Elemental Magic (Tree Elves only)

Undead: Necromancers & Spirit Magic (can also have Ward Magic – all races)

Vipers: Assassins & Potion Masters (all races, except Dwarves)

Viper Phases:

1.   Ursinii (Ur-Sign-Ee): young, no training, just joined the Vipers
2.   Aspis (Ass-pis): Initial training, basics, Pit induction
3.   Walser (Wall-Sir): Late training, ShadowMarks
4.   Berus (Bear-Us): 5 Years of Training, running assigned Marks & training lower Vipers (2 assigned Berus and 2 assigned Aspis)
5.   Ammodytes (Am-O-Dye-Tis): Top Vipers, "Pit Leaders", 1 for every 3 Berus, choose their Marks and assign the others
6.   Fangs - Leader and 2nd in Command

Locations

Realms: Mortal, Demon, Spirit, and Realm of The Divine

Aquanalis (Ah-Qua-Nal-Us): City on the Water, gateway to The Aqu'immensi

Atri'anima (A-Tree-An-Ee-Muh): The Halls of Souls, Spirit Realm

Castellum In'Caelo (Cast-El-Um In-Kai-Low): Fortress in the Sky

Castle Oblitori (Oh-Blee-Tore-Ee): Castle of the Forgotten

Città Dellalun (Sit-Uh Dell-La-Loon): City of Moonlight

Cylendri (Sy-Lin-Dree): Mortal Realm

Cylendri Forest: center of map

Ess'Magis (Ess-Maj-Us): Realm of The Divine - Home of the High Gods & The God Forge

Est'alda (Es-Tall-Duh): The First Tree

Fini'via (Fin-Ee-Vee-Uh): The town at the End of the Road

Forge of Giants: Original God Forge, built before the creation of the Elves, abandoned in the First Age (Age of the Elves)

Infernus (In-Fur-Nus): Demon Realm

322

Lapidis (Lap-Id-Us): Stone City

Library/Sanctuary of Cylendri: Largest collection of the Histories at the Castellum In'Caelo

Lyria Village (Leer-Ee-Uh): Kara's home Clan, Keepers of the Sacred Harmony, direct descendants of the first independent Clan

Mira'lyn (Meer-Uh-Lin): Elven Village (half Terestralis), direct descendants of the second independent Clan

Terastra (Tair-Uh-Struh): Southern Desert, independent tribes, the Terastralis

The Aqu'immensi (Ah-Qui-Men-See): Boundless Waters (great Ocean)

The Citadel (Sit-Uh-Dell): base of operations, sits at the crossroads of all Realms

The Crypta (Cript-Uh): Death Mage's prison

Other Terms

Magics:

Death (Destruction, Death, requires sacrifice)

Spirit (Transfiguration, Creation)

Ward (Protective Enchantments & Healing)

Elemental (Manipulation of Earth/Air/Fire/Water)

Meads:

Honeymead, Berrymead, & Melonmead – Traditional, sweet, classic flavors: brewed exclusively by Elves

Rootmead – Southern, tart and less sweet with hints of spiciness: brewed exclusively by Terastralis using Dryroot and Citrus flavors

Travelers or Trufflemead – dry/more bitter with almost no sweetness: a common favorite of Merchants who brew it in small batches using foraged truffles, and not fermented for very long

Deep Mead – Only found in Lapidis, no sweetness present (strong, dark, and more bitter): brewed exclusively by Dwarves using hops and mugwort

The Risen: Demons pulled from Infernus by Mormagi and Summoning Crystals

Travel Stones: Created by the Dwarves, can only travel by them if you have a Dwarf with you, or have a Stone Charm, which are very rare (excludes Spirits, who can tap into any magical item)

Terastralis (Tair-Uh-Strall-Us) or Tera: Of Terastra, the Southern Tribes

Old Elvish:

Alis Aquilae (Al-Iss Ah-Quill-A): On Eagle Wings (to gain Gryphon wings/gold eyes)

Beni'dea (Ben-Ee-Dee-Uh): Blessings of the Goddess

Con'sial (Kahn-See-Al): Advisor

Deavita (Dee-Uh-Vee-Tuh): Goddess - in reference to the Mother of all life

Dis'cutia (Dis-Cue-She-Uh): the Shatter Spell

Esselda (Ess-El-Duh) & Esseld'iel (Ess-El-Dee-El): The First Elf & Daughter of The First Elf

Ingr'essi i'namli Deavita (In-Gres-See Ee-Nam-Lee Dee-uh-Vee-tuh): I request entry in the Goddess' name

Legati Pri'mas (Le-Ga-Tee Pree-Mus): First Lieutenant

Mag'nicelo (Mag-Nee-Sell-Oh): The Veil between Realms

Mai'ngolo (Mine-Goal-Oh): Well of Magic (the old magic)

Mi'filia (Me-Fill-Ee-Uh): Daughter

Mi'matia (Me-Maw-Tee-Uh): Mother

Mi'promit'ia (Mee-Pro-Mee-Tee-Uh): I Pledge Myself

Sacri'Sanguis (Sack-Ree-Sang-Wee): Blood Sacrifice

Scali'perius (Skal-Ee-Pair-Ee-Us): The Slicing spell

Dellalunian (Old Elvish Variation):

Dulci puer'mea (Dull-Chee Pure-Me-Ah): My Sweet Boy

Flessial, Adatil, Ni'Riveael (Fless-Ee-Al, Ah-Duh-Teal, Knee-Riv-Ee-Ale):
Flexible, Adaptable, Undetectable (the Viper Creed)

Giard'in Capallina (Jiar-Din Cap-Uh-Lean-Uh): Garden Pasta, Traditional
Dellalunian Dish

Me'amata (Me-Uh-Ma-Tuh): My Beloved

Reli'Sanguis

Book Two

Salvation of Cylendri

Coming Soon!